THE FRENCHMAN

A BENNETT SISTERS MYSTERY

LISE MCCLENDON

THALIA PRESS

THE FRENCHMAN

A BENNETT SISTERS MYSTERY

© 2017, by Lise McClendon
Published by Thalia Press
USA

ONE

The headlines were ridiculously easy to spot by now, on the newsstands around Manhattan. ***The Power of Sister-hood***, the magazine blared. Merle Bennett paid for five copies of the inane rag and rolled them under her arm. She was getting good at this. Over the last two weeks she'd disposed of at least seventy-five copies of ***Society NYC.*** Her sisters wouldn't be happy. But that article about the five Bennett sisters had to go.

She dropped the magazines into the trash bin on the corner, near the Greenwich Village offices where she worked for Legal Aid for at least one more day. Inside she got to work, cleaning out her desk. She dropped the chipped white vase into the box on the floor. Two years ago she'd brought it home from France. Should she take it back, set it on the mantle, add a pink rose from the garden? That seemed cheesy. Merle was not the sentimental type and yet here she was, planning her getaway with roses and nostalgia, while cleaning her desk for her replacement.

Six months wasn't long. She'd be back here kissing up to high-powered lawyers for *pro bono* money in the new year.

If everything goes as planned.

The words popped into her head. She frowned. As if her planning was soft, unformed, and unreliable. It was not. It was firm, credible, and solid. That was who she was.

Two months earlier Merle told her boss she was taking half a year off. While unhappy, Lillian Warshowski took less than a week to find a young attorney willing and able to hold her job in the interim. Lawyers were always looking for something to break the tedium of desk work, brief-writing, research, and stale coffee. Her job, wining and dining white-shoe firms for services for indigent clients, might look glamorous from the outside, like one big party, but Merle had had enough rich food and drunken lechery for a lifetime. She needed a break. France in all its simplicity, in its golden light and slow days, was calling.

Her bags were packed. But Tristan was dragging his feet. She texted her son quickly to begin, definitely, today. In three days they would fly to France and there were hundreds of details she had to attend to. The one thing he could do was pack his own suitcase.

Of course, Tristan would rather spend his last bit of summer partying with his friends before heading off to college than traipsing around a musty old French village with his mother. What 17-year-old wouldn't? He was driven, very much his mother's son, but lately — since his college acceptance — he'd disappeared into a social world she didn't even know he had, full of cute young things and who knows what. It worried her, but so far, he'd kept himself out of trouble. *Three more days, Tristan. Hold on.*

This summer trip to France would probably be their last together. She hoped not but knew better. She would return in late August to get him moved into his dorm then back she'd go, footloose in France for months and months. The open time caused a knot in her stomach even though she had a very detailed plan of renovation, cavorting with Pascal, her French boyfriend, and — *yes* — writing.

She would write her novel. No big deal. Everybody was writing novels these days, and lawyers who wrote novels were a dime a dozen. It was a vanity project, no doubt about that, but it had grown into a slight obsession since her last, short visit to France. There it had come in a dream of sorts. No, it *was* a dream — call it what it was. A dream about a goat herder, a young woman during the time of the French Revolution.

It was silly, childish, thinking about it so much. As if she'd gone into this misty corner of her mind, a playground full of lovely toys, walled off from the practical, rational side where duty and desk loomed in all their grownup glory. Well, once in awhile you had to do the thing your childish mind demanded. She shivered in the warm office at her newfound rebelliousness.

The small, red leather-bound notebook sat in her lap. She'd bought the journal earlier in the month and had been scribbling ideas into it ever since, tidbits about the French Revolution, ideas about characters and events, anything to keep the idea of writing the novel alive until she got back to France. She opened it and peeked inside. On the first page she'd marked out five or six possible titles. The one that remained was 'Odette and the Great Fear.' It had a nice *double entendre* feel to it. The Great Fear happened during the French Revolution when food riots raged and commoners thought the nobles were trying to starve them.

But what was a young woman's 'great fear?' There were so many things to fear when you were young, and yet so many choices. Living in the midst of turmoil was tenuous, and made your choices more stark. Did a girl's ambitions matter? Was staying alive all there was? The words 'great fear' made you want to think about what life means and— stuff. Now that was a literary phrase.

She closed the notebook, bringing herself back to reality, listening to Lillian talk rapidly on the phone. This beautiful old brick building in the Village was her home away from home, but now she had another one. Her cottage in the Dordogne.

The photograph sat on her desk, front and center, as if she might forget. The stone house with the azure shutters didn't have a name — yet. (It was on her list: *Name the house.*) The front door's shutters were broken and mismatched. There was a patch of stucco hanging from the corner wall and a broken flower pot in the street. She hadn't even gone there this spring with Pascal. She was too busy at his house, farther south in the hills outside Toulouse. The list of renovations and repairs was daunting but she vowed to complete them. Being in France would make everything possible, even plumbing and literature. It gave her such a lift. France made her optimistic, it made her smile, it made her feel sexy and alive.

France was a drug, and she wanted it all the time.

The tapping of Lillian's heels across the hardwood floors brought her back. Her misty mind was getting bossy, showing her scenes of an 18th Century village in southwestern France, far from the Paris cobblestones but teeming with intrigue, scents of the bakery, and wild places.

Stop it. Three more days.

Lillian had a strange look on her face. Was that a smile? She was walking and smiling at the same time. Merle braced herself.

Her boss in her tailored blue shantung suit tapped her manicured nails on the edge of Merle's desk. "Have time for a coffee?" She turned toward the door then looked back. "Let's walk."

Grabbing her purse, Merle hurried down the front steps after her boss. Lillian was ten feet ahead and showed no sign of slowing until she reached the door of the espresso bar on the corner. Short with a severe helmet of platinum hair, Lillian waited for Merle to open the door for her. It was a bit annoying. And Lillian was still smiling. Odd, to say the least.

They ordered cappuccinos and found a table in the sunshine. July in New York City could be hideously hot and smelly but this summer had been mild. Not that Merle would be staying in the city any longer than necessary. This was definitely her last day of work. She felt the promise in that phrase and took a sip of her coffee, dabbing the froth from her lip with a paper napkin.

Lillian reached into her bag and pulled out a magazine, smoothing it carefully. She smiled more, even showing teeth. "This is so lovely," she said, almost purring.

Merle's heart jumped in her chest. The magazine in question was familiar to her. The one and only **Society NYC**. Glossy and shallow like most gossip magazines, a city version of *Town and Country*. It was to her shame that her photograph was in it, along with her four sisters. Just the sight of it made her angry. How had she missed this particular copy on the newsstands? Lillian beamed at her, cheeks glowing with pride.

The older woman leafed through to the article. There it was, the headline that read: **THE POWER OF SISTERHOOD: Five Legal Brains Set Sights on New York.** The photo underneath showed the five of them in Times Square with their arms linked, smiling like goons. That day in March when none of them realized what the story would be like. They'd gone out to lunch first at a swanky downtown restaurant and someone had ordered champagne. Maybe two bottles, hard to keep track. Some sister started criticizing another's choice of dress and shoes. Another wanted to know where a sister got her hair done because it looked like a rat's nest. But they had laughed, all of them. It had been fun and they were all buzzed and loose and rosy when they got to Times Square.

Where had the magazine's editors come up with the idea that the Bennett sisters were on some crusade, out to rock the foundations of the city, swing battle-axes through legal worlds? From Francie? She might say something wild like that, off-the-wall explosive, just for laughs. Or was it Annie who had just moved to Manhattan and was starting her own consultancy? It didn't sound like Stasia at all, although she was the most high-powered lawyer amongst them. Elise, the youngest sister, only pretended she worked in the city for the article.

Whoever had blabbed, whoever had given that stupid writer the idea for that atrocious article, they were keeping their mouths shut. Merle had interrogated her sisters and they all denied it. Four out of five sisters were thrilled with the publicity if not with their photographs inside. Merle was the exception. She abhorred it. Since the issue had hit the newsstands two weeks before she had tried to buy up all the copies she could find and burn— er, recycle them. Obviously, her subterfuge hadn't worked.

"This is a really good photo of you, Merle," Lillian was saying. "You look so relaxed and happy. This one of Elise is unfortunate. I know she's prettier than that. You should have let me help. My cousin's son takes the best casual portraits. But, well, what's done is done. At least your photograph is excellent. Is this at your home?"

Lillian had never been to Merle's home in Connecticut. Not that she'd been invited. Was that what she was suggesting, that Merle should be more social? If Lillian had visited she'd know the sunshine on Merle's cheek, the stucco walls behind her, the lavender at her side were all obviously not the Connecticut suburbs. Merle spun the magazine toward her. But that *was* her home, her house in France. She smiled, longing to be there again.

"The Dordogne," Merle said. "Where I'm headed soon."

Where was Lillian going with this? Because in the years they'd worked together she'd never invited Merle out for a coffee. They were not that type of work colleagues. They socialized by taking big-shot attorneys out to big-deal dinners.

"Of course. That French light," Lillian murmured, a bit wistful. She read the headline out loud triumphantly. Merle glanced around the half-empty coffee shop, glad no one was sitting nearby. "So. What are you going to do with your power, Merle?"

"My— ?"

"Power. Your intellect, your drive. You probably don't realize how talented you are, Merle. That's part of your charm. It says in the article your name has been floated as a candidate for various public offices but you have always said 'no.' Is that true?"

"I've only been asked to run for school board. No one wants that job."

Lillian scoffed. "As if your children go to public school."

As if Lillian even knew her *children*. There was only one. "Tristan went to public school last year." When the money from the so-called inheritance ran out. Lillian was such a snob. Merle smiled a smile that she knew didn't reach her eyes.

"Tristan. Lovely boy." Lillian had the decency to look embarrassed, mixed liberally with pity. "Would you run for something else? State legislature? Congress?"

Merle shook her head. "I don't think so. Would you?"

"Me?! Oh, no." Lillian tipped her head coyly. "I am thinking of retiring though."

Merle sat back in her chair. Retire? What would Lillian do with herself? She was a workaholic of the first order, and Merle would know. Although, Lillian must be in her late sixties. The window light highlighted the crosshatch of wrinkles on her cheek.

"Are you surprised?" Lillian chuckled. "I see you are."

"I never thought of you not working," Merle said softly. "I mean, I'm glad you're considering it. You deserve it."

"I do." Lillian preened for a moment, running a finger over a perfect eyebrow. "Merle, I'd like you to take over the office when you return from France. If you could get back by September, October at the latest, that would be ideal. I could get you up to speed on all the details— you know most of them anyway. Then by December you'd be in charge."

"I — what?" Merle never stammered, yet, now she was.

"Be in charge, dear girl. Of the entire office, the fundraising, the arm-twisting, all the Pro Bono events. Call the shots, make the plays. The power position."

Merle shut her mouth which had been hanging open. "I'm not into power, Lillian."

"Don't be silly. Everyone is *into* power." Lillian pushed away her cup. "That's how things get done. How change happens. How the world is made better. I know you're *into* that."

Merle blinked, feeling trapped. Of course she wanted the world to be better, for justice to happen, for progress to be made. It was her mantra: make that list and check things off. But this, what was this really about? She'd never aspired to Lillian's job. Not in a million years. Lillian embodied it; it fit her like a glove. And she was *so not* Lillian.

"I'm planning on returning after the holidays." Merle tried and failed to make her voice firm.

Lillian waved that off. "You can change that. I'll pay the airline change fee if that's the issue."

"It's not that." Merle stared at her boss, with her stiff bearing, her squared shoulders, her head like an emperor's on a Roman plaque, all golden crown and granite glance. "I have plans. We agreed to my coming back in January."

"Plans to do what exactly?" Lillian had stopped smiling.

Merle felt her words like a blow to the chin. She always had plans, lists, agendas, duties. To have Lillian question her organizational skills, her forward thinking, like she was a matron on a cruise with nothing to do but browse the all-you-can-eat buffet, was insulting. With a mild shock of embarrassment she thought of her novel, her gothic romance. She couldn't tell Lillian about it, not now, maybe never. Did that mean she was ashamed of it? Was the project ridiculous? What about Odette who she loved like a sister, who she might have been if she'd been alive in France in the late 1700s? This was her plan, her project, and it had no bearing whatsoever on Lillian and *her* 'plan.' Merle had every intention of exploring Odette's world in depth and at length, as frivolous and unimportant as it may seem to, well, anyone.

"Does it matter?" Merle said. She was suddenly over caring about Lillian's retirement.

Lillian's eyes flashed in anger, and she closed the magazine with a slap. "I was mistaken. I had thought you would take a considerable, and very lucrative, promotion in the spirit of generosity and admiration that was intended. But I see. You have *other plans.*"

MERLE SAT in the coffee shop for fifteen minutes after Lillian had gone. All the pleasure and anticipation of her trip to France had vanished. Lillian had complimented her by offering her this job but it also seemed to be all about Lillian, *her* schedule, *her* time off. Had she envied Merle's long break? Had she purposely disrupted Merle's plans to punish her? It all seemed very possible.

Before stomping out, Lillian had mentioned the salary. She'd said it triumphantly, almost gloating, like it was so massive that it would bowl Merle over. The figure was much higher than Merle had imagined, especially for a non-profit like the Legal Aid Society. That sort of money *would* make a difference to her life. She could buy a new car for instance. But it wouldn't make her abandon France, or come back three months early. As a bribe, it fell a little flat next to endless, golden hours in the Dordogne. Whether Lillian's timetable was a deal-breaker went unsaid.

Glancing at her watch, Merle saw she had ten minutes before the meeting with her replacement. The lawyer was eager and bright and had excellent people skills, according to all his recommendations, a real social animal. All things, Merle realized, she lacked. Youth, no more. Energy and excitement— nope. Social animal? She was holing up to follow her imagination down a rabbit hole. Was it time to give her job to someone who actually enjoyed it?

With a sigh she stood up, stuffed the **Society NYC** magazine into her purse so no one would see it, and stepped onto the sidewalk into the afternoon sunshine.

Her last New York afternoon for awhile. What possessed Lillian to offer her the job she obviously loved so much? Would she really retire? Could it be she, Merle, *was* like Lillian: driven, cold, and obsessed with a hard agenda that stopped for no man or woman? Who used a non-profit job benefiting the underprivileged as a cover for unbridled ambition?

Merle blinked, stunned by her own question. Was she that sort of person? Cold and unfeeling? Hiding under the guise of a do-gooder? The fact that she couldn't answer that question made her wary. Maybe deep down she was lacking in some way. Her marriage had been a sham, a source of sorrow. Could France fix whatever she lacked? Was it the drug she needed to make herself whole, to make her warm, to make her human?

Nothing would help Lillian Warshowski; she would never change. But Merle still had a chance to be a better person, to love deeply, to open like a rose in the golden French sunshine. France would heal her.

But would she ever work in this town again?

TWO

PARIS

The teenager was groaning again.

It was almost a week since her last day of work in the City. Merle Bennett felt energized and alive in this town, Paris, the City of Light. It felt so natural, so right, to be back in France. Despite the summer heat and the constant drag of a seventeen-year-old, she was here, in France, where miracles can happen to your soul.

She hadn't given Lillian Warshowski an answer to the promotion offer. They'd left it hanging that last day, with polite hugs and good wishes for the future. The fact that the lawyer replacing her at Legal Aid was a strapping young man who flirted mercilessly with Lillian was a blessing. It made leaving much easier.

Taking a leave of absence from work would be a joyous, freewheeling time for most people, and Merle felt that too. But her sense of duty and responsibility weighed heavily on her shoulders, especially as a single parent now, making the pleasure fleeting. The last details of closing up the house in Connecticut, doing paperwork for Tristan's college, setting up everything to run like clockwork while she was absent; It was a headache that left her sleepless. That is until she got on that airplane.

It took one day in Paris to forget all that. Her list of must-sees was long because of research. Things she wanted to see up close, even if she never used them in the novel. The days had been full, and this was the end of the third and final day. So naturally the teenager was dragging his feet.

Merle Bennett stared up at the medieval building, situated next to the Seine, with newer Renaissance parts, slate turrets that glistened in the aftermath of the morning shower. The oldest part of Paris, smack in the middle of the river. Tristan was sitting on the wall along the riverbank, head in his hands.

"Not another museum. Please, Mom. You're killing me."

"Have you seen this one? The *Conciergerie?*"

He didn't look up. "Probably. Aunt Stasia took us to six every day."

Merle hadn't been in Paris that time—she'd been ordered to stay in Malcouziac by the police— but she remembered marveling at the ambitious nature of Stasia's sightseeing. And here she was, doing the same thing.

"This is the last one. I promise." She got out her museum passes and touched his shoulder. "You enjoyed the Hall of Mirrors and those gardens at Versailles, didn't you? This is much smaller. Tiny in comparison. Then after, it's that famous ice cream place. It's close by."

He stood up slowly, unfolding his tall frame until she stood in his shadow. "Let's get it over with."

Bribed by the promise of cool treats he entered the old building. Merle wanted to see this museum, rather obscure by Paris standards, because it was one of the few remaining buildings where events of the French Revolution took place. The Bastille was gone, torn down soon after the mobs stormed it in 1792. Versailles was all about the royals, not the revolutionaries. They had wandered around the Marais district, looking for the location of the Temple, a medieval fortress built by the Knights Templar that was used as a prison during the Revolution. Not a speck of it was to be found, torn down centuries before.

Also, it had rained.

At least today was sunny. Until they stepped inside the Guards Hall of the *Conciergerie*, an enormous, shadowy room with fancy gothic ceiling arches like hot air balloons suspended from the sky. It echoed, eerie and empty. Leaded glass windows lined the sides. Tristan said in a loud voice: "Another church?"

"A prison. They called it Death's Antechamber. Everyone who came here was sent on to the guillotine."

"Cool. Do they have one here?"

They had a blade but no guillotine structure. The French had a complicated relationship with the humane beheading of their people. They hated the guillotine now even though it was used until the '70s. No more though. Out of sight, out of memory.

It only took twenty minutes to see the dungeons of the *Concierg-erie* and they were back on the quai, overlooking the river, hoofing it back down the *Île de la Cité* to find *les glaces*. With ice cream in hand, Tristan's grimace lifted. "When is Pascal coming? If he *is* coming."

It was a good question. Before they left home, her boyfriend, if you can call a 40-something man a 'boy,' said he would show them around Paris. Then he bailed at the last minute. Merle had been texting him but he wasn't answering. He'd gone completely silent.

"I guess he's working." Pascal couldn't talk about his undercover work. That had to be the reason. It couldn't be that he'd gone cold on their relationship. Could it? Their affair— or whatever you called these things today— was so sporadic, a week here, then months would pass, then another week somewhere else.

"Right," Tristan sniffed. "So much for Pascal, huh?"

Merle frowned at the pavement as they walked back across the bridge to their hotel in the Marais. Was it the end? It didn't feel like it. It felt like Pascal was busy and couldn't answer. But maybe she was deluding herself. They'd had some romantic times. That weekend in Brantôme for instance. She'd never forget that. But the excitement was hard to keep going across oceans.

They were both professionals. He was a policeman attached to wine fraud. She was a lawyer attached to— what was she attached to? Her son, her job, her country? Her son at least. And he was going to college. He didn't need her any more. She felt suddenly— again— bereft. And very alone. There were BIG LIFE THINGS happening that she was apparently not ready for.

Tristan threw his free arm around her shoulders. "Sorry I'm such a grump."

He read her so well. "I'd probably be a grump if I had to play tourist with my mom, too. In fact, I was." She'd come to France for the first time with all her sisters and her parents, the year she graduated from high school. Just like Tristan. But instead of seven squabbling relatives they were just two. Tristan's father should have been here. Harry had been gone two years now. Sometimes, with Tristan, the loss was still fresh. Harry had missed so much, and Tristan, despite what he claimed, missed his father very much. "Did I ever tell you about that trip?"

He nodded, licking melting ice cream. "You got lost at the Eiffel Tower."

He didn't want to hear it again. "Have you thought any more about your major?"

"You mean, am I going to do pre-law?"

"No! Really, Tristan, don't go into law. It's boring, tedious, and soul-sucking. Unless you want to."

He laughed. "This family. So transparent."

They were all lawyers, her grandfather, her father, all five sisters. The youngest generation was unformed as of yet. Merle secretly hoped none of them became lawyers. It was time for an engineer or an astronaut or a shoe salesman in the family. Anything.

Their last dinner in Paris was a casual one: no fancy French food for Tristan. He wanted pizza on the sidewalk near the Centre de

Pompidou and he got it. He laughed, as he always did, when the waiter asked "*Gaz? No gaz?*" and replied, *please God no gas.*

"Did you ever call Valerie?" he asked with an edge in his voice, emboldened by his mother's compliance to his whims.

"I talked to her mother." Valerie was Albert's grand-niece. Albert was their neighbor in Malcouziac, a retired priest and teacher. Valerie and Tristan had a little summer fling last year. "She's doing an internship in Brittany. Something about oysters."

"Oysters!" Tristan made a face. "The French are so weird about food."

"They'll eat almost anything," Merle agreed.

The pizza arrived, looking bland and American.

"You liked oysters at Christmas," she reminded him. He shrugged, stuffing his mouth. "Did you know that lots of French people nearly died of starvation back in the sixteen and seventeen-hundreds? That was part of what started the French Revolution. There was a famine. The people were hungry but the nobles had plenty of rich food."

"Is that why they eat anything they can get their hands on, like horse meat? Ugh."

"Probably. Remember Marie Antoinette supposedly said: 'Let them eat cake'? Wasn't her. But somebody said it. The royals were not very in touch with the common people."

"So they chopped off her head?"

Merle nodded. "The revolutionaries got a little carried away. They even sent the people who started the whole thing, their friends, to the guillotine."

"Geez."

"Lots of infighting in the first republic. Chaos, really. Everyone wanted the power, and they were willing to do almost anything for it." She thought of Lillian then and her mention of 'power,' and how everyone wanted it. Maybe that could figure in her novel somehow. She pulled her notebook from her purse and scribbled out a few lines about the pursuit of power.

Tristan set down his slice. "So what's the deal with Pascal? He can't even come see us? Will he even be around in Malcouziac? Because, no offense, mom. I may go home early if it's just you and me the whole time."

She felt the stab in her chest. *"No offense?"*

"I didn't mean it that way. It's just... you know. No Valerie. No Pascal. I've seen everything there is to see in Malcouziac, right? What am I going to do there? And don't tell me about your list of chores."

Merle dismissed the thing she was thinking of saying, about painting and sanding and patching. "You could try fencing again with Albert."

"No."

"You have books to read." He had a long list of books for Freshman English loaded on his tablet.

He rolled his eyes and ate more pizza.

"All right." Merle crumpled up her napkin. "If that's the way you feel. You can go home whenever you want. I'm not going to lock you in the dungeon."

"Or cut off my head?"

She gave him a half-smile. *The verdict was still out.*

As she handed over her credit card to the waiter, her phone blipped. A text from Pascal— finally.

So sorry, chérie. Buried in work. You arrive tomorrow in Bergerac, oui? I will pick you up. Tell me the time.

She texted back when their train arrived, adding a heart like a silly girl. Her mood went from the dungeon to high in the tower. She smiled as she re-read the text.

"Is it Pascal?" Tristan asked.

She hesitated then turned the phone to him so he could read the text.

He smiled, chewing as he scanned it. "So he hasn't dumped you after all. Smart."

THREE

LANGUEDOC, SOUTHERN FRANCE

Pascal d'Onscon adjusted the floppy necktie, tucking it into his waistband to keep it out of the way. In the process, the ridiculous hat fell off, rolling in the dust of the vineyard rows. The sun beat down on his neck as he bent to retrieve it, smashing it down on his head. The Panama hat didn't fit him any better than the necktie. But the assignment here was nearly done and the clothes had done their job.

He wandered down the vines, inspecting them in case a field worker was watching. He'd asked the *proprietère* if he could go out alone and look at the grapes. The owner of the vineyard was an elderly man of the old school. Still sharp, still working hard, but he was nearly ninety and half-blind which allowed others to do as they wished. Two sons, one grandson, and other scattered relatives all worked the vineyard, a vast sea of grapevines undulating over the mostly flat plain near the mouth of the Rhône River.

Pascal figured he'd walked nearly two miles in the last hour, up and down the rows, over to the far section of Chardonnay vines far from the offices and caves. He was finishing his inspection, tasting a grape here and there for sweetness, and deciding where to go next when the grandson appeared, skidding to a stop in front of him.

Antoine-Luc Gagne was breathless and appeared relieved to find Pascal. The policeman squinted at him, on alert if there was an emergency. "What is it?"

The young man with sandy hair and a guileless expression gulped a breath. "Ah, there you are, sir. I've been up and down the rows." Pascal waited for him to gather his wits. "My grandfather says you are to come in for refreshments when you are finished. Or—" He consulted a wrist watch. "Right now, if you please."

In his fictional role as a grape buyer for a large conglomerate, Pascal felt little need to please or cajole the proprietors of *les vignobles* like this one. He was an honored guest at the vineyard, a sudden new member of the clan, because of his supposedly fat wallet. The growers would be happy this year. It had been a good one and unless an early frost turned everything to ice wine, everyone would make a decent return. He wiped his brow as he followed young Antoine-Luc down the row toward the main tasting rooms. It was much too hot here to entertain the prospect of an early frost.

So, if everyone was so happy, why was the wine fraud division of the *Policier Nationale* taking a close look at Domaine Bourboulenc? There had been talk among workers, wine agents, and other spies, that the Domaine was planting cheaper varieties of grapes, fast-growing ones, and switching them at the time they sold product to the high-end wineries like the Bandols and Châteauneuf-du-Papes. Simply sending the real Bourboulenc variety out of the AOC wine-making region was grounds for an investigation. The switching of varieties made the crime much more grave.

So far Pascal hadn't seen anything out of the ordinary. He could recognize many of the 50 or 60 varieties of grapes on sight. Others he needed photographs to take to headquarters for identification. This was his third day at the vineyard and it was beginning to look like a dead end. It was difficult to catch a switch of varieties under any conditions.

His boots were no longer black but the color of the earth, filthy, chalky. He thrust his hands in his pockets as the boy got farther ahead. At the end of the row he waited for Pascal.

"It will be a good harvest, yes?" Antoine-Luc asked affably.

"Should be. But one never knows." Pascal had seen more than a few good growing years ruined by thunderstorms, unseasonable heat, and other rogue events. Grape-growing was a mercurial business, depending on unknowable factors like weather patterns, thus the unsavory nature of criminal activity to make up for lost profits. When all the stars align, many fortunes are made. When they don't, it is often disastrous.

The tasting room of Domaine Bourboulenc was a disused, musty room lined with empty plastic jugs and centered with a rustic wooden table. A rock propped up one leg. A dirty glass pitcher sat at the downhill end. Antoine-Luc grabbed it.

"This way. Into the kitchen," he gestured toward a door in the back of the room. "We are very casual here."

Pascal followed him through the door into a darkened space with two grimy windows. He could make out an ancient range. An old refrigerator rattled in the corner. On the other side of the low-ceilinged room, three men stood around another wooden table, drinking wine and eating cheese and fruit. The grandfather and his two sons. They smiled at Pascal and waved him over, offering him a glass of red wine.

The small talk around the table was strictly agricultural, giving Pascal no new data for his investigation. It wasn't until Antoine-Luc escorted him to his car an hour later that Pascal got a glimmer of information. The young man had enjoyed a glass or two of wine himself, perfectly normal. He seemed loose and happy.

"So, you will buy many tons of grapes then?" Antoine-Luc slapped him on the back. "Of course you will! There is no better grower of the delicious Bourboulenc than right here. Everyone knows it." He swung toward Pascal and moved in to speak confidentially. "It is true. Everyone knows it, monsieur. Even those *tapettes* over at Châteauneuf-du-Pape."

Pascal eyed him. "I have some competition?"

"*Bien sûr!* The fancy domaines buy our grapes for their *grand cru*. They are the best. If only grandpapa would ask the right price. He nearly gives them away for free."

"Would he sell to me at the same outrageous price?" Pascal asked.

"*Absolument!* He will make you a deal you won't believe. A steal. And, I shouldn't say, maybe for you an even better deal than the others." Antoine-Luc grinned at him. "I would much rather sell grapes to you, monsieur. I can tell you are a real Frenchman."

The boy kept up his patter as Pascal climbed into his car, rolled down the windows, and turned on the air conditioning. Antoine-Luc waxed on about the beauty of the old green BMW sedan, how powerful and beautiful it was even at its age with the sun spots on the paint, and on and on. Pascal thought he would never shut up. Finally, he looked at his watch and it really was time to go.

He had a train to meet.

FOUR

The man in the blue coveralls paused in his chores, his cycling cap pulled low over his eyes, watching the green car blow up dust as it wound out of the vineyard and turned onto the highway. The sound of the gears grinding faded as he squinted into the sunlight bouncing off the rear window.

It couldn't be. Probably not. No. It was just a similar automobile. Although green was an unusual color. So maybe he sold the car to this man who came to look at the vines. The man in the straw hat who walked up and down the rows, checking grapes like he was a buyer or a winemaker.

Léo Delage knew he could ask someone. Maybe the little man— what was his name? The grandson. But that guy had no time for field workers, flitting here and there like a butterfly. He was just like his father and grandfather, looking down on the common man. Sometimes Léo wondered why his ancestors had bothered to overthrow the nobles all those years gone by. The common man — the dirty man, the coarse, uneducated, and ill-dressed man— what had they called them? *Sans-culottes?* Had they worn no pants? That was a stupid name. Or knee breeches? Léo couldn't remember. Maybe they were truly 'without fancy pants.'

Pants or no pants, the common man was still treated like dirt in this country. Everyone knew it even if they had giant televisions and big bank accounts to distract them. Those people knew it because they dished it out every day to the little people, their cleaners, their waiters, their farmers. He had gotten no help, no encouragement during his years 'away.' No training, no new vocation. He was jettisoned onto the street like yesterday's garbage, with only a cheap set of clothes and twenty Euros. That hadn't gone far.

He had gone to South America on a freighter. He had liked that, being on the ocean. For awhile it was good, until the incident that sent him jumping another freighter for France.

The country hadn't exactly welcomed him back. Perhaps they were hoping they'd seen the last of him. At least he had work now. The old man knew his old man, that was the way things still worked. Another thing that hadn't changed since the Revolution. France was a constant, a river that kept flowing no matter what happened around it. Ah, the old man would like that, he loved poetry, and France. Léo's father had died while he was away. Missing the funeral was not a burden that weighed on him.

It was the man in the green car who annoyed him.

Léo walked down the vines with his secateurs, trimming off errant growth. Now, mid-July, the energy from the sun needed to go to the swelling grapes as they entered the homestretch toward harvest. Many were still impossibly tiny. But they would grow and ripen under the Mediterranean sun. Léo felt no emotion toward grapes. Why would he? They weren't his, they would not feed him. They were not children, or dogs, or even friends. They were just grapes and would soon feel the boot heel of the master like Léo so often had.

If the man in the green car was who he thought he was, well, it appeared to be an omen. He had gotten out of prison at the perfect time, he had found this vineyard at this moment, it had to be a sign that things would turn around for him. It was about damn time.

No, *past* time. He had little left to waste.

FIVE

MALCOUZIAC, DORDOGNE

When Pascal turned his car into Rue de Poitiers, Merle felt the warm rush of familiarity run through her. This was home. She loved this little village with its ancient walls much more than her actual hometown in Connecticut. Was it the cobblestones? Was it the sunlight on the golden facades? Was it the collection of colored shutters down the short block — sky blue, turquoise, burgundy? Was it the disreputable jumble of stones at the end, where the *bastide* wall had crumbled centuries before?

It was everything. She felt her shoulders sink into the leather seat. She loved France. It was going to cure everything, all her ailments, her worries, her heart.

"What the hell?" Tristan growled from the back seat. Merle blinked, coming back from her French daydream. "Oh my god."

She turned to see what Tristan was looking at. Something on his phone? "What is it? Bad news?"

Pascal glanced at her, his brow furrowed. "Don't worry. We will make it right."

"Make what right?"

He pulled the car up to her *maison de ville*, a two-story stone and stucco townhouse with blue shutters that were falling apart. At least the roof was repaired, and she had plumbing and electricity. So much had been done that first summer, it still amazed her. So much left to do, yes, but—

Tristan was out of the car, swearing. Pascal turned off the car and patted her arm. He also climbed out. Merle unclipped her seatbelt, worried now. What had happened? Was it the house? She could see a little of it and—

No. She stood by the hood of the car, hand over her mouth. In shock. Someone had vandalized the front of the house with spray paint, swirling circles and lines of purple and orange and black, then used it as a paintball target. Splats of fluorescent paint in orange, pink, and green pocked the beautiful stone from the sidewalk right up to the eaves. The door shutters had been ripped off their hinges and hung limply, still attached in one place. More paint splatters covered the glass panes and raised panels of the door.

She blinked, trying to clear her vision. Trying to make this sight go away. This was a dream, wasn't it? She hadn't been to her house for a year, not since she and her sisters had taken a walking tour together here. And when she returns, this slap in the face.

"*Connards,*" Pascal spat, wiping a hand across his brow. "Dirty scum."

He looked back, frowning at Merle who stood frozen, eyes wide. A tear threatened to stream down her face and she quickly brushed it away. Tristan was silent now too, a worried look as he glanced at his mother. Pascal took her hand.

"It will be all right, blackbird," he soothed. "It can be cleaned."

"But why— ?" she began. "What did I do?"

"It is the act of *voyous, les bons à rien,* good-for-nothings who have nothing better to do with their pathetic lives."

Her first days in Malcouziac flooded back, painful memories she would rather forget. Trying to evict a squatter, the awful policeman, the horrible mayor, a murder, unfriendly people at every turn. Things had improved eventually. Hadn't they?

"Do you have the key, Mom?" Tristan asked as he pried the door shutters out of the way and tried to peer inside. "We better check everything."

As she handed her son the key, Madame Suchet stepped out onto her stoop, wearing a plum-colored dress and her ever-present pearls. She lived directly opposite, at the end of the street. Merle turned toward her and the old woman nodded, lips clamped together in a half-grimace. She waited, hands tightly clasped, eyes flickering over the spray paint on the front of the house.

Merle told Tristan and Pascal to go ahead. She greeted Madame Suchet with a smile.

"*Bonjour, ça fait longtemps.*" It had been a long time since they'd spoken.

"*Bonjour, madame.*"

Madame Suchet looked the same, full makeup, heels, and manicure, except she had a new haircut. Before she wore her hair piled high in the old style. Now she'd had her steel gray locks cut short, grazing her chin. It made her look younger.

In her emotional state Merle struggled with her French, managing to ask if she knew when the vandalism on the house had occurred. Madame Suchet expressed regret over the whole business and said it took place in the night, several weeks before. Had she seen who did it? She shook her head.

Merle squinted up at the ugly mess. Weeks had passed. And no one thought to tell her? But then, who would? Another neighbor, Josephine, was tasked with occasional garden maintenance in the back but she might never come down the street at all, only using the alley gate. And, come to think of it, Merle hadn't heard from Josephine in months, since before Christmas. Once in awhile, every few months, she would get a postcard. But nothing recently.

Madame Suchet was now saying she didn't have a phone number for Merle in the United States, and anyway, it was too expensive to call.

"Has the *gendarme* been around? Does he know about this?"

Madame S had no idea. There was a new gendarme, someone from elsewhere, not a good sign. No one really knew him.

Merle shook herself and began to come to her senses. This could be cleaned up, as Pascal said. It would be all right. The door shutters were misfits anyway. She would order new ones.

"I'm so sorry this happened," Merle told Madame Suchet. "For you to have to look at this out your windows."

The old woman nodded in a friendly but sad way. Merle felt she had said the right thing for once. Madame Suchet looked as pained as Merle felt.

"You will tell the other neighbors that I am very sorry I was not here to stop this. To fix it right away?"

Madame reached out and patted Merle's arm. It was as kind as anyone had been in this village besides Albert. Maybe vandalism was a local problem. Maybe others had been hit as well.

THE INTERIOR of Merle's townhouse was musty and dark with that closed-up smell. The old fireplace, huge and blackened, contributed to the odor. Maybe this year she would get it cleaned. The long, rustic table, too large to remove, was covered with dust. The window over the horsehair settee was filthy, barely letting in light.

With a sigh Merle did a quick inventory. Everything seemed to be in place. She plugged in the little fridge, kicked the door shut, and sighed in relief as the motor started up. The water wouldn't have been turned on yet. She would have to wait for Pascal to help with that. She could see him with Tristan in the back garden, and made her way outside.

Their heads were bent together and both had their hands stuffed into their pockets. They looked up at her in unison.

She paused, another blow hitting. Her beautiful, secret garden. It had been vandalized as well. The green metal table and chairs were gone. In their place were broken flower pots, torn-up plants, and garbage from some kind of party: soda bottles, wrappers, sacks, and bottles. It littered every corner of the garden, once a sanctuary but now defiled.

Merle kicked trash as she walked across the stone patio to the low wall surrounding the acacia tree. Sinking down on the wall she finally looked up at the back of the house. Thankfully there was no spray paint. But the espaliered pear tree that grew against the wall was damaged, some limbs broken and the lattice frame ripped out.

Why. The word reverberated in her head: why had someone done this? But she knew Pascal was right. Just bastards with nothing better to do, that's all they were.

Tristan had gone inside, emerging now with a garbage bag. He began silently picking up trash. Pascal poked around behind the old *pissoir*, a stone outhouse that Merle had hoped to make a laundry room. She noticed the back gate hung open a crack. Jumping up she stalked angrily to the gate and pulled it open. On the other side, in the alley, was more trash.

How had they broken in? Then she saw the key that hung on the *pissoir* wall was gone. Someone must have climbed the wall and unlocked the door, letting the party inside. More than once. Where had they taken her patio furniture? She would have to get new chairs. She would need the locksmith again.

Across the alley another gate opened. It was Albert, in his workmen's blue jumpsuit, a straw hat on his head, and gardening gloves on his hands. He raised his arms, smiling in welcome.

"*Bonjour! Bonjour!* You have returned at last!"

At least someone in the village was happy to see her. She felt stiff with anger as she and Albert exchanged cheek kisses. He burbled on, asking her about her travels, her winter, how was the boy, and so on. She pulled him over to her back garden and showed him what had happened.

"*Mon dieu,*" Albert breathed. "Ah, Tristan! *Bonjour! Content de te revoir!*"

Setting down the garbage bag Tristan allowed the old priest to clap him on the back and kiss his cheeks like an old friend. Pascal popped out from behind the *pissoir* and got the same treatment.

Albert linked his arms through Merle and Pascal's. He beamed happily. "We are all together again. *Tout va bien.*"

Merle glanced at Pascal. Everything was not well. But showing Albert the vandalism on the front of the house seemed unnecessary.

"We are so happy to be back in the village," she said instead. "It's been too long. But I will stay through the fall this time. Long enough to get lots of work done on the house."

And work it needed. In its neglected, vandalized state it didn't look promising. It didn't look like the house in her memory, full of laughter and friends and sisters, wine and boyfriends and goat cheese. At least Pascal would be around. She eyed him again. Would he? He would probably leave for work assignments and she'd be here alone, waiting for the next gang of hooligans to break into her garden.

It wasn't a comforting thought.

"We have some unpacking to do, Albert," she said. "Shall we go out to dinner later?"

He agreed and waddled back out the gate. Merle watched Tristan pick up ugly soaked newspapers and broken beer bottles. How long had they sat out here in the yard— months? A year? Was it the same bunch that painted the front of the house? Albert didn't mention a party; had he seen anyone? She called to Tristan: "Do you see a date on those newspapers?"

Her son blinked, surprised. Then he fished a soggy paper out of the bag and squinted at the masthead. "July fourteenth."

"Bastille Day," Pascal reminded her. "Many celebrations."

A week ago. She bobbed her head, worn out by all the travel and lists and prospect of work ahead. She felt all the optimism drain out her fingertips, leaving her as dusty and dry as this summer's day. Pascal took her chin in his hand and tipped it up. "No fretting, blackbird. We can fix all this. It will be better than before. You have the insurance, *oui*?"

"Yes. I think."

Why couldn't she remember about the homeowner's insurance? She must have it, she wouldn't be so careless... She was just tired. She shut her eyes. She hated this. For a moment she wanted to leave it all, go home, forget she ever inherited this stupid, unlucky, dark, antiquated house in this godforsaken village. Go back to Paris, run home to Connecticut, go to Spain or Italy or the Greek Islands. Anywhere but here.

Then Pascal pulled her in, wrapping her in his strong arms and pushing her head against his shoulder. She couldn't bring herself to raise her own arms. They hung limp at her sides. But the gesture, the warmth, made the urge to flee lessen, the pain diminish. As she breathed into his shirt, expelling air from her lungs, she knew she was still alive. And that meant she wasn't going to give up on her dream. She wasn't going to be chased away.

"It will be all right, won't it?" she muttered into his shoulder.

"*Ah, chérie, bien sûr.* Do not worry, blackbird. It will all be fine."

THE REST of the afternoon was spent taking photographs of the front of the house, the damaged door shutters, the paint on the stone and door. Then itemizing the damage in the back garden: missing furniture, damaged plants and containers, some bent pieces on the ancient metal cistern that sat on ten-foot legs, collecting run-off water from the roof. Inside the pissoir there was a disgusting mess better left to the imagination. Merle decided not to mention it to the insurance agent, whoever he was.

She wouldn't be able to search her online records for the insurance company until she had a wifi signal. She would find one somewhere this evening, in the village. Tristan finished picking up trash in the back and in the alley, loading broken flower pots to the bag and setting it outside the garden gate.

Pascal came down from the second story and announced that

everything was fine up there. "Some small visitors, *chérie*. But you put your mattresses in the plastic things so all is well. I swept up the tiny calling cards."

"Did you find the sheets and pillows?"

"Just where you left them. I put them on the bed." He leaned in for a kiss. "For you."

Tristan cleared his throat. "Did you put them on my bed?"

Pascal laughed. "You can do that yourself."

"I cleaned up all this crap! And I can't even take a shower yet. Look at my hands!"

"Can you turn the water on, Pascal?" Merle asked. "I'll plug in the water heater. You can clean up after dinner, Tris. Until then, use the rainwater and we'll go get a nice dinner."

They met Albert at *Les Saveurs*, a small, intimate restaurant with an enormous cornucopia of plastic fruits and vegetables spilling onto a dusty sideboard. They managed to sit far from the garish decor by requesting an outside table. The small patio overlooked the acres of vineyards and the ruins of a chateau atop a distant hill. Last year the Bennett sisters had taken a quick tour of the ruins. Merle wanted to go back and look around more this year. Albert insisted on sitting with his back to the setting sun, something about eye strain.

It felt good again, to be back in the Dordogne with sunlight glancing off tile roofs and the smell of herbs wafting up from kitchen gardens. Merle decided she would plant more herbs this year, to fill in the holes where some of her favorite plants had been yanked from the earth. That yellow rose, for instance, had been lovely. At least the wisteria was too cumbersome for the little fuckers to mess with. Merle smiled to herself. Once in awhile the term did seem appropriate.

Just as their food arrived so did another group of diners, entering the small patio and taking the table next to them. Three men, all middle-aged, they looked like they were on business. No smiles or small talk, dress shirts, long silences. Now that he was eating, Tristan was happy again, filling his stomach with pasta and truffles and babbling to Pascal about his plans for college, the town he would be living in (a small one in Pennsylvania), and a few hopes and dreams. Pascal was attentive. He liked Tristan as much as the boy liked him, and had told Merle that he missed Tristan at the family wedding that spring in Scotland. Merle asked Albert a few questions about his life in the village. Nothing much going on, as usual, he said with a smile.

The man sitting opposite Merle at the next table kept looking at them, making her uncomfortable. Was he suspicious of English-speakers? Although he didn't look particularly old and had all his hair, his face was hard. On one cheek a scar ran from just below his eye to his jawline. Merle's imagination went into overdrive: how had it happened? A knife fight? A war wound? Why hadn't he had some cosmetic work done? Was it a badge of honor?

Pascal reached for her hand under the table. He squeezed it as if saying: *Come back.* Had she been staring? Oh, dear. It was hard to take your eyes off that horrible scar.

Tristan was still talking. Albert looked off over the hills, twirling the stem of his wine glass philosophically. Was something on his mind? He seemed different this year. He was older of course, his white hair thinner. He always seemed so vibrant and engaged in life. It worried Merle seeing him like this. It was like when he got bashed on the head by burglars. He seemed back to normal last summer.

Tristan asked him about the fencing club. It took him a minute to respond, still daydreaming, staring into space. "Albert?" Tristan asked again.

"Ah, *oui,* it goes well. This summer not so many boys but we always have our ups and our downs."

"Any girls?" Tristan asked.

Albert turned toward him then. "Eh?"

"Any girls in the club this summer?"

"*Les jeunes filles,* yes! There are three sisters, little stair-steps. Also from Paris, like Valerie." He mimed their heights. "Seven, ten, and thirteen. Not very good but oh well." Albert squinted at Tristan. "You will come, yes? Maybe help me this year with the little ones?"

"Oh, I— " Tristan looked surprised.

"He'd love to help, Albert," Merle said. "He doesn't have too much time but I'm sure he can squeeze in an hour or two."

Albert slapped Tris on the back. *"Parfait!"*

Tristan shot his mother a look then smiled at the old man. Merle knew she'd hear about this later. The three men at the next table declined dessert and left. They must not know about *Les Saveurs'* amazing pastries. The man with the scar looked at her with his flinty eyes as he rose to leave. Was she staring again? Blast.

Pascal eyed the dessert menu. "Who will share something *chocolat* with me?"

THEY ALL WALKED ALBERT HOME, down the next street over from Rue de Poitiers. The evening was warm, the stars bright. Merle wanted to ask him if he knew who the man with the scar was but it didn't seem like the time. Albert was tired. Why it seemed urgent to her was confusing. Until she dreamed about Odette again that night.

She'd been writing notes in her journal, scribbles really. Nothing more. She could see the beginning of the story in a vague, misty-mind way. Was that enough to start? She had no idea. She hadn't even read a book about writing a novel. It was dumb, she knew, but she hadn't had the time. She took out her phone and searched online for something appropriate. Tristan and Pascal were outside, rebuilding the pear tree lattice and trimming dead branches in the dark.

This man with the scar— could he be in the story? He was memorable. She couldn't keep her eyes off his deformity, which was embarrassing. But it was more than that. Something else.

Pascal came inside and dragged her upstairs to bed. It was late, after midnight, but as they made love she felt energized and alive, the way he always made her feel. Loved and even adored.

And yet her mind drifted back to the Revolution, to Odette, her little goat-herder.

ODETTE AND THE GREAT FEAR

PART ONE

As they rounded the hillside, the fifteen goats in their patchy black and white coats, their bells jingling around their necks, Odette felt her stomach clench and she doubled over in pain. She had been hungry so long. Her insides had shrunk to nothing and her clothes hung on her like sacks.

Now she had food. Bread even, a miracle. She patted the parcel slung across her shoulders, the hunk of hard bread, the bruised apple, the bit of cheese. It was a miracle, this food, but one her stomach wasn't prepared for. Her body had prepared for the end, for starvation, for no more sustenance. Shutting down the juices, she called it. When food came again, so unexpectedly, her body didn't know what to do.

Her mind did. *Drink some water from the goatskin.* She obeyed her mind, hoping the pains would go away soon. She'd been in the southwest now for two months, after the long and dangerous journey from Paris. Along the way she'd seen so much deprivation: dead children, wandering women out of their minds, men in fancy silks chased by peasants with pitchforks. She tried not to think of it. Instead she concentrated on the kindness of the family who had taken her in, given her work. They gave her food and a reason to keep living.

The autumn was coming but slowly. She wished she knew how to find the famed truffles under the ground, or had a pig to do the digging. She poked her staff into the dirt under the oak tree. How did the pigs smell through all that dirt? It was a mystery.

Not much sustenance in a stinky truffle but some cash perhaps. She had exactly two sous to her name, sewn into her skirt hem. Once, with her family in Paris, there had been plenty of food and even money for sweets. Her father knew a sugar importer but the man had disappeared, arrested and sent to prison by the revolutionaries. Her father was also a merchant, had been forced to house so many rebels in their modest townhouse that the brigands stole or broke everything of value. He and Odette's mother had fled to the north, to the coast, where it was said one could subsist on fish and pears.

She tapped the upturned tails of the goats, moving them around the hill. Why had she not gone with them? She missed her parents but it was time. She was grown now. Everything was changing in Paris. Life would never be the same. She begged to stay behind and then that decision turned against her.

Below the hill were vineyards already yellowing with autumn. The harvest was poor, she'd been told. The weather had been odd since the mountain had blown up in Iceland, a volcano sending ash and clouds to cover the usual sunshine. Although years had passed, the countryside had still not recovered. The weather had changed. Wheat had withered and died. Odette had heard of people eating potatoes but the thought of it was repugnant. Bread was the engine that ran France. For bread, wheat was necessary.

Then came the Great Fear. The people of Paris became hungry then alarmed. The nobles were trying to starve them out, hoarding wheat or burning it so that the *paysans,* the common man, would die. Would not have the strength to rise up in anger. Was it true? She didn't know but it didn't matter. The panic seized them all.

Odette had marched with the other women to Versailles, to tell the King to stop the nobles' evil plan. It took them two long days to walk from Paris in the crowd. At first, they had been full of indignation and fury. Then they were hungry and their feet were bleeding. After arriving at the magnificent palace they still had to walk home.

She looked down at her feet now, in the yellow grass of the hillside. Her shoes had worn through four times as she walked south. She lined them with paper, strapped them with twine. Finally, they fell completely apart. These boots were a gift from the family who had rescued her. They were too small and pinched her toes but she didn't complain.

Paris seemed so far away. Occasionally a tax collector would come by the village and give them news of events there. But mostly they lived out their country lives like they had for generations here, raising chickens, picking fruit, milking goats. It was both a blessing and a curse to be so far from Paris. Country people could be so insular, so ignorant of events that would overtake them if they weren't careful.

She looked at the sky. It was later than she thought, she must have been daydreaming again. A dark cloud was headed for her hill, and it wasn't far away. A gust of wind smelled like rain. The goats jerked their heads up in alarm. Two suddenly bolted down the hill, causing the others to panic and follow. Odette swore, calling to them to stop as she ran after them.

Goats did not like to follow orders. This was something she'd learned in the last two months. Through the vineyard rows she ran after them. They split up, going in several directions, bleating loudly. The hill flattened out for awhile then she realized it dipped down again. The goats disappeared over the edge, kicking up their heels in the chase.

The heavens opened, a hard, cold rain falling. Bits of ice mixed with raindrops. They pelted her arms, her head. Odette had never heard of ice falling from clouds before. Damn Iceland! She felt sure it was the end of the world.

Through the rain she saw the old chateau ahead. It was rumored to be vacant, that *le comte* or his son or someone had gone to Paris for the revolution and never returned. The peasants wanted his property, that was evident. They wanted him to be sent to the gallows or whatever new death sentence the rebels dreamed up. The guillotine, that was it. They hoped he was now headless and they could take his land. It wasn't an original idea.

She ran under an arch, a carriage *porte* of some sort, huge stone thing. She had to huddle against the main wall of the chateau, in the door frame, to get out of the rain. It slanted in with such velocity, kicking up pebbles and ice. She was drenched to the skin, shivering.

And the goats were lost.

Oh, mon dieu, how would she explain this? She had to find the goats. But in this rain? This strange icy storm of autumn?

She took strong breaths to calm herself. The shivering continued. She wrung out her skirt hem and her cuffs. Then, without warning, the door she was leaning against opened, sending her tumbling backwards into the chateau.

SIX

MALCOUZIAC

Merle put the cap back on her pen. The rock she was sitting on at the chateau was hard and she couldn't write any longer. She stood up, stretched, and took another look around the old walls. The roof had fallen in ages ago but the rough outlines of the original building remained. If only they could talk. She wandered through the empty spaces, the grass growing up through cracks in the stone floors. Why had it been abandoned? So many grand houses had been restored, or made into museums. Chateau Biron, not far from here, was a grand old place, fit for a lord, or a romantic poet. But not this one.

She closed her eyes and tried to imagine what Odette might have found here in 1793. Scenes swirled in her head, from old movies, from photographs, from somewhere inside her head. She was lost for a moment in her dreams then jerked awake. She looked at her watch, time for the insurance adjustor. She had just enough time to walk home, if she hurried.

She looked at the sky, cloudless and blue, the picture of summer.

No ice from the sky today, Odette.

~

THE INSURANCE ADJUSTOR was not pleased.

Her name was Madame Vaux. She carried a large black handbag and had the look of the permanently displeased: a flushed face with loose jowls, lank hair dyed almost purple but not quite, and small, hard eyes. When Merle arrived she was standing in front of the house, glaring at Tristan. He had a bucket of water and a rag in his hands. He'd been washing the windows on the front door, his shorts sudsy and damp.

"What's she saying?" he asked Merle when Madame Vaux barked at him.

"Something about waiting until she'd seen the damage."

M. Vaux turned to stare at Merle then. "You are American?"

"*Oui, madame.*" Merle smiled. "You speak English. Thank you. My French is not the best."

"Still, you have a house in France. You need to be learning the language."

"Yes. *Oui.*" French lessons were on her list.

"Is this the damage then? This— paint?"

"There is a little more in the back," Merle said. She led the woman back through the house. Her high heels clacked on the floors. Madame Vaux's age was a mystery, somewhere between 35 and 70.

When they reached the garden, Merle explained that her table and two chairs, plus two lounge chairs, had been stolen. She opened her list on her phone of the broken items, dead plants, and general trash. The adjustor looked around the yard, walking carefully in her stilettos, and turned suddenly when Merle finished.

"That is all?" she asked sharply.

"Also, the gate, madame. It was forced open. It needs repair and will require a new lock."

Madame didn't bother to look where Merle pointed. She had a small notebook out and scribbled in it with a yellow pencil, pausing to lick the point now and then. Merle was quiet, letting her work. Finally, Madame Vaux lowered her hands and grimaced.

"Madame Bennett, you have a policy which does not cover outdoor furniture at all. You left your belongings in the yard all year, yes? Without covering or protection?"

"The gate was protection."

"But not much, eh? The jumping over the wall takes a moment. However, the cleaning of the front of the house will require professional work. Not a boy with a bucket."

"I understand."

Madame Vaux stepped closer to Merle. "This will not please you, nor does it please me. But, what can I say? It is business. The professional cleaning will be close to seven-thousand euros. The workers bring a— what do you call it? The shooting of the sand against the rock. It is expensive. But you have a ten-thousand euro *franchise*, ah, how do you say? Deductible on your policy, madame."

Merle squinted at the woman. "So, nothing?"

"*Rien. Dommage.*" The woman sighed dramatically, as if she was so very sorry when obviously she was just saving the company a lot of money. "If you had called me first, madame, and told me the items of destruction you were claiming, I could have avoided making the trip from Bergerac. In the heat of the day." She threw her notebook in her handbag and snapped it shut. "Now, is there somewhere pleasant for a woman to eat in this village? Do you eat French food? I suppose you would like a McDo, wouldn't you? All those greasy hamburgers—" she shuddered, repulsed— "are not for the French."

Merle opened the garden gate and told her about a fictional place in the center of the village. She closed the gate with a bang as Madame Vaux wobbled down the alley in her heels. Merle leaned against the wooden gate and closed her eyes. Maybe she'd never understand the French. Maybe they were just as annoying and diverse as Americans. Maybe there was no *'bonne civilisation'* or whatever they prided themselves on as French culture.

Tristan's voice came from the house. "Can I keep going now? Is she gone?"

"Yes," Merle called back. "Carry on."

She sat on the wall under the acacia tree. She knew exactly how much money was in her savings account. Not enough to cover a professional sand-blasting clean-up. There had to be another way. Ladders? Scrub brushes? Chemicals? She shuddered at the thought.

Odette's adventures bounced around her mind, keeping her from caring much about house cleaning. France was a royal mess back in the revolutionary days. It almost ceased to exist. Except for some fancy-pants intellectuals it probably would have fallen apart. Napoleon wasn't much help either. For a merchant's daughter with no means of support, no friends in the countryside, it must have been horrifying.

Merle couldn't wait to get back to her story. She considered running away again but this house needed her. Tristan needed her guidance. He had only a couple days left before they took him to Paris. And from there, home. These last days had been bittersweet, dinners with Pascal and Tristan, walks in the countryside, wine, plus chores of course. Tristan wouldn't miss her massive to-do lists in college.

The old stone *pissoir*, an outhouse with a sordid past, stood squat and solid, ready for a new future. It would make the cutest laundry room if she could figure out how to get water and sewer and electricity to it. No small feat and sure to be expensive. Everything on her list had a price bigger than she imagined. The gutters were a mess. The window frames were splintering. The door shutters were toast.

She eyed the huge old water cistern. Should she take it down? And how? It was enormous, standing on ten-foot legs, reaching up to the second floor eaves. She stood to go examine it just as Pascal stuck his head out the kitchen door, waving a baguette.

"Good news, *chérie!* I am chef tonight."

SEVEN

PARIS

On the train to Paris a few days later, students and tourists chattered, exclaiming about the countryside or staring at their phones. Merle sat across from Pascal, their knees touching. He had surprised them by coming along on these last three days for Tristan in France. Tris was over the moon, talking animatedly with the Frenchman, waving his hands around like a real European. It made Merle smile to see them together.

Pascal had been busy somewhere most of the time they'd been in Malcouziac. She never asked him about his work, most of it was undercover and he couldn't talk about it. She wondered, of course, who he was when he was on the job, what lies he had to tell, what roles he had to play. He'd played a roofer very well in the past, she knew that personally. What other professions did he know? Who did he charm?

Merle smiled at herself. Her imagination was running wild. This writing thing had made her suspect everyone and their motives. *Bad Merle*. She didn't like to live her life that way, especially with Pascal.

Before they left she had tried to contact Josephine, the elderly woman who had tended her garden for the last two winters. She had lived in Merle's house once upon a time, before the war. If nothing else, Merle needed to get the key to the garden gate as hers was now AWOL with the vandals.

Josephine's tidy house was three blocks away. It was small, a doll-house with old Tudor-style half-timbers. And closed up, shutters tight on windows and doors. The plants in the pots on her stoop were dead. Merle looked up and down the street. Did she know anyone who lived here? She hadn't made many friends in Malcouziac. That was another bullet point on her list: *meet the neighbors, make friends.*

She tried Josephine's phone number but there was no answer. Merle didn't have time to snoop around the village, looking for her friend. But she was worried now. Had something happened to her? Where was she? Had she moved? Had she died?

No answers at present. She added 'Find Josephine' to her growing to-do list.

IN PARIS, Pascal, Merle, and Tristan checked in to a small family-run hotel in the 14th Arrondisement. After wandering through the Tuilleries and doing next-to-nothing in the slow French manner, Pascal led them to a bistro that served Belgian food. It was noisy and lively and perfect. They ate sausages and drank beer.

They had just stepped back out onto the sidewalk in the summer twilight when Pascal got the call. He frowned, looked away, and muttered something. He began to walk toward the Seine, phone on his ear. Tristan followed him. Pascal spun back at him, face stony, and held up his hand for him to stop. Merle joined her son and they watched Pascal stalk toward the corner.

"What was that about?" Tristan asked.

"Work probably."

He glanced at her and frowned, biting his lip.

"What?" Merle asked.

"I thought I heard a woman's name."

"Well, he probably works with some women," Merle said. Pascal was still walking, across the street, dodging cars, then down the next block that ended at the river quai. He seemed hell-bent on putting distance between them. Why did he need to go so far? She glanced at her watch. Their hotel was in the opposite direction. Where was the Metro stop? She dug around in her purse for her map. "Do you remember where the subway is?" she asked Tristan.

"Not really. Hey!" He pointed in Pascal's direction. "He's waving — come on."

Ot the Pont Neuf, that graceful old bridge, looking down the Seine at the golden lights sparkling off the dark water, the dark outlines of the Louvre and other venerable buildings against the purple sky, Merle listened to her two favorite men discuss women, Paris, strange food, drinking, and university life. Then, Tristan asked Pascal who had called.

"Was it top secret stuff? You can tell me. I can keep a secret," Tristan said, grinning.

Pascal glanced at Merle. "No, it was not secret stuff. It was a woman."

"Ah-ha. I told you, Mom."

"It was my ex-wife. She lives here in Paris."

A small pause as they all adjusted to that reality. Pascal had never discussed his ex with Merle. It was her assumption that they had no contact, that she had broken his heart by running off with her piano teacher, and he hated her. But, no. They spoke on the phone, perhaps even saw each other in Paris.

"What's her name?" Tristan asked cautiously. "You've been divorced a long time, right?"

"Nearly ten years." He raked his hand through his hair. Was he nervous about something? "Her name is Clarisse."

Merle cleared her throat, determined to be an adult. "It's nice you can still be friendly after all this time."

"Friendly?" Pascal barked a laugh. "No."

Later that night, in their hotel room with Tristan sleeping next door, Pascal told Merle that Clarisse had been calling him recently. He didn't know how she got his number. She was a little bit crazy, he said, dismissing her. He kissed Merle on the neck, and other places, and told her to forget Clarisse. She was ancient history.

TWO DAYS later Merle took Tristan to the airport in a taxi, an extravagance Pascal thought was silly. But she wanted comfort for these last few hours together. Tristan gazed out the window, thoughtful. They talked a little about the house in Malcouziac. Merle promised to go to the gendarme and report the vandalism when she returned. Tristan reported that he had looked up how to remove spray paint from rock and sent her a link to some alternate solutions, mostly chemical. He told her to be careful on ladders this summer.

He acted, she thought, very much like a husband. Light scolding about safety, suggestions for future action, silence in the face of leave-taking. He was growing up. He would be on his own while she was in France this fall.

"I'll be back in September," she reminded him.

"You don't need to come back, you know." He glanced at her guiltily. "I can move into the dorm myself. You already bought me all that crap, the sheets and the mini fridge."

"But how would you get there? Besides, I want to get you settled. Make sure you have everything. Give your roommate the once-over. It will make me feel better about— everything." She grabbed his hand and squeezed it for a second.

"Aunt Stasia and Uncle Rick said they'd take me," he said. He'd already discussed it with her sister, Merle realized. "Willow goes back to school the same time and my college is on the way."

"I'll be back," she said, hoping to end this talk of her sister taking over. Tristan looked at her. She saw relief in his eyes and realized he was testing her. Making her choose between him and Pascal in a way. "I'll always be there for you, Tris."

At the sprawling Charles deGaulle Airport, they stood in the various lines together, until it was time for him to go through security. He turned to her, serious now.

"Mom. Are you and Pascal going to get married? Like this fall?"

Merle startled. "What? No. What gave you that idea?"

"I wish you would," he said quietly, hanging his head.

"Tristan. Honey. I will discuss anything like that with you. We're not getting married but if we talk about it I will tell you right away. I will never do anything without you." She hugged him to her. "Never." She held his shoulders and looked him in the eyes. "You are going to do great in college, you know. Your dad would be so proud of you. Make tons of new friends and study like mad. Now, go. Don't miss your flight. Either Stasia or Rick are picking you up. I'll see you in September."

"That's a song, right?"

He began humming as he walked backwards, waving goodbye as he disappeared into the crowd.

EIGHT

PARIS

Pascal sipped his *café* at the sidewalk bistro and watched Merle eat a big English breakfast of eggs and sausage. How did she find the energy? It was too early for such a large meal, he thought. She caught him staring and offered him some toast.

"*Non merci*, blackbird. So, what is on the agenda today? I am at your service."

She explained a complicated tour of various historical sites she wished to see. Something about this book she was writing. She appeared to be obsessed with it, talking constantly about the history of France, the revolution, and various devastating side channels such as famine and beheading. It was a tumultuous time, no doubt fascinating to an American. But so long ago, Pascal could not get excited by history so far back.

His own family was involved in the revolution. He had heard the stories for years as a child. How many *grand-pères* back was it? He could count them if he cared. He knew about each generation of d'Onscon, at least back to the 1750s. Branches went this way and that, died off, remarried, changed names when females carried the line. Merle was much more interested in genealogy than he was. He knew that from her snooping around at the church in Malcouziac. Finding the true nature of her husband's birth. That, he supposed, could get someone interested in musty old dead people. He, Pascal, however, was alive now.

"What are you thinking about?" she asked, pushing her plate away. She'd cleaned it well. He liked a woman with a good appetite even if it was a gigantic breakfast. So many French women were concerned about their looks a bit too much.

"Your excellent appetite." He smiled.

"No, something else. Tell me. Was it Tristan?"

He blinked. "Sure. I was wondering if he had a safe journey."

"No, you weren't. Come on."

"You are a mind reader now, *chérie*? All right." He sighed. "I was thinking of my *grand-père*, many generations back, who lived here in Paris during the revolution."

Her eyes sparked. He must try to make her eyes spark more often. It was charming.

"Really? Where did he live? What did he do? What happened to him?"

And so the day began with a visit to the city archives to track down the address of his *grand-père,* Guy d'Onscon, from the 1790 records. It was tiresome work but Merle did most of it, head down, reading endless computer screens. She shrieked when she found old Guy. They were scolded in the archives and ran out into the summer morning with the address in hand.

It was in an alley in the Marais where they found the spot where *la famille* d'Onscon resided above their shop. A small, dirty building with paper over the windows and a faded blue door, it was impossible that anyone lived here today. It looked like a storehouse for the restaurant next door.

"Well, it's a bit sad," he said, staring at the narrow, two-story stone building.

"Do you want to go in?" Merle asked, rattling the handle.

"Not necessary."

Merle looked at him. "Is this interesting at all?"

"*Un peu*. But how does seeing this little place make any difference now? You know what happened to him? It happened to everyone. He lost his business, went broke, his son became a partisan and fought with the revolutionaries. It went nowhere, *chérie*."

"How can you say that?" She glared at him, hands on her hips. "The revolution may not have lasted. The First Republic, I mean, but it had lasting effects. All over the world. It was the beginning of the end of kings, of divine rights. The beginning of the rights of man."

"Of course. I have read my history." He didn't want to argue about his country. "But it is the history of real people. Certain persons related to me, not an abstract philosophy. That is what the revolutionaries didn't understand. They got their heads so far up their asses that they ended up killing each other."

"Well," she said. "Yes. They did." She shrugged. "What happened to *grand-père* exactly? What did he do here?"

"He was a wine merchant. A successful one so the story goes. Isn't everyone in the past successful?"

"He was into wine, just like you?" She took his arm and led him toward the Place de Vosges, an open plaza with orange gravel and sparse trees, surrounded by arcades of shops and restaurants. "Is everyone into wine in France?"

"It is rather popular. You may have noticed."

They found a bench in the shade. The day had begun to heat up. Paris in the summer could be a cooker. *Quel soleil*, as the ladies would say. *What sunshine.*

"What happened to him? He had a son? A wife?"

So, Pascal told her the family stories. He knew them by heart and to stop telling Merle would only make this whole topic endless. Get them over and done, he thought.

The violence of the revolution was pervasive, on nearly every street in Paris, then spreading into the countryside. Guy d'Onscon was a merchant of wine and spirits, cheese, and other sweet meats, with contracts with nobles and therefore vulnerable to the partisans.

He was forced from his home with his wife, his business looted. His whereabouts after the revolution are unknown. His son, however, joined the partisans. He was injured in violence in the following year.

"He was a hero of the Revolution!" Merle squeezed Pascal's arm, delighted. "Keep going."

The son, named Pascal—

"You're named after a Revolutionary hero!"

Pascal the elder was injured badly. He was sent by someone, relatives perhaps, who knows, to the south of France to recuperate. He married his nursemaid and stayed in the South. For his health, obviously.

"Where?"

"I believe it was the Luberon but I am not certain."

Old Pascal had a son who joined Napoleon's Army and was killed at just sixteen. Pascal and his wife had two more sons. The third son was very clever, got back into the wine business in some way, and made a lot of money. Probably as a distributor or merchant like his *grand-père*. But as these things go, that man's son was a stock speculator, a gambler and wastrel, and lost all his inheritance speculating on railroad stocks.

"Bummer."

"*Oui*. We could all be massively rich by now. Shall I go on? We are up to the late 1800s."

"I am all ears."

"What? All right. I will continue."

When the gambler's son is born— there are many sons in this story— he goes back to Paris as there is nothing for him in the South with total bankruptcy. He ends up selling tickets at the Eiffel Tower. Then *his* son is Pascal's *grand-père*, who fought in World War I, barely old enough so luckily joined the war effort late. Then Pascal's father is born in 1930 in the Alsace, then—

"*Voilà. Moi.* So, a happy ending after all."

Merle set her head on his shoulder. "Thank you. It's wonderful that you know so much about your ancestors. I only know a little about mine. What did your parents do? Are they still alive— I never asked. I'm sorry."

"My father was also in the wine business. He was a distributor and a collector of fine wines. I learned everything from him. He was a friend of Père Albert. They knew each other from their youths somewhere." He paused. "He has been gone ten years. And my mother five years."

His phone buzzed in his pocket. He pulled it out and cursed under his breath. It was Clarisse again. He considered not answering it but that wouldn't stop her from pestering him. He apologized to Merle and stood up.

"You must stop this nonsense now, Clarisse," he said in rapid French.

Clarisse purred: "Ah, where are you? I will come by and give you many *bisous*."

"No. Please do not call me again."

"Wait, Pascal, I am in trouble. Please, I need your help. It is Yves."

He paused. Her *amour*, the piano teacher, the one she ran off with. Had they ever married? He thought not. Pascal never liked the man, for obvious reasons. Was he hurting her?

"What about him?"

She began crying noisily. This was a common tactic with Clarisse and unfortunately Pascal was not immune to it, even after all these years.

"Stop crying, Clarisse. What has he done?"

She sniffed. "He is so cruel. You would not believe it. He has told me to move out and he gives me only until the end of the month to find somewhere to live. I have nothing, Pascal, nothing." Her voice broke and there was more crying.

"Do you have money?"

"I have nothing, Pascal."

He swore again. "I can help you with some money then. That's all. Come by the Hôtel Paris on Rivoli, tonight at six. Wait for me in the lobby." The crying stopped and the thanking began.

He turned back to Merle. Had she heard, or understood, what was said? "I am sorry, *cherie*. It is my ex-wife again. I must give her a little money to find a new place to live. Her piano teacher is throwing her onto the street."

She stood up and smoothed her skirt carefully. Was she angry? Didn't she smooth some piece of clothing when she was trying not to be upset? He tried to decode her expression. He wasn't getting any message. Women— as hard as he tried he would never understand them.

"It's all right, Pascal. What else could you do? Was she crying?"

"Could you hear that?"

"You said: *Arrête de pleurer*. I understand a little French." She put her arms around his neck. "And you, my revolutionary hero, are just an old softie."

She kissed him then, out in the open, like a French woman. She tasted a little like sausages. He guessed she wasn't angry after all.

MERLE SAT in the small reading room off the lobby of their hotel, her notebook open, staring at the words. It was a small room with dark wood paneling, sunken velvet chair cushions and a worn carpet. It smelled like cigars and old dogs. But Merle wasn't really there. She was time-traveling.

Odette had found her goats, wet and nasty, but also the stranger, the owner of the chateau. It didn't seem quite right though. Gothic romances were supposed to be like this— castles, rainstorms, threatening older men, young innocent girls. But something was off. She just wasn't getting into the story the way she hoped. Maybe because there was absolutely no way Odette was going to fall for that old codger.

Sitting back she sighed, letting her head fall against the seat back.

Pascal was upstairs, curled into a ball, curtains drawn, napping. She had dragged him all over Paris today and he claimed he was tired. Strangely she felt energized, alive, despite all the walking. She loved hearing Pascal's history and imagining the events that fictional Odette or his ancient grandfather, Guy, might have seen. Pascal was much more accommodating to her demands than Tristan. They'd had a long lunch with wine before heading back here mid-afternoon.

The day had warmed dangerously, as August in Paris can. Merle sipped the remnants of her *café au lait*. The sun moved across the notebook in her lap. Out on the sidewalk an elegant older woman walked her small dog, pausing at every post and pillar for a sniff. In old France, the entire afternoon would be spent eating a midday meal with family and taking a siesta, then back to open the shops for awhile in the cool of early evening. She'd run into that in some areas of southern France. It annoyed tourists though and was mostly abandoned. Tourism reigned supreme, along with wine.

Wine. She closed her eyes and tried to imagine Pascal's ancestor's little shop. Wine in racks, cheese in the cellar where it was cooler, some jam and tins of meat on shelves, a little man in a blue apron. He had Pascal's black, curly hair and intense eyes. Then the picture fractured. Partisans entered, stole wine, beat him with sticks.

Well, that wasn't a very pretty dream. Maybe Pascal saw it that way, too, that was why he wasn't interested in re-living the Revolution. To Merle it was turbulent but fascinating. But very distant.

The bell on the lobby door jingled. The sound of footsteps came through the adjoining doorway. Merle saw a woman and a young boy. The woman was blond and pretty, around forty, and the boy with her looked about nine or ten. He had his hands stuffed into his pockets and sulked, his eyes flicking around the hotel lobby.

The woman walked to the reception desk on high heels. She wore a beige trench coat, unnecessary on such a warm day, with a colorful scarf. Her hair was twisted up on her head. The boy wore baggy shorts, a soccer shirt, and worn athletic shoes. She rang the bell and tapped her nails on the desk impatiently. The boy said something to her and she shook her head, mouth in an unpleasant line.

The boy wandered into the reading room. He paused, seeing Merle there, then flopped on a sofa with a bored expression. In the lobby, the woman now was punching her mobile phone.

"*Oui? Je suis ici.*" She had told someone she was here. Merle's senses tingled. She checked her watch. It was nearly six o'clock. Was this the ex?

It took Pascal a few minutes to appear at the door leading to the stairway. He opened it cautiously, spotting the woman as she turned to him.

"*Bonjour, Pascal,*" she said in a sing-song voice. He nodded to her and stopped in the middle of the lobby to extract his wallet from his back pocket.

"I can give you two-hundred euros. I'm sorry, that's all I have," he said in French.

The woman, who Merle knew was called Clarisse, stared at him. She said something in a low, hissing voice, very rapid.

"That's it," Pascal said, holding out the cash.

She erupted with what sounded like insults, spinning toward the parlor. She paid no attention to Merle but stomped in, looking for the boy. "Come here," she said to him sharply. "Hurry. *Vite.*"

The boy dragged his feet across the carpet. Clarisse spun him toward Pascal. "Here," she said. "This is why I need money for a new apartment. Here is your son."

The look on Pascal's face was stunned disbelief. Then he blinked, staring at the boy. Merle looked away, embarrassed to be here in this very personal moment. The naked emotion on Pascal's face was so intimate. Did he know he had a son? Had Clarisse kept the son a secret? The questions roiled through her mind.

She glanced back. Pascal had bent down toward the boy. "What is your name?"

Clarisse was squeezing the boy's shoulders. It looked painful with her long fingernails. The boy paused then cleared his throat. "Didier, *monsieur*."

Pascal glanced up at Clarisse. "Didier?"

"I named him after your dear father."

Pascal looked rattled now, wiping a hand across his eyes. "And what is your father's name, Didier?"

Again, the boy paused and when he spoke his voice was barely audible. "I don't know my father. He left before I was born."

Now Pascal's face reddened with anger. A muscle in his jaw twitched. "And I suppose you are going to say you are ten years old?" He stared at Clarisse. The boy said yes. "And you waited ten years to tell me I have a son? Do you take me for a fool?"

He pounded a fist into the door frame, rattling the room. Clarisse jumped back a step, losing her grip on the boy.

"You expect me to believe this charade, Clarisse? Suddenly I have a son? When I haven't seen you in ten years? This boy isn't mine any more than you are. Get out of here."

"But the money," she whined.

"Find some other—" He used a word Merle didn't know. She imagined it was a word for 'sucker.' They didn't move. The boy looked up at Clarisse, his eyes filling. Had she told him Pascal was his father? That they would be a happy family? Was this all an act? Merle felt sorry for the kid either way.

"*Sors d'ici!* Get out of here!" Pascal shouted. He pointed at the door. The boy bolted through the lobby and out onto the sidewalk. Merle watched him slow to a walk with his head down. Then he looked up, smiling at the sky. He pulled some coins from his shorts, counting them, and dropped them back in his pocket.

Clarisse gave Pascal a few well-chosen words and lifted her chin, marching out. The clicking of her heels on the tile floor faded as the bell on the door chimed. She looked back at Pascal through the window, hatred in her eyes. On the sidewalk, she looked up and down the street for the boy, calling his name. He had vanished from

Merle's view. Clarisse called out for him to wait before running down the block.

Merle stood up behind the velvet chair, holding its back. Pascal had his forehead against the door frame now, fists clenched at his side. He glanced at her and stood up straight.

"So that's Clarisse," she said.

"All the crazy parts of her."

"How long were you married?" Merle asked. She didn't really care. But maybe he needed to talk about it finally.

"Two years. Not long, but long enough. Truthfully I would have paid that piano teacher to take her away by then."

She wondered if he wasn't just saying that to cover his broken heart. But it didn't matter now. "So, she's a gold-digger?" He frowned, not understanding. "Someone who uses people to get money?"

"She wasn't always that way." He glanced out the window where she'd disappeared. "I looked her up this afternoon, her address, her record. She hasn't lived with Yves for years. She's lived in six different apartments and owes money all over the city, for rent, meals, all sorts of things."

"How does she support herself?"

He sighed. "It's a mystery."

"I saw the boy examining some coins from his pocket. In a happy way."

He grimaced. There was pain in his voice. "We tried to have children. She has forgotten that she told me she was unable to bear a child. I didn't believe her. I thought she was secretly taking the pills, you know? That would be like her, to lie about something like that. She wasn't though, the doctor told me. And now she expects me to forget that, to think that I have a son she conveniently forgot to tell me about."

"How could she? That is too cruel."

Pascal stepped over to her then, and put his arms around her, pressed his cheek against her hair. "That, *chérie*, is Clarisse."

~

THE NEXT DAY Merle had arranged to spend several hours at the American University in their library. Pascal had been sullen at dinner the night before, his mind obviously still on his ex-wife. He drank more wine than usual. He was sweet with Merle as always, but preoccupied. There wasn't much she could do about his mood. She decided to carry on with her research plan and left him to go into his headquarters at *Policier Nationale* and do whatever cops did in the office.

Their last night in Paris was better. Merle was on a little high from finding so much good information about France in the late 1700s, about the Revolution and the social changes, translated into English. Plus, she had written six pages in her notebook on the next part of *Odette and the Great Fear*. She felt the French air on her face, the delicious food on her tongue. The restlessness and anxiety that formed her American self was falling away the way it had two years before. She was slowing down, enjoying little things, the way the sunlight glanced off the rooftops, the pots of red geraniums on every balcony, the colored sails of the boats on the ponds all over the city, the flap of the tri-color flag.

At dinner that night she confessed to Pascal that she considered France a drug. That it cured people of their illnesses, erased the worst of the modern age, the crass commercialism, the puritanical outrage, the hyper-religiosity, the need to constantly judge other people. Pascal was drinking a soft Cotes-du-Rhône as he listened. He stared at her for a second when she stopped then burst out laughing.

"Blackbird, *tu es très touchante*. You are so earnest, is that the word? But you don't mean that."

"Yes, I do. There is a definite therapeutic benefit from just being in France."

He eyed her, smirking. "It cures you? You are changed? Through the air?"

"Absolutely. It cleanses you of the ills of modern life. Opens your senses."

He eyed the wine label. "How much of this have you drunk?"

"Not as much as you! You don't see it, because you're French. You don't understand how the culture and society and the way the French live is a balm for the soul."

"We made it that way on purpose. It didn't just happen."

"So you agree! France is a drug."

"I think you may have overdosed already. And you are here until Christmas." He patted her hand. "I will try to keep you anxious and busy. Working on your endless lists. No sitting around watching the people all afternoon, full of the bliss."

"Why not? I would love to do that. I adore bliss." As soon as she said it Merle realized she would be bored to tears, sitting in a sidewalk café for hours on end, doing nothing.

"Only people without jobs do that, blackbird. College students or old drunken men or the chronic lazy. Or people who work in clubs."

Visions of purple strobe lights popped into her head. Possibly she had drunk too much. "Should I get a job in a nightclub? That sounds like fun. Is it very French?"

"No, blackbird. It is very American. Rock and roll, what you call it? Techno. Rappers. All your exports. You like hip-hop?"

Merle frowned. "You're killing my buzz."

He looked at her from under his thick eyebrows. "France is not a drug, ma chérie. The people who think France is a gastronomic Disneyland full of sunflowers, they are the ones who will take us back to the past, to an age that never happened except in their minds."

"Back to Madame Guillotine?"

"And worse."

She fingered her wine glass, wishing he would pour her a little more but worried he thought she drank too much. Was she drunk? Was she being an idiot? Did she say France was perfect? No. Just a lot more livable than most places. It suited her. Was that a crime? Did it make her anti-American? No. She would always love America.

Right now though, she needed a hit of *la belle France* in all its life-changing glory.

As they enjoyed dessert, an éclair with a heavenly filling, a thought pushed in from the edges of her mind. Maybe Pascal was right, in a way. Not that France wasn't a gastronomic Disneyland full of sunflowers, because, seriously, it was. Every tourist knew that.

But maybe she wasn't worthy of it.

Maybe she didn't deserve her French dream. Maybe it wasn't hers.

France was Harry's legacy, his birthright. Her husband who died after marching up seven flights of stairs on four shots of morning espresso, Harry who had betrayed her yet loved her, Harry who she had not loved enough: France was his. He could have returned in his old age, retired in his quiet village, enjoyed his dark, little cottage as his birthright. She could see him, waddling around with his pot belly proud, tipping his hat to the old ladies. But it was all taken from him.

Was she unconsciously living out Harry's dream? It seemed liked her own adventure, her own dream, but maybe it wasn't. Maybe she had just co-opted her late husband's life in some twisted sort of revenge for his cheating.

But, honestly, she didn't care about the cheating any more. Yes, he had done it, yes, he had a child with another woman. You can't hate someone who is dead. They've paid their price. It would always nag a little, the jealousy. But she didn't blame the child. It was done. Over.

Pascal was looking pensive too. Maybe thinking about that boy that his ex-wife claimed was his. He was an adorable child when he wasn't scowling. He didn't look anything like Pascal with those blond curls though. Pascal always wanted a child, he'd told Merle. He loved Tristan like a son. What was he thinking now? That he wished she was young enough to give him a child? A deep ache in her belly reminded her that was impossible, even if she was younger. With Tristan she was one and done.

Did Pascal even want a child? They'd never discussed it. He

didn't believe in marriage any more, he'd made that clear. *Why beat yourself up, Merle?* What they had was what they had. And it was plenty.

She knew she was being silly and a little ridiculous about France being a drug. She *felt* silly and playful, and very happy tonight. Who wouldn't, having a mouth-watering meal in Paris with a handsome Frenchman? Of course, France didn't cure what ailed you, unless what ailed you was a pasty complexion and a hankering for goose liver.

Still, ridiculously, she clung to her hope that being in France would transform her into the person she wanted to be. She didn't believe in magic. But change, that was possible, wasn't it? She so wanted to be someone besides one of five lawyer sisters. Someone who was buttoned up and rigid. Someone who made lists obsessively. She wanted to be calm, and herself, individually— not one of five. To be creative, free, not caring what others thought. France must be able to help with that.

Her sister Annie claimed that turning fifty was a watershed, the beginning of the 'Fuck you Fifties' when you stopped caring what people said or thought about you. When social judgment rolled off your back like a tattered garment you no longer needed. When you were truly free.

But Merle had turned 51 already and she still had all these anxieties about how well she was doing at work, how well her child was doing at school, how other lawyers viewed her, what her neighbors thought, how her sisters viewed her— how *everyone* viewed and judged her. She still cared what her people were thinking.

"Yoo-hoo. What are you thinking about, blackbird?" Pascal asked, tapping her hand on the tablecloth. "You look so serious."

France and me, she almost said. *France and me and you.*

ODETTE AND THE GREAT FEAR

PART TWO

The goat sheds smelled a little too rank for a girl from Paris. They were clean enough, they had to be for the milking, but still there were many smelly animals in close proximity.

Odette was learning to milk the goats, an intense, near-constant activity on the farm. The ones she took out to pasture in the hills were the young kids and males. They didn't have an immediate function to the farmer, Odette's employer, the Daguerre family. She was entrusted with their safety. That had gone fairly well, except for rainstorms and getting lost once or twice.

She hadn't told the Daguerre's that she'd met *Le Comte*. The Count was the man who opened the door behind her at the chateau, as she cowered there during the strange icy rain. The man with the scary face. He was tall and broad-shouldered but stooped a little like the weight of the world sat on his shoulders. He might have been handsome once but now he had a horrible scar from the fighting, he said. A duel with another noble over some perceived slight.

She must have been staring at it. She couldn't help it, it was a long, angry scar that went from his lower eyelid to his chin. He seemed self-conscious about it, turning away from her eyes. He wasn't particularly friendly but he did talk to her for a moment before sending her back outside in the rain.

The only person she'd told about meeting *le comte* was Margot, who ran the milking shed. A pleasant, smiling girl who taught Odette everything there was to know on the farm, Margot had promised to keep her secret. Everyone would want to know that *le comte* was back from Paris. It wasn't common knowledge but if they found out Odette had met him she would be deluged with gossips. He was an important man, but hated by some. Odette didn't mention the scar; Margot didn't have time for gossip. She needed Odette to learn milking fast because they'd lost another farm worker. He had run off to Spain where he heard things were better. Where he'd got that information was unknown.

Odette gripped the teats of the goat as she'd been taught. The animal twitched and attempted to get away but she was tethered well. Odette patted her neck and spoke soothingly, the way Margot had taught her. A calm goat is a good producer, she said. Soon Odette was expressing milk into the pail. The rhythmic sound of the liquid hitting the metal was very satisfying. She forgot about the heavy odor of the animals completely.

Late that night she stepped out of the kitchen to check on her herd. Just because she was milking in the morning and evening didn't mean she could neglect her regular responsibilities. She was tired but it was good to be helpful and she didn't mind the hard work. A ten-year-old boy could tend the goat herd but there wasn't one available. So many men had been conscripted into the Army or gone to fight with the partisans. Or run off to Spain.

She walked past the milking shed and the grain store. The summer crops had been a disappointment. At least no nobles had come to confiscate their wheat— yet. There were tales circulating of heavy-handed tax collectors and hated elites who either burned the wheat stores to the ground or confiscated it. Did *le comte* do horrible things like that? She had no one to ask. The harvest here wouldn't go to market. There wasn't enough. They would grind it and make bread for the farm. Odette wished she worked in the kitchen sometimes. She adored making bread with her mother as a child, the texture and sweetness of the dough.

She reached the gate that led to the pastures. The light was fading and she could only make out a group of six goats in a nearby field. She kept walking, making the little clicking sound that sometimes made them come to her. More often they ignored it but it was worth a try.

Odette hadn't heard from her parents in over a year. They were in Normandy then but said they would soon move on as there was no work. They didn't know where she was either. She'd had nowhere to write to them. It was very sad. She'd had one letter from her younger brother who was attending classes in Lyon. Somehow, during all the turmoil, the university kept its doors open and its students fed. It was a blessing. Her brother was so smart. Odette's heart swelled, thinking of him as a scholar and a thinker. He would be a great man one day. When all this was done, she hoped to go to Lyon. She wanted to see him in action.

Something moved off to the left by a copse of trees. How could the goats have gotten so far on their tether? They were full of mischief. She headed across the pasture and reached the trees. Shadows were deep here. She paused, peering into the dark.

"Come here, my pets," she cooed. "Time to go home."

A grunt came from behind a tree, followed by the rustling of leaves and a groan. She startled. "Who's there?"

"*Aidez*—" A voice, male, whispered. "*Aidez-moi.*"

Who needed help? Odette couldn't see anyone. She stepped toward the voice. "Where are you?"

"*Ici.* Here."

She almost stumbled over his leg, outstretched from behind a tree trunk. "Oh. *Pardon.*" She leaned down. He was slumped to one side, holding his other leg. "Are you injured?"

"My leg," he whispered.

A cloth was wrapped around his thigh. His face was taut with pain. His long hair was tangled with leaves. How long had he been out here?

"I'll be back in a moment. Stay right here," she said stupidly. He wasn't going anywhere. She ran back to the barn, struggling to open the heavy door. She found the wheelbarrow tipped up in a corner, righted it, and pushed it outside.

The old thing was heavy and clumsy to maneuver through the lumpy pasture. Finally, she was back at the copse. She left the wheelbarrow and stepped in to the darkness, hoping the man was still alive.

"*Allo? Monsieur?*"

"I am here." His voice was very weak. "Can you help me? I need water."

"We must get you inside. I have the wheelbarrow if you can stand—"

"Not inside. Too many questions."

Was he a criminal? How had he been injured? Where was he from?

Those questions.

She was able to reassure him that she would only take him to the barn. It was too cold to spend the night outside in his condition. She would bring him food and water to the barn and keep his presence a secret, if that was what he wanted. For some reason he believed her.

With her help, he rose on his good leg and hopped to the wheelbarrow. He was tall and muscular, easily a foot taller than she was. It was awkward with him draped over her shoulders. She pushed him into the wheelbarrow. He moaned in pain but held on to the sides as she managed to get him back across the bumpy pasture, through the gate, and into a little-used fruit store that smelled of fermented plums. It was clean enough and she brought over some hay from the barn for him. Then she went back to the house, let herself in the kitchen and pumped water into a bucket and stuck a small piece of cheese in her skirt pocket.

He was asleep, or unconscious, when she returned, his dark hair splayed across his face. It was a handsome face of a man not old but not young either. His hands were black with dirt, the way hers had looked while she walked south. Water was for drinking not washing. She set down the bucket and left the cheese wrapped in a handkerchief. If only she had a blanket, she thought. The nights were getting cold. But he was well-dressed in a wool coat and trousers. She straightened his coat to cover him better. His boots of good black leather looked much nicer than her walking shoes. She looked at his wound under his hand. Old blood stained the tourniquet around his thigh. Tomorrow, when he was rested, she would see about getting him help with that.

"*Merci, mademoiselle,*" he croaked as she stood to go. "*Beaucoup.*"

NINE

MALCOUZIAC

The Dordogne sun shone bright and hot on the table where Merle sat sipping her second *café au lait* and re-reading what she'd written. She'd been back in the village for twenty-four hours and was still looking through her research notes from her productive day at the American University. And then there was Pascal.

His call during the train home from Paris had put him in an odd mood. Another one. Was it Clarisse again? He wouldn't say. If it wasn't Clarisse wouldn't he have said? She had never encountered this with Pascal before, this moodiness and secrecy. Of course, everyone had moods. Life gives a person moods. Smooth sailing life was not. But Pascal's mood deepened on the train and when they arrived in Bergerac he announced abruptly that Merle must get a rental car and get herself home. He couldn't take her after all. He had to work.

And that, the suddenness of it, the quick goodbyes, had put Merle in a bit of a funk. The honeymoon period was over with her Frenchman. When they run off like a husband on a business trip, all preoccupied and brisk, ready to be gone, off into action in the world instead of being happy at home with you—? It pained her. This was an awkward patch in their relationship, she realized, maybe even a turning point where they could go forward or not. Seeing Clarisse had made that clear. He still had some feelings of responsibility toward her, maybe something more, even if she was trying to extort money out of him. And the boy had rattled him too.

Was it a midlife crisis? She sighed. Male midlife crises were so predictable. He was probably the right age for one. Did Frenchmen have midlife crises, or just take a new lover and call it good? Did they buy red convertibles and grow snazzy beards? Was Merle his midlife lover? Was there someone else? What did that mean?

There were too many questions without answers.

Maybe she would go see Irene who owned the goats and get away from the questions in her head. Yes, she would call the goat farmer tonight and see when was a good time. But could she stay at Pascal's like before? He hadn't given her a key to his cottage. It was a dreamy little place on the top of a hill north of Toulouse, shabby, dusty, and isolated: there was nothing to dislike about it. Last May she'd zoned out in the garden, watching apple blossoms fall to earth. And learning about goats from Irene. That's where she'd dreamed up Odette and her French revolutionary adventures. It would be an excellent place to work on the book.

The waiter came by. He was young, new to the village, or at least not someone Merle recognized. With fewer than 500 residents she recognized many of the young ones; Malcouziac was nearly seventy-five percent elderly. This man was not 30, scrawny, with pimples and thin, mean lips. She caught his eye.

"I think I'll have some lunch," she said. He brought her a menu. It was nearly lunch time and a few more tables filled with diners, enjoying the summer sunshine on the terrace of the café. The waiter got busy with the other people, bringing them menus and napkins and salt shakers, adjusting umbrellas, finding chairs. She laid her menu down to wait, having decided again on the *salade de campagne*, the country salad, a fabulous sort of chef's salad with bacon and hard-boiled eggs.

She looked up at the man sitting two tables over, facing her, and startled. It was the man with the scar again. He was alone this time, perusing the plastic-covered menu. Merle looked away, uncomfortable to be so close again to him. Who was he? He had made his way into her story as the face of the Count. Her character couldn't keep her eyes off the scar— and neither could she.

How embarrassing. Maybe she should go home for lunch.

The waiter arrived. "Madame?"

She mumbled her way through her order, splurging on a glass of bubbly Gaillac Perlé. Pascal had introduced her to it. She kept her voice down and the waiter had to bend closer to hear her. For some reason she didn't want the stranger to hear her American accent. When the waiter took away her menu she went back to her notebook, head down, eyes down. The classic pose of someone who doesn't want to be interrupted.

She picked her way through her salad, sipping the dry sparkling wine and looking at birds in the fountain nearby. For nearly an hour she sat curled over her work and her lunch, biding her time. She ordered another coffee. The man with the scar finished his meal and rose to leave. She watched him throw down some money and glance at her, then he wound through the tables. He rounded the corner on the plaza and disappeared.

When the waiter returned with her coffee she asked him if he knew who the man was. He looked confused. She pointed at the now-empty table and made a quick gesture to indicate the scar. The waiter shook his head.

"*Désolé, madame*. I am new here," he said.

"*Je m'appelle* Merle Bennett," she said, introducing herself. She held out a hand. He looked embarrassed but took her hand limply. "I am American but will be living here on Rue de Poitiers for a few months. Until Christmas."

The waiter couldn't have cared less about her residency in the village. He nodded politely and disappeared with her dirty dishes. Well, she tried. Maybe he'd make it through the summer and they'd meet again.

Still, she wanted to know who that stranger was. She couldn't say why exactly. He played some part in her story so maybe they were meant to meet. He didn't look like a friendly person, not with those intense eyes and that sneer. He looked about sixty, with gray hair. He wore ordinary clothes, like a farmer would wear when he came into town, plain but serviceable. Was he a farmer? He must live around here.

Her mind was on overdrive again. Something about that man made her imagination run. Her musings kept her mind off Pascal and Tristan, what they were up to, how they were doing, why didn't they call, why didn't they write. She didn't want to be that sort of lover, or mother. She would give them space.

In this room of her own, here in Malcouziac with time to burn, she could wonder about strangers. Make up imaginary lives for them, conjure up scary counts and goat herders and men with bad legs. A sinister-looking stranger in real life was almost as fascinating. How had he gotten that scar? Was he also in a duel? Maybe a knife fight. Where did these knife fights take place? She could see him in her imagination, crouched, snarling, throwing a long knife between his hands menacingly.

Oh dear. Too much coffee?

She pushed back her cup and gathered up her notebook and library print-outs. She'd copied out an article in an obscure library journal from the 1960s. The author made the case for the gothic novel, or gothic romance, as part of a long history of slightly-scary, mildly-romantic stories told around the campfire for millennia. One of the author's points was the use of physical appearance as a ruse, a foil, either to distract the reader or lead her astray. To make the point that everything is not as it appears.

Was the scar on the man— or the Count in her story— hiding something? Was he not really a bad person after all, but perceived that way because humans are so quick to judge by outward appearances? Was it his mask, in a way, like the *Phantom of the Opera*? Or his deformity like the *Hunchback of Notre Dame*? Did it keep the world at arms' length, and did he want it that way? Was it up to the rest of the characters to learn how to see past the exterior and see the inner goodness?

Was this the real meaning of the gothic novel? That people perceive what they want, see what they want to see, judge others on the wrong criteria, and are often wrong? Wasn't Jane Austen's *Pride and Prejudice* based on that? It had, after all, originally been titled 'First Impressions.'

Such a common, even dominant, trait in humans. We see people, and despite whatever opposing information we learn later, those first impressions take root. Then the gothic novel is a story of immaturity, or the fallacies of impressionable youth, that then must be taught the more adult way to live.

She jotted that down, quite pleased with herself. She had no idea if it was right or wrong, but did it matter really? Every writer probably had some half-baked idea of what fiction was about. What *humanity* was about. She would make a large card with that theme on it, and hang it on her fireplace near her laptop.

After she paid her bill, Merle went into the café to use the restroom, sauntering slowly through the small interior to see if she recognized anyone who might know the man with the scar. Her literary ramblings hadn't diminished her curiosity. Behind the bakery counter was the young woman who often waited on her, a sweet-faced brunette with very blue eyes. After using the toilet, Merle passed her again, remembering that the girl's English was nonexistent. It would be difficult to explain in French over the huge display case why she was so curious about a stranger.

Back outside Merle decided to visit her neighbors. One of them must know who the stranger was. She'd hardly seen Albert since she'd been back, and hadn't located Josephine yet. Her elderly neighbors made up her entire social circle in Malcouziac, at least when the chic Parisians next door weren't around.

Josephine's small half-timbered house looked the same: shuttered and empty. Merle knocked hard on the door shutters and tried to peer through the crack. Still no answer. She looked around to nearby houses and picked the one to the left where a small tricycle sat abandoned on the front step.

Children's voices came from inside as she knocked on the freshly-painted red door. A young mother arrived, baby on her hip.

"*Bonjour, madame,*" Merle said. "*Je cherche Josephine Azamar.*" *I am looking for Josephine.* She gestured to the old woman's house.

"Ah—" The woman rattled off something very fast that sounded like Josephine had been gone for some time.

"*Pardon.*" Merle shrugged helplessly. "*Je suis Americaine. Parlez-vous anglais?*" *Do you speak English?*

The woman's eyes rounded in surprise as the baby wiggled in her arms. "A little. Do you want me to repeat?" Merle sighed in relief. "Madame left in the springtime. To live with her sister in the Nîmes. Half-sister, I think. We were all so very happy for her as she was lonely and recently took a bad fall on the cobbles. And Nîmes is said to be very pretty."

"I'm sorry I missed her." Merle frowned. "She had a key to my garden. I'm sorry, I'm Merle Bennett. The last house on Rue de Poitiers?"

"Oh, *le beau jardin*— the beautiful garden. Josephine tells me this."

Now not so *beau.* "She was taking care of it. Did she perhaps give you the key?"

"No, *madame,* I am sorry." She turned and said something in French to another child who came to get the baby. "I do have access to her home though."

She led Merle through her happy, toy-strewn house and out the back. Her garden was simple, also full of children's toys and tiny furniture. They went into the alley, then the woman unlocked

Josephine's garden gate. Her garden was small but breathtaking, full of roses and pots overflowing with pink and white geraniums.

"I tend the garden for her until her return," the woman explained. "Just watering. It is no trouble."

"She is a fabulous gardener."

"*Ah, oui.* Now where would your key be?"

They spread out in the tiny garden, looking for a key hanging somewhere as the other one had in Merle's yard. It only took minutes to determine it wasn't there. The house was locked up tight and the woman didn't have a key.

At the door, Merle had a thought. "I am looking for someone to remove a cistern from my garden, and to build a small addition, and to renovate a laundry. Can you recommend anyone in the area?"

The woman, Laure Thibaud, was pleased to say that her husband had a construction company. She gave Merle a business card and told her to call him, that he would be most happy to help.

So it wasn't a complete waste of time, Merle thought, pocketing the card as she rounded the corner to Albert's house. The old priest came to the door looking as if he had been napping, all three hairs on his head wild, wiping his glasses on his shirt hem.

"Ah, Merle, come in, come in." He escorted her through his monk-like, tidy house to the kitchen where he made her sit and have tea and cookies which he called biscuits like the English. After all her coffee today she was floating away on hot drinks. They chatted about the weather and her trip to Paris, her research into the French Revolution. Albert told her a few things about Robespierre and the Committee for Public Safety that turned against him, sending him to the guillotine. Unlike Pascal, Albert, who had been a teacher at a private school, wasn't squeamish about the period, giving her lots of juicy details about the Reign of Terror.

"Do you remember a man sitting near us at dinner the other night, at *Les Saveurs*?" she asked after a lull in the conversation. Albert seemed more alert today, not like that night at the restaurant.

He seemed distracted then and she'd been a little worried about his mental state. "He had a terrible scar on his face, down one cheek?"

Albert set down his cup and frowned. "No, I am sorry."

"He was sitting near my end of the table. I was just wondering if you knew who he was. How he got that scar."

"Scar?"

Didn't he know the word? She raised her voice a little. "He has a scar, an injury, a line down his face." She traced a line down from her eye. "Like this."

Albert said nothing, just shook his head.

"You never saw him?"

"No. As I said." He looked over her shoulder at his plum tree. "There are many people with strange faces, are there not?"

"Of course. I was just curious." Which was a little weird, her morbid fascination with a stranger. Best to drop the subject. There were many people with scars and deformities, as he said. No reason to obsess about one.

Unless you were writing a gothic novel that featured a man with a scar.

Her long to-do list rose up in her mind, as it often did. On it was prominently placed: *French lessons.*

"Albert? Would you tutor me in French? I can pay you of course."

The old priest blinked. "Me? No, I am too old for such things." He touched his chin dramatically, the picture of the thinker. Then his eyes widened. "Ah, yes! You remember *Madame* Armansett?"

Merle shook her head. "Does she live here?"

"Yes, she helped you with translation. In the— the jail."

Merle had been held briefly for murder two years before. It was all a big mess, a fight over her house. The entire village seemed conspired against her. The translator, *Madame* Armansett, was an elegant older woman with upright bearing who looked like Catherine Deneuve.

"Oh, yes. Is she tutoring?"

"She teaches English here in the village. I will ask first then give her your telephone."

Merle thanked him. She wondered if she'd ever hear from *Madame*. She seemed a bit haughty to be lowering herself to tutoring. But a teacher would be good for learning the language.

"When will Pascal be back?" Albert asked.

"I'm not sure. He's working somewhere." She smiled. "You know how he is. Top secret."

They talked a little more about goings-on in the village. A *fête*, a new pharmacy, the Thursday market. Merle invited him to her house for dinner the next night and he accepted. Maybe he would remember the stranger between now and then.

Or maybe she'd see him herself.

LÉO DELAGE WAITED in the shadows near the old arcades, where pigs and chickens were once sold. Now it would be specialty lettuce and *foie gras* and fine speckled eggs, he supposed. He wasn't interested in the fine foods of France. They had lived in his dreams for many years. But no more.

He watched the American come out of the café and look around. He'd been following her since morning when he'd made his way from his old van where he'd spent the night. The car park for the village was tucked away outside the ancient walls. No one bothered him there. It had not been convenient that she recognized him at the café. He had been foolish, too bold, to bring his co-workers to that fancy restaurant the previous week. He'd had to make himself scarce that night but no matter. He was acting on instinct now.

The search for the man in the straw hat, the one who drove the green car, had been laughably easy, once the little man— *l'imbécile*, Antoine-Luc, got drunk and started ranting and prancing in the village. Getting him drunk had been fairly straightforward, though expensive. Then the grandson of the vintner told him the man was a wine buyer named Paul Duguay from Lyon. There was, naturally, no such person.

Léo knew that policemen often used false names similar to their own, and he knew the name of his nemesis. He knew he had the right man. Pascal d'Onscon was not listed anywhere either, of course. As a policeman, he would be very careful about that. He did, however, give the grandson a mobile number. And that was his mistake.

The police thought criminals were stupid, and, it was true, many were. But Léo Delage, he was different. He had two years at the *École Nationale Supérieure Agronomique* in Toulouse before he was called home to learn the wine trade at his father's knee. He knew how to find someone, just as he knew how to hold a grudge, how to honor vengeance, and how to fight like hell.

That policeman had no *grande école* education. And he thought himself so superior.

The woman walked briskly in her short summer dress, past the fountain, to the west out of the plaza. Léo pushed himself out of the shadows, watched her disappear, and followed.

TEN

The vandals came back.

Merle had been coming and going through the alley, working on the gate's handle, patching broken slats, repainting the gate, installing a cheap new metal bistro table and chairs, finding a nursery for new plants. She was so obsessed with (yes, obsession was one of her issues) on returning her garden to its past glory that she didn't see the damage in the front right away. It took Madame Suchet tapping on her front door to get her to notice.

Her neighbor was wringing her hands and muttering in French, a pitiful grimace on her kindly face. Merle was confused but tried to calm her. Mme Suchet pulled her outside and waved her arm at the front of the house.

The vandals had used different colors this time: yellow, blue, and green. They weren't quite so artistic as last time, or tall, concentrating their mayhem on the ground floor walls. Several of the tags looked like symbols but of what, she couldn't tell. What the hell was wrong with people, Merle thought, covering her mouth with a hand to keep from cursing aloud.

"I am so sorry, Madame Bennett," Mme Suchet said. "I did not see them again. At least you had not completed the cleaning yet or there would be another cost to you."

"Yes, that's lucky," Merle mused, feeling anything but lucky in this unlucky little *ville*. "Now I really have to talk to the police."

"Oh, *absolument*. We can hope they will catch the bad men. Whoever they are."

"Do you have any idea who might be doing this?" Merle asked.

Mme Suchet shook her head, biting her lips as if trying not to speculate. Merle waited her out. "There has been some talk, in the village."

"About what? A certain person?"

A Gallic shrug. "I will ask at church. Someone must know."

Merle reassured the woman that she would take care of it. Mme Suchet told her the police were now stationed in Sulliac, a larger village ten miles away. To the east, she explained, pointing to the west helpfully.

There was only one problem. Merle had no car. In the past she'd borrowed Albert's ancient Deux-Chevaux, a classic Citroën that offered a wrestling match with the gear shift rather than an easy drive. But Albert had told her that his 2CV was out of commission and it was too costly to fix so he was just letting it gather dust until he could decide what to do with it.

The day had arrived. Merle Bennett would buy a car. It was time. She'd be in France for months this trip and would often have the need for her own wheels. She'd have to find a place to park it, a garage or at least a permanent parking spot outside the walls. She glanced up at the mess the vandals had left her and hoped they wouldn't do the same to her as-yet-unknown vehicle. She had calculated this cost into her trip and hoped to spend no more than € 5,000 on something that had four tires and an engine.

A small used car lot crouched by the only gas station in Malcouziac, about a quarter mile outside the old walls. Close enough to walk to, that was key. Merle took a few more photographs of the vandalism for the police, changed into slacks and walking shoes, and headed toward the southern gate of the village as her watch turned eleven.

The ESSO station was an eyesore, a slab of cracked concrete and asphalt with antiquated pumps, a dilapidated garage where two vehicles were up on lifts, greasy spots everywhere, including on the scalp of the man who greeted her. Jean-Paul, last name not required, was middle-aged, short, and swarthy, a highly-oiled individual of the used car salesman species. He wore a short-sleeved blue shirt and a thin black tie, and walked over to her briskly as she looked at his magnificent selection of autos.

Merle recognized the type of salesman, even though she'd never bought a car before. How embarrassing, at her age. She had no idea what to look for, how to deal with pushy salesmen, how to negotiate, how to avoid getting swindled. That last was impossible, she decided, watching Jean-Paul bounce on the balls of his feet and rub his hands together. To him she was fresh meat. He strung a rapid line of French together.

Did he speak English, she asked yet another French person. Thankfully he did.

Seven vehicles graced the side lot where weeds and grass went untrimmed. Most were fairly late models, no real clunkers, she assumed, seeing Peugeots and Renaults and a couple of British Vauxhalls with the steering wheel on the wrong side. Those were out, so now there were just five.

Jean-Paul steered her to the most expensive one, a black, heavy-bodied Mercedes that looked like it had seen a few mafia wars. It reminded her of her lawyer who'd helped her navigate the inheritance of Harry's house, and his flashy Benz, and not in an appealing way. She moved on, asking him about the next, a late-model Citroën in a lovely shade of blue. At €12,000 it was too much. Jean-Paul was delighted to explain the size of the engine, the number of miles on the odometer, and other, faintly pertinent details. She kept moving.

The last three were more ordinary French vehicles, two Renaults and one Peugeot. She pointed to the cheapest one, a Peugeot with several dents. The faded sign in the window said €7,500. Over her budget but the cheapest car on the lot. Obviously, she knew nothing about car prices.

Jean-Paul shook his head sadly.

"No, no, madame. That will not do. It has been in a crash, you see. My manager said not to sell it under any circumstances. Not until it is safe to drive. You need something immediately, no?"

"Yes, but— Why is it out here with a price on it if it's not for sale?"

He continued his lament. She could see what he was up to, trying to get her to buy something more expensive. But now she really wanted that Peugeot.

"What year is it?"

It was seven years old, maybe more, he said, and the odometer was not reliable. It said just 70,000 kilometers but was no doubt wrong. That was too low. Someone had fiddled with it. Besides, it had been a horrible crash. Lives may have been lost, he suggested vaguely. He nudged the side mirror to demonstrate. It wiggled slightly.

"How much will the repairs cost?"

"Oh, many thousands," he said, frowning. "At least four-thousand Euros, I am guessing."

Merle rounded the car which was dark gray and creased with long, horizontal scratches as if the owner lived down a narrow road in a forest. There was a large dent on the right rear fender, plus a smaller one on the driver's side door. The tires looked new. She opened the door and stuck her head into the passenger side. Someone had cleaned it with a fragrant potion. The seats were worn but clean and not terrible.

"Do you have the keys?" She held out her hand.

He shook his head violently, almost angry now. He refused to let her start the car and got red in the face when she insisted. He glanced back at the garage, put his hands on his hips in a comical fashion, and told her unequivocally that this car was not for sale.

Merle had had enough. She thanked Jean-Paul and hiked back

up the hill in the noon-day sun, sweating through her shirt. She'd hoped to find something she could live with but obviously buying a car wasn't something one did willy-nilly. She was much too practical to just buy anything a man like Jean-Paul pushed on her. Maybe there was another used car business nearby with more reputable people.

As she reached her fancifully decorated *maison de ville* her cell-phone rang. It was Madame Armansett, the English teacher. She was pleased to offer her tutoring services. Perhaps Madame Bennett could come by her home this afternoon to discuss the fee?

Happy to have at least accomplished that item on her list, Merle had a leisurely lunch in her garden and a quick shower before going to the Armansett residence. It was a lovely townhouse similar to hers but more modern with window boxes, green shutters, and spotless off-white stucco. The teacher opened the door, dressed in a tight, short-sleeved blouse tucked into a full skirt, a get-up that could have served June Cleaver well. Her makeup was flawless, her platinum hair done to perfection.

"Madame Bennett. Sit please. We meet again under more, shall we say, optimal circumstances."

They arranged themselves in parlor chairs covered in a riot of paisley. Sunshine poured through the windows, setting off the gleaming wood floor. The sweetness of lavender floated in the room. Merle had a moment of house envy.

They discussed schedule and fees, both of which seemed reasonable to Merle. They would meet twice a week here at the teacher's home unless one of them was out-of-town, then arrangements would be made. All was completed in minutes, no refreshments offered or required.

Merle stood to leave. "I could have used you this morning," she said, smiling. She liked Jacqueline Armansett, she decided, who was just a more formal person than most Americans. Maybe one day they'd be on a first-name basis. "I need a car but they wouldn't sell me one."

Madame blinked. "Where was this?"

"At the used car lot by the gas station. I assume the station owns it? I talked to Jean-Paul, do you know him? His English is pretty good."

The teacher straightened up, nostrils flaring. "I'm afraid I do know him." She stared at Merle then raised a finger. "One moment." She walked into the kitchen and spoke softly to someone. A man followed her out, wiping his chin with a napkin.

"My husband. Madame Bennett." They shook hands. His name was Hervé. He was tall and broad-shouldered, with a neat graying beard, wearing a suit. "She needs to buy an auto. She has talked to Jean-Paul."

"I see." Hervé spoke excellent English. "Madame, the ESSO is mine. Perhaps I can help."

And so it happened that Merle bought the Peugeot for more than she wanted to pay but much less than the sticker price, out from under Jean-Paul who had designs on the vehicle for himself. Merle couldn't hear what Hervé was yelling through the glass windows of the station, but it wasn't good. She didn't see Jean-Paul again.

Hervé assured her that the car had not been in a crash, that it had very low mileage plus new tires and shock absorbers. The only thing necessary was the dents pounded out. Perhaps a paint job. She didn't care about dents. Compared to her old mini-van at home this car was a palace on wheels. The financial arrangements were made, a complicated overseas financial transaction involving two banks plus several translators and currency exchanges. In two days she was the proud owner of a beat-up Peugeot the color of low-hanging rainclouds. Her first car purchase at fifty-one years old. She was so proud.

The morning after she took possession of her vehicle, Merle set out to find the police station in Sulliac which appeared to be more like twenty miles away and to the south. Apparently Mme Suchet had never actually been there. At any rate Merle had GPS on her phone because the roads in this section of France were poorly marked with little white arrows pointing to this town or that highway. Too bad if you weren't going that far or didn't know what the big city was in the direction you needed to go.

Sulliac was one of those 'most beautiful villages of France'-type places, with luxuriant hanging baskets of flowers on every lamppost and a long green park next to a slow-moving river. The river itself was on the brown side of picturesque but it did make a pretty picture with ducks swimming and children running alongside. No *bastide* walls here, just winding avenues and more tourists than in Malcouziac.

The police station was tucked away behind the *mairie*, the town hall, just as Malcouziac's had once been. She wondered why her village had lost their *gendarme*. Because he was a criminal? (He was.) But that was two years ago. Was the lack of a gendarme what led to petty crime like vandalism? Their last policeman had been horrible but at least he kept his nose in everyone's business, strutting around, discouraging crime. Merle hadn't liked it then but it was possible she missed at least a little police presence.

Inside the small, industrial-style building she explained in French what had happened — twice — to her house to a woman in a police uniform behind the counter. The woman was blond and attractive, with a wary coldness in her glance. She nodded, filling in blanks in a long form, asking a few questions as to when, why, where, and who she was.

"You are not a French citizen, madame?"

"No. I am a homeowner, however." Merle didn't like the way this was going.

"Are you the sole owner of the house?"

She started to say 'yes' but remembered the way the estate had been divvied up. Her son Tristan owned half, per French law. "With my son. We both inherited it from my late husband who was a French citizen."

"We require your son's signature on the complaint," the policewoman said primly.

Merle explained he was in the United States. The policewoman

said it could be mailed to him and returned, although she acknowl-
edged that would take weeks as the government did not send by air
mail. Merle got out her phone and showed the woman the
photographs. She nodded gravely, as if she cared about the state of
Merle's house. "*Ç'est dommage*," she muttered, eyes like ice.

"All right," Merle said impatiently. "Give me the form and I'll
mail it to him." She wasn't going to let bureaucracy keep the police
from doing their duty. They obviously discouraged complaints this
way, especially from foreigners. "In the meantime, does anyone need
to see the damage, or, I don't know, come over to Malcouziac to look
for culprits? While there's still a possibility of evidence lying
around?"

The policewoman pushed a slice of gum into her mouth and
chewed slowly, keeping her cold eyes on Merle but not answering.

After a long stare-off Merle turned to go. "Thank you for all your
help, *madame le gendarme*. You've been most kind."

On the sidewalk Merle crumpled the form and dropped it cere-
moniously in a trash bin. Would they do nothing? She had filled out
another complaint form.

What Sulliac lacked in crime-fighting it had in shopping. There
was a large complex with both a grocery and a hardware store just
outside of town. Merle stocked up on things she couldn't get in
Malcouziac: frozen vegetables, crackers, hummus, light bulbs, scrap-
ers, rags, and a big can of paint remover. Two large padlocks, one for
the gate and one for the front, along with several potted plants that
she couldn't resist.

As she was pulling out of town she saw a *brocante*, an antique
shop, with a side yard full of junky household items like ancient
refrigerators, chipped sinks, and rusty ironwork. Her heart leapt a
little. Admiring Madame Armansett's lovely house had made her a
little crazy to fix her place up, make it shine. Harry was right, she
supposed. She did love old houses, as he'd posited in his will. She
loved transforming them into something they had lost. It felt like
bringing back the dead.

Wandering the enclosed yard she spotted a pair of tall shutters with curved tops, just like her original ones. The blue paint was a faint memory but they appeared intact. She picked through the appliances and doorknobs and pulled them out. They might be too tall— she hadn't measured the doorway— but that half-round top was perfection. The owner helped her tie them on the roof of her trusty new vehicle. He cautioned her to drive slowly, not that he needed to. She could barely see the road with the shutters dangling over the windshield.

This Peugeot car was just the best, she mused, rubbing the steering wheel as she passed a field full of sunflowers, nodding to the eastern horizon. Just like France.

LATER THAT NIGHT, after a light meal in the garden, after wrangling the awkward shutters off the roof of the car and getting them into the garden, after finding a place to park the Peugeot far away in the public lot, Merle heard from Pascal. It was a text, not very personal, and too short for her liking, but it was something.

My blackbird, how are you? I apologize for my abrupt leaving at the train. I have had to return to Paris but will see you as soon as possible. P

What did you reply to that? It didn't actually require a reply, did it? She stared at it, annoyed. Then she was annoyed with herself. Of course Pascal had to work. He couldn't hang around painting shutters and patching the roof the way he had when he was undercover in Malcouziac, spying on winemakers. There were bad guys to catch everywhere. Why had he gone back to Paris though? Was it Clarisse or work?

Meeting his ex-wife was probably not a good idea. When she was just a ghost from the past, the ex was a concept without much power.

But as an attractive blond, with high heels and a tight skirt, she entered Merle's imagination. Where there was often fertile ground.

Stop obsessing about lovely Clarisse. He doesn't love her. He loves you.

That little self-lecture warmed her until the stars popped out. The very smooth and saucy Pinot Noir she'd splurged on at the store in Sulliac didn't hurt either.

Merle took her notebook to bed. She glared at her to-do list, hoping to bully it into submission. Very few items had been crossed out yet. She was falling behind. And yet she wanted to keep writing the novel. Maybe she should it put it off until the weather turned cold?

Merde. She was going to need a source of heat in this house. Something besides the fireplace. She scribbled *Woodstove?* on the bottom of her very long list.

Then she turned to her notes about the novel. Carefully she re-read the chapters she'd written, making notes on the side for changes, additions, ideas. It was so comforting to live in another world where the mundane was an afterthought, where pain was just a word, where one had control of all events, and the author was a god.

She fell asleep dreaming of Odette. And Pascal. Just a little about Pascal.

ELEVEN

PARIS

Pascal was not pleased.

Several days earlier, he had been summoned to the headquarters for *Policier Nationale*, a big buff-colored block near the Tuilleries in one of the finest ancient parts of Paris. Clean and efficient on the outside but it was never a good thing, being called back. Like being sent to the principal's office as a student, something that happened quite often in his youth. He liked to fight, he admitted once to a headmaster. Truly there was nothing better in his youth than a good dust-up. If someone picked a fight with him, he wasn't going to say 'no.' And more often than not it was his mouth that started a fight.

He'd learned to curb that tendency. His superiors at the *Policier* didn't like criticism, and his co-workers were too busy, often stretched to the limits of their time and abilities to solve crimes, locate perpetrators, and juggle court appearances. He'd learned much from them, and no longer, after these many years in the service, gave any of them a bad time. Some were even friends, and he trusted his life to any of them.

Still, he was not happy. The building was grim, utilitarian.

Nothing about it conjured up his silly description of France to Merle, a gastronomic Disneyland of sunflowers. No flowers here. No funhouse rides. Just the smell of burnt coffee.

He found the conference room on the third floor and let himself in. He hoped he hadn't done something stupid. But if he had, what could they do? The union would protect him. He felt a smirk forming on his mouth and wiped his lips to remove it.

The meeting, as it turned out, was a dull affair, the annual round-up of expenses, caseloads, arrests, convictions, and failures of same. The entire wine fraud division, minus a few lucky sons-of-bitches who had good excuses, was present. Some officers were commended, others berated. Pascal skated through unmentioned, and was pleased about that. The gathering of the division was held every year, after the end of the fiscal year, and somehow Pascal always found a way to miss it, even to the point of forgetting that it occurred. He was deep into field work this time each summer, looking for action in the down-time before the *vendange*, the harvest. A fertile time for criminals, when the anticipation of a poor harvest drove some to fraud.

Why was he not there now? How had they managed to trick him into attending this tedious afternoon? He slouched, tapped his pen rhythmically, and yawned. Finally, the meeting ended with all his fellow officers dashing from the room like freed prisoners. Pascal jumped to his feet as well. Then the director called his name.

He skidded to a stop near the door. The director, a burly man of sixty, once an ace undercover detective himself, nodded to him. "A moment, d'Onscon?"

Ah, he thought. *Now I get the strap.*

He walked back slowly and took a seat next to his boss. "*Ça va, Étienne?*"

"Can't complain. If I did no one would listen." He squinted at Pascal. "How is the Domaine Bourboulenc operation going? You did not answer my inquiries."

"I'm sorry about that. I leave that cellphone in my car while I'm working, as I'm sure you did as well when you were in the field?"

The director nodded cautiously. "And—?"

"They are cagey. The grandson is the key. He is keen to be my friend and I have been cultivating him."

"No evidence yet? Have they moved grapes to Châteauneuf?"

"Not that I've seen. But the *vendange* comes soon. I will keep a close eye on their operation."

The director understood the wine business, its schedule, the demands of weather, the flow of events, better than anyone. He knew the harvest would not be for several weeks at the earliest, depending on the rains and cold.

"Good," the director muttered. "Now, something else. You remember one of your first successes, the arrests made at Le Grand Vinon?" He looked at a sheet of paper in front of him. "It was before my time as director but I heard of it of course. You nabbed the scion. A nasty piece of work he was."

Pascal would never forget. It was his first big case and he had found and cultivated the players himself, worming his way into their confidence over many months. It was in the Sancerre, a rolling *terroir* in the Loire Valley. He still remembered those odd little wine caves built into chalky cliffs where ancient humans had once lived. And the delicious taste of gunflint in the white wine.

"Of course. Fifteen years ago."

"The son, the one masterminding the fraud, was one Léo Delage?"

Pascal nodded. He would never forget the nights spent playing cards and drinking with the man who was at least a dozen years older but acted like a reckless lad, boastful and careless. And he would also never forget arresting him with a team of uniformed police and their dogs. The trial was short but vicious.

"He received a ten-year sentence as I recall."

"And got out in eight. Ten was a bit long." The director smiled, softening the criticism. All policemen liked a good, long sentence for their arrests. "And then he disappeared for awhile. We assume he went overseas because we lost track of him."

"Good riddance," Pascal said.

"*Oui.* But four months ago, he returned to France."

A chill went down Pascal's spine, causing the hairs on his neck to rise. "Did he?"

"He entered through the port of Marseille. He used his passport, though it was expired. They confiscated his documents but he jumped the gate there while the officers weren't looking. He got lost in the crowd."

"This was four months ago?"

"In April. We only heard about it in a quarterly report where the names, or possible identities, of persons entering the country illegally are listed. As you imagine it takes some time to track down the names. Their identities are often *faux.* Most have no papers at all. The refugees for instance."

Pascal frowned, trying to calculate the risk of the man he'd arrested all those years ago. Would he still be a threat? "Where was he for those years?"

"We don't know. A man like this, he may use several names, with more than one passport. He made a lot of unsavory friends in prison, I'm told."

PASCAL PUSHED THROUGH THE DOORS, out into the sunshine. Paris hummed along, warm and humid, a bit of odor blowing off the Seine but looking no worse for its criminals, terrorists, and scam artists. Tourists snapped photos, mothers pushed babies in strollers, it was calm and unsuspecting.

And seemed, in that moment, to hold danger behind every well-trimmed shrub and polished streetlamp.

The director didn't have any wise words. He didn't tell Pascal what to do about this potential threat, the man he'd once befriended and betrayed. Pascal knew how he'd feel if someone spent months pretending he was your pal only to suddenly turn you in to *les flics.*

He had a pretty good idea how Léo Delage was feeling, after spending eight years behind bars for his part masterminding a classic counterfeit wine swindle.

Not happy. Not happy at all.

The question was whether that unhappiness had simmered so long that it had hardened into contempt. Or revenge. Or hatred.

Or all three.

Where was Léo Delage now? Still in the Marseille area, working as a dock worker where no one asks questions and the shipyards are run by organized crime? Or back in wine country, using his skills to rehabilitate himself? If Pascal had to guess, Léo had wandered home. Possibly he was working at his old winery, although that was forbidden under the terms of his sentence. He wasn't to set foot on the place, let alone work there. His son now ran the business, the director had told Pascal, and was doing a fine job of running it into the *terroir*, so to speak. He had left the seminary and his dream of the priesthood to try to save his inheritance. But maybe with Papa home from his travels things were looking up.

Maybe it was time to pay a visit to the Le Grand Vinon again. Yes, a sip of *Sancerre*, full of mineral and citrus, shining gold as the sun, well, that would go nicely too.

TWELVE

MALCOUZIAC

Merle had been working her way down her to-do list, replanting her garden, having the door shutters cut down, applying paint remover to her stone house, installing new locks, and discussing projects with Laure Thibaud's husband, the contractor. She was feeling good about her progress. She had two weeks before she would head home to get Tristan situated at school and was working hard to get things rolling for when she was gone.

Then someone named Louise Fayette called. It took a moment for Merle to remember Irene's daughter, Louise. The neighbor of Pascal, Irene raised goats and had let Merle help with the birthing—actually called 'kidding'— last May. Merle had never known Irene's last name. Louise, normally a quiet, shy college girl, was agitated about something and her English was failing her.

"*Je*— I cannot do it," she stuttered. "It is too much."

"Slow down, Louise. What is too much?"

"*Ma mère,* my mother, she has, um— surgery. On the leg, the knee."

"I'm sorry to hear that. Is she all right?"

"Ah, *oui*, as bossy as ever. But she must stay off her leg for four weeks more."

"That would be hard." Irene was an active though plump woman of indeterminate age. Louise was college-age so Irene was probably not sixty yet. Apparently, they mostly did everything on the goat farm themselves. "Who is milking the goats?"

"*C'est moi, bien sûr.* I do it all, madame. But I must go back to college. I have found someone to do the work on the farm until my mother is back on her feet. I am worried though. She will not use the crutches. She will not stay in her chair."

Merle made some sympathetic noises. What did Louise want?

And there it was: "Can you come? Just for three days or so? Cook her some meals, make sure she eats and stays off her leg? I am so worried she will need surgery again if she doesn't behave as her *docteur* says. I have asked everyone who lives near here and they are so busy with harvest and such. Her sister lives far away, in the Savoie."

"Oh." Merle looked at her notebook, sitting on the new metal garden table. Would she have a chance to write there? Irene couldn't be that much trouble. She'd been meaning to go see her. And it was just three days. "Of course I can come, Louise. When do you need me?"

Louise sighed in relief. "*Merci beaucoup, merci, madame.* Can you come tomorrow?"

IT WAS late afternoon the next day when Merle rolled up the hill where Pascal and Irene lived in close proximity but idyllic isolation, in an area full of fruit orchards, pastures, and a vineyard or two, outside of Toulouse about fifty miles. Once again her GPS had saved the day, and her new Peugeot was a steady companion, its new tires crunching through the dirt and gravel in the approach to the goat farm.

Louise was packed and more than ready to leave, springing to her feet, thrusting a list of instructions at Merle, and giving her a quick hug before making her escape. She would return in four days, she promised. Merle frowned. She'd said three days but what was one more? The young student jumped in her compact car and roared away to her university in Toulouse in a cloud of dust.

Merle set her bag down and shut the door. She hadn't even gotten inside and she was in charge of the invalid. She listened for signs of life and when she heard none, poked her head into doors leading off the hallway in the back of the house. In the first one she found the woman, snoring slightly, propped on pillows, with one leg in a brace. Merle shut the door quietly and went to unpack.

According to the scratched-out instruction sheet, Louise had given her a bedroom in the back, a spartan space suitable for monks and housemaids. At least Merle thought this was the bedroom described hastily by Louise. She looked into the other room and it seemed to belong to Louise, with clothes and perfume and lipstick and books strewn all over.

Back in the roomy country kitchen, Merle got out her notebook and tried to work while the house was quiet. She got a little done, stood to stretch, when Irene's voice screeched from the back: "Lou-lou! *Où es-tu?*"

"*Bonjour, Irene,*" Merle said, pushing open the bedroom door. "*C'est moi,* Merle Bennett."

It was then that Merle remembered Irene spoke no English. This could be interesting. But good immersion into French. Or a disaster of miscommunication. Take your pick.

Irene looked haggard and disheveled, her graying hair out of its customary bun and spread over the pillow. She pushed herself upright and stared at Merle.

"Who are you? What have you done with Lou-lou?" she demanded in French. "Get out of my house! Lou-lou!"

Merle introduced herself again and told Irene her daughter had to go back to college for a few days. Why hadn't Louise explained it all to her mother? What would happen, Merle wondered, when the term began? Would Irene be mobile by then? How long had it been since her surgery?

"I'm a friend of your neighbor, Pascal. We met in the spring. I helped with the births of the baby goats, remember?" Merle smiled gamely. What the hell had she gotten herself into?

Irene fell back against the pillow. "Oh. Yes, Louise told me you were coming. How is Pascal? We never see him these days."

Merle relaxed. "He's fine. Working somewhere. He works very hard."

Irene swept her arm at Merle as if to say, *right, sure, he works hard. But not as hard as I do.*

Which was probably true. Irene must have worked herself into a state and then hurt her leg or knee or something. She was hungry, she exclaimed. "Bring me some water and some cheese," she demanded, closing her eyes.

Merle scurried around the kitchen, finding a wooden tray at the ready and putting a glass of water and *un peu de fromage* on it. When she returned to the bedroom she found she was required to help Irene into a true sitting position, arrange many pillows, find a new pillow for under her knee, set the tray on the side table, search for her pills, and many other directives.

By the end of the first evening with Irene, Merle understood Louise's rush to leave. Merle already felt like a handmaiden to a queen, and a most unpleasant one at that. She had heated up the soup that Louise left for supper but it wasn't hot enough for Irene. It wasn't spiced correctly and there was no bread on her tray. The woman ate in bed, staring out the window of her bedroom at the barn where the goats were milked. Merle would have liked to go out there but she didn't think she should leave her patient. Maybe tomorrow.

When she went to get the tray, Irene told her to turn on her bedside lamp. The weak glow was barely enough to read by but Irene put on small reading glasses and demanded a magazine that she could have reached herself. Merle smiled patiently, handed it over, and picked up the tray. One meal down, eleven to go?

"Where is César? I must speak to him."

Merle paused. "Who is that?"

"César! Bring him in. I must speak to him about tomorrow's milk delivery."

Irene might have explained who this person was and Merle missed it. Irene's French was very brisk and laced with patois. Merle went to the door and looked for someone working in the goat shed or pastures. Flashes of Odette and her injured man danced in her imagination. The evening was still, a tender purple in the sky, the birds twittering in the fruit trees that lined the drive, and the occasional bleat of a faraway goat.

She stepped into the twilight. She'd forgotten the views from this hilltop, the sunset now charming the western range of trees and vineyards. A pink light caught a chimney top; there must be a house on that far hill, sheltered by ancient trees. It was so quiet, almost sacred, this rarefied moment of calm.

Then Irene hollered from inside the house, yelling for César. Merle straightened up and repeated his name at volume.

A man appeared from the goat shed. He was short, wearing a black apron that went almost to his shoes. He had a bandana tied around his head. He waved at Merle and waddled over slowly as if his knees or back hurt. As he got closer Merle realized he wasn't wearing a shirt. The apron front hung over his bare chest then was criss-crossed and tied in the front. It looked like leather and was well-worn, the sort of thing a blacksmith might wear. If you ever ran across a blacksmith these days.

He stopped a few paces away and looked shyly at Merle. He nodded, smiling.

"*César?*" He nodded again. "*Je m'appelle Merle*. I am taking Louise's place for a few days. Taking care of madame." Her French was crap, she knew it. She waited to see if he could understand her. His slightly goofy grin, complete with missing teeth, didn't falter. She continued, telling him Irene wanted him. He winced, shrugged, and loped into the house without a word.

He didn't stay long. By then it was time to help Irene to the bathroom and get her pills. When all that was accomplished, Merle said good night and left the woman to her devices.

She'd only been on duty for four hours and Merle was exhausted. The woman must be in pain, she decided, and it was making her grumpy and demanding. Merle had never been in this situation before, and to suddenly take care of someone that she didn't really even know was not ideal. She took a hot shower and went to bed early, hoping Irene slept through the night. It would be good for both of them.

The next morning she found César sitting at the kitchen table, eating a peach and drinking coffee. He was still shirtless in his black apron, his chest hair popping out saucily from behind the top. He was a curious man, swarthy with thick, muscular arms and thinning black hair and deep-set eyes. Perhaps Italian with a name like César? Merle was still in her robe. She nodded to him, checking her watch. It was six-thirty and full light. The sun rose early on a hilltop.

It seemed a little odd that Louise didn't mention César in her instructions. She said she'd hired someone but made no other mention of him. But Irene was in charge and, apparently, he knew goats. As Merle made herself coffee he said something about it being a good morning and made milking gestures. He held up his thumbs to say all done, or all good or something. Merle gave him a vague smile and went to get dressed.

The next two hours were busy, making and serving breakfast, getting Irene dressed, and all the chores related to helping an invalid. The woman complained about her leg, moaning when moving about, but refused to use the metal walker or crutches or even a cane, all of which perched near her bed. Merle didn't argue. She wasn't going to be here long. Louise could deal with her mother's recalcitrance later.

César appeared for lunch and Merle gave him a bowl of the soup from the night before. He used sign language and a grin to make his wishes known. Merle settled Irene back into bed for the afternoon. Her back hurt from propping up Irene.

Tucking her in again, fluffing her pillows, Merle straightened and sighed. "Okay?" Irene grimaced, arranging her leg on another pillow.

"*Ça va*," Irene grumbled. It goes, literally. Yes, it did just keep going.

"What's with César?" Merle asked in French. "Is he new here?"

"Louise found him somewhere. God knows where. But she says he's good with the goats."

"Is he French?"

"Greek. From some island. They know their goats there." Irene gave him grudging respect.

"I've been feeding him. Is that part of your arrangement?"

"Of course. Now I must rest." She shut her eyes. "Close the curtains."

Merle wandered back into the kitchen and looked at what was available in the tiny refrigerator for dinner: green beans, eggs, cheese, and something in a bowl. Her culinary skills were really not that advanced. Green bean quiche? Hmmm. And Louise had left without doing any marketing or instructions for meals.

She popped her head back into Irene's bedroom. "I need to go into the village for food, Irene."

Without opening her eyes, the woman waved a hand, a sweeping 'get-out' motion.

One trip into the village should be enough for the rest of her stay as live-in helpmate to the cranky Irene. What would make the woman happy in her state of pain? Merle would buy whatever they had and figure out what to do with it later.

The short trip down the hill to the village was a nice break. The sun shone hot and dry on the rocky hills. Irene's farmhouse crouched low against the landscape, dark with small windows. It was getting claustrophobic. The small store in the village was more of a convenience store than a true grocery, lots of beverages and some sad looking produce. Was there an outside market here? The village wasn't much more than a collection of houses. Limp lettuce it was then. Plus, frozen chicken and duck breasts, sausages, orange juice, and, of course, a couple bottles of wine. Maybe a little evening sip would put Irene into a better frame of mind.

When Merle returned with the groceries an hour later— she had taken a coffee break at the *boulangerie* and treated herself to a chocolate croissant— she noticed the front door was standing open. She startled, looking around the yard. Where was César? Had someone come while she was out?

She hurried inside. Nothing seemed out of place in the sitting room and kitchen. No humans to be seen. She rushed to Irene's door, still closed. A low moan came from inside and she pushed the door open. Irene was lying on the floor by the bed, writhing in pain, and cursing.

"Oh my god, what happened?" Merle said, helping her to a sitting position, then hoisting her up onto the bed with a grunt from both of them. "Are you all right? And your leg?"

Irene batted away her hands, still cursing. At least that's what Merle thought the words were, spoken with such venom. She stepped back.

"Get my pills. And ice."

Merle did her bidding, wrapping some ice cubes in a dish towel and getting her a glass of water and her pill bottle. Irene gulped down a pill and scooted back onto the bed, swinging her bad leg gingerly into position with her hands. She arranged the ice pack then fell back on the pillows and covered her face with her hands in a dramatic fashion.

"Irene?" Merle whispered. "Are you okay?"

"That bastard," she spat. "That Greek bastard."

"César?"

"Of course, César! What other Greeks do we have on the farm?" Her damp eyes were fierce and angry.

"Did he hurt you?"

"I heard him. Out in the kitchen, searching all the drawers. You must check. Go look in the bottom drawer by the sink. Bring me the wooden box!"

Merle backed out into the hallway and hurried to the kitchen. All the drawers in the large Welsh cupboard by the sink were closed, the doors, too. She kneeled down and began opening them, one by one. In the bottom drawer was a box that looked African, carved and inlaid with mother of pearl. She carried it back to the bedroom.

"*Donne le moi*. Give it, give," urged Irene, holding out her arms. Merle handed it to her and had a sinking feeling. She never should have left Irene to go to the grocery. She never should have gone anywhere. If César had stolen something it was her fault, for leaving Irene and the farm undefended.

The box was empty. Irene cried out in pain and fury, covering her eyes again. Now she wailed, sobbing that all the money from the last three markets was gone, that the Greek bastard was a thieving *connard* and that she was going to starve here alone, abandoned by her daughter, her friends, and, while she was at it, *La Republique*.

Merle eased onto the side of the bed, hoping to comfort Irene somehow. The woman was nearly hysterical, pounding her fists into the bedding and ranting on about thieves and Greeks. Where had Louise found the man?

Louise. Of course, Merle must call her immediately. But first she had to put her groceries away, make some dinner, and get some calming wine into Irene. She went to open a bottle of Provence rosé from the shop, a cheap one but she liked it. She brought Irene a healthy pour and sat with her as she sipped it gratefully, her face wet with tears.

"What should I do?" Merle asked. "Call the police?"

"Yes! They will find *la crapule*." Whatever that was. Irene got angry for another minute then it went away. "They are so far away, and I don't even know the man's last name. I fear he was illegal. I didn't ask."

"Maybe Louise knows. Where did she find him?"

"Who knows?" Irene closed her eyes, defeated but at least calm.

"Did he have a car?" Merle had seen an old van, the little white ones everyone used in France.

"I—" She shook her head. She grabbed Merle's arm in alarm. "*Il a volé la camionnette*. He has stolen the van! Go see— oh, I know he has stolen the van."

In the yard Merle looked around, trying to remember where the small white utility van was usually parked. A square of yellowing grass next to the barn was a clue, as were the tire tracks through the dirt, but no van was there. Was it parked in a barn? She looked in the goat shed. It was empty, and fragrant. All the goats were out in the field, munching grass.

Oh, no. *No, no, no.* Who would take care of the goats?

Merle had another sinking feeling as she made her way back to the farmhouse. Louise really needed to come home.

Because there was no way in hell Merle Bennett was milking goats.

ODETTE AND THE GREAT FEAR

PART THREE

Dawn was breaking over the eastern hills when Odette straightened her back, stretching, and massaged her painful hands. Milking took hand strength she never realized, and obviously never had. Sustained clenching of the fists, the squeezing down of the teats, the endless teats: it was tedious labor, probably why it was usually given to women. She frowned at the goats as she untethered them, one by one, and led each one back out into the pasture to graze. They were slave masters, these goats, demanding creatures.

She was sitting in the kitchen, nursing a cup of milky chicory, warming her sore hands, when she heard the shouting. One of the farmhands, an older man with a bad limp, was excited about something outside, calling to Monsieur Daguerre, the farmer. He came at a trot, with another man at his heels.

Odette stepped to the window. The three men rounded the goat shed and walked quickly toward another barn. Her heart skipped when she realized they were heading directly to the old fruit store where she had hidden the man. *My* man, she thought possessively. *My patient. No.* What were they going to do to him?

She ran outside, following them around the milking shed. When she rounded the corner of the weathered fruit store she saw the three men standing in front of the open door, the very door she'd opened last night. The wheelbarrow sat next to it. She hadn't put it away last night.

She pushed aside a man from the village visiting M. Daguerre. He was dressed like an important man. She apologized but moved in front, peeking over the farmer's shoulder. Why hadn't she moved the man this morning? First thing, she should have seen to him, brought him more food, moved him somewhere safer. But the goats... the damn goats needed milking.

The farmer crouched down on his haunches and touched the man's neck. "Warm," he said quietly. "Not dead, Alfred."

The man with the limp, Alfred, stepped closer. "No? Ah, *bon*."

"He is injured, monsieur," Odette said. "Look at his leg." Better that they think he wandered in on his own.

M. Daguerre brushed bits of straw off the man's leg, exposing the stained bandage. "Come. We must take him into the house. Madame will nurse him."

It took the four of them to carry the man across the yard into the house. Odette might have mentioned the wheelbarrow but instead took his bad leg and brought up the rear. The man didn't wake. His skin was very pale, almost blue, and he looked like death. But maybe they could warm him up and treat his wounds. Maybe it wasn't too late.

There was much commotion inside the house with the arrival of the unconscious stranger. The house maid, Perrine, was a silly thing but she set about boiling water and taking the man's boots off. Madame Daguerre set up a folding cot near the big fireplace, stoking the flames with more logs. The men lifted the patient carefully onto the canvas cot and grimaced at the poor devil. They left, satisfied they had done everything possible for him, even though all they'd done was move him.

Madame not-too-delicately cut the leg off his trousers, exposing a gaping wound congealed with blood. The treatment of the wound made the man come round, groaning and thrashing in pain. Odette held his shoulders down while Perrine took his feet, letting Madame clean and do whatever it was she did to the wound. It looked like a gunshot to Odette, a round hole similar to the musket ball wounds she saw in Paris. But she kept her speculation to herself.

The next days went by in a whirlwind. Odette still had to milk her goats, get the milk to market or to Madame Daguerre's oldest daughter who made the cheese at her own farm down the road. Madame herself was chief nurse to the man they simply called 'L'E-tranger,' the stranger. They asked him his name several times while his eyes were open but he was out of his head with fever.

Between milking chores Odette tried to help with the nursing. On the third day, in the night, the man's fever broke. His eyes were clear that morning as she arrived after milking to wash at the pump. She turned to him, drying her hands, and was surprised to see him eyeing her back. His eyes, she couldn't help noticing, were an intense dark blue.

"You look better," she said, smiling. His skin had color again. "Feel better?"

He propped himself up on his elbows and looked around the kitchen with its smoky fireplace, whitewashed stone walls, and small, leaded windows. It was a pretty space to Odette, although rough. Was he used to something more grand?

"Where am I?" he said, his voice scratchy. "Where is this?"

"You're in Périgord, monsieur. Is that where you were headed?"

He flopped back on the cot as if disgusted with the countryside, or just Périgord, then threw back the blanket covering his injured leg. He poked at the bandage experimentally.

"It was a bad wound. Madame Daguerre, the farmer's wife, treated it with various pastes and poultices."

He wiggled his toes, poked some more, and covered his leg again. "And who are you, mademoiselle?"

"My name is Odette. I, too, came down from the north, escaping the violence." He glared at her accusingly. She was a stranger too, a foreigner from the city who didn't belong here, who had memories from terrible times. Did he not remember her wheeling him out of the woods into shelter? "*Pardon, monsieur.* I make too many assumptions."

She turned away, folding the hand towel over the edge of the sink. Now that the man was cleaned up, his face washed, his hair tied back with one of Perrine's blue ribbons, now that he was awake and alive, his eyes seemed too bold to Odette.

"I did come from the north," he said finally, without detail, she noticed.

"And what is your name, monsieur? You have been with us four days and we know not your name."

"My name is Ghislain. That is all I can say."

"And why is that?"

He smiled. "Because you have only given me your first name."

For a man only recently out of his wits he had gotten them back quickly. How old was he? Impossible to say but no child. He was tall and, if not for his injury, no doubt hale and hearty. His shoulders looked very strong. She offered him soup and bread and helped him sit up on the cot to eat it. He asked for more.

"Did you make that yourself, Odette?" he asked, lying back again, eyes closing. "That delicious stew?"

She took the dishes to the sink. "No, monsieur. I am the goat girl. I herd and milk the goats. I do not cook. Of course, I know how to cook—"

But he was asleep again, snoring, his hands laced over his blue coat. She adjusted his blanket. His eyelids were bluish and delicate, papery thin, a dark beard growing on his robust chin. She watched his chest rise and fall, like clockwork, reassuringly. In another time, another place— well, no spilt milk, *ma petite*. This was the time they had. If the last two years had taught her anything, it was that this moment, this present time, could be all anyone had on this earth.

At supper that night the whole staff of the farm, some seven of them including Perrine and another young girl who helped in the house, talked to Ghislain, exclaimed over his recovery, joked and poked him, and generally treated him like a curiosity, something from a traveling show. He seemed to enjoy the attention, charming the women, but gave them few details of his journey except to say that there was much fighting in the streets of Paris, street by street, block by block. The news sheets had been full of it, even though they were months old by the time they reached Périgord.

No one, not even Perrine who tried with all her might, could get Ghislain to tell about his part in the fighting, or how he ended up in their fruit store with a hole in his leg. Was he a partisan? Was he a soldier? Was he brave? Did he kill the other man? Did he lose his horse somewhere? What sort of hat did he wear? The questions went from serious to ridiculous. Did he crawl into their fruit store? Where had he been previously? How long was he there? Odette stayed silent on that note. He didn't remember her part anyway.

Too painful to recollect, he said of his travels and travails. His wound was also off-limits as a topic of discussion. Madame Daguerre demanded he tell her if it was a knife or a musket ball or the horn of a cow or a sword blade or a pitchfork. But he did not, would not answer. This made the Madame a bit angry. After all, she had worked hard to nurse him back to health and felt she deserved answers, a juicy bit of story to explain her sacrifice to her friends, to burnish her nursing reputation, to make both of them a little heroic. But he said nothing. That made Madame curious. Her eyes narrowed as she walked away from him that night, hands on her hips. Odette could see her mind whirling: he is a fugitive, a criminal, a deserter. Someone with something to hide. Even a murderer on the run.

And perhaps he was. It was not up to Odette to say.

But the next morning when she got up in the dark, made her way out of her hard bed under the rafters, stepped down the many stairs, tossed the piss-pot outside, pushed through the kitchen toward the door, glancing where he slept, Odette knew one thing about Ghislain, her stranger.

He was gone.

THIRTEEN

IN THE DORDOGNE

L ouise Fayette returned to the farm in the morning, her hair sticking out in all directions and looking as frazzled as Merle felt. Irene herself had finally kicked into action to save her goats the night before, finding a neighbor willing to come over and handle the milking for one time only. Louise was a little late for the morning milking and Irene let her know how she felt about that. But at least she had arrived, and was right now in the shed with the nanny goats.

Merle had cajoled the older woman into moving from her bed to the kitchen table, using the metal walker that she despised. It made her feel so old, she grumbled, shuffling along, leaning heavily on the arms of the contraption. Nobody wanted to use a walker, Merle explained. They did it because they had to, because getting mobile again is important. Merle had no idea where she got her little inspirational speeches. They just came out.

And they worked, thankfully. Irene sat down with a thump on the wooden chair and raised her leg onto a nearby seat. Merle poured them both coffee and sat across from her.

Irene had let Merle brush her long hair and wind it into a bun, poking the bobby pins in to keep it in place. Irene had washed her strong, weathered face with a warm cloth and asked for her face cream, smearing it onto her cheeks and forehead. She looked better, less like a wild woman of Borneo.

"What shall we do about César then?" Merle asked. "What does Louise think?"

Irene sighed. "She does not know his full name, as I suspected. She found him on the computer, you know?"

The Internet, Merle presumed. So that was that. Money gone, thief on the run. "I'm sorry."

"The government needs to do something about crime. It has come from the cities into the countryside."

"We had some vandalism in my village as well. They spray painted my house," Merle said, grimacing. Irene was shocked. "But nothing that can't be cleaned," Merle said cheerfully. No point in getting all down in the dumps about *la belle France*.

Irene set down her cup. "I must call the doctor about my next appointment. It can't be too soon that he gets me out of this brace. Bring me the telephone."

Merle pulled the old phone over from its place by the door. It was at least forty years old with a rotating dial. The cord didn't quite reach to Irene. Merle dialed the number for her, an activity that brought back her grandparents' house, pushing the heavy dial around, waiting for it to return, then repeating. She handed the receiver to Irene who had to bend forward to listen on it.

While Irene talked to various people at the doctor's office, Merle stepped outside. Louise was in the yard, hosing down a goat with fresh water, speaking to the animal in a low, loving voice, ruffling her coat. Merle took out her phone and snapped a photograph. Louise was somehow like Odette, an urban girl on a farm, doing her best. What was Louise studying? Something important, like medicine or astrophysics probably.

How much the world had changed in two hundred years. Stability, more or less, between the bloody wars, a couple Napoleons and five republics, had made such a difference in the lives of people like Louise. She grew up on a goat farm like someone in the 17th Century, but went to college and had all sorts of possibilities open to her after, things that a woman like Odette could never dream of. A woman of the French Revolution could protest her lot, could march to Versailles and shake a fist at the King, but she had no voice in government. No vote, no education, no power.

Louise looked up and smiled at Merle. She was a good daughter. She had come home when she probably had a million things going on, things more pressing than milking a goat. What would happen now? Would she find another itinerant goat farmer on French Craigslist? Who would take care of Irene?

Merle was due to go home the day after tomorrow. Her own to-do list was waiting and she couldn't stay here with Irene forever. Maybe it was time to get busy and help figure out the Fayette's dilemma. For everyone's sake.

In the house Irene was stretching her arm out to reach the base of the telephone, grunting. Merle took the receiver and replaced it.

"*Bon.* They send the nurse tomorrow to make an evaluation of my stitches, and also the *aide à domicile.*You can go home, Madame Bennett." Domestic aide? Ah, someone to help around the house. Perfect. Irene smiled at her. "Finally, they do something for me for all those taxes. Maybe I get some decent meals, eh? Something I don't have to gnaw with my teeth."

"I never said I was a good cook. Or a French one," Merle said, smiling. A great chef she was not. But she could leave with a clear conscience. What a relief.

"Louise will be happy," Irene said, crossing her arms like the captain of the ship at the helm. "She is a very bad cook. And she snaps at me. Well, I am not a very good patient."

"It is hard to be a good patient."

"I am always running here and there. I hate this—" She pointed out her bum leg. "It is not me."

"Your leg is better? No pills?"

"I won't take any more." Irene dusted off crumbs from the table. "Now, who will do the milking? We must find someone reliable."

"What if I call Pascal? He might know someone around here?"

"Pascal? He is a *policier,* not a farmer." She shrugged. "But go ahead. The government should be good for something."

Merle went out into the yard and called Pascal. She left a long message then walked over to the milking shed. Inside Louise was still milking, down to her last two goats. Merle watched, impressed with her skill and speed.

"You're good at that," Merle said as Louise untethered the goat and let it go into the pasture.

"I should be. I've been doing it since I was six."

She sounded less than thrilled about that. Merle said, "How can we find a replacement for César? Do you have anyone else you can ask?"

Louise just glanced at Merle, an angry glance, and went back to milking. Well, it wasn't really her responsibility, was it? She left the shed. Pascal called back as she walked toward the house.

"You are at Irene's?" he asked, surprised. "Is she all right?"

"She had knee surgery. She's not a happy patient. And then the worker they hired to milk the goats stole their money and their van. I went into the village for an hour and he took advantage of my absence."

"*Connard!* Who is milking then?"

Merle explained the problem finding someone to do the milking, someone more trustworthy than César. Louise must go back to school. He said he would try to find someone. And he would look up the van's identification and submit it to Motor Vehicle Theft. Maybe they would find it somewhere. No doubt the dastardly César had sold it to the North Africans by now. But for the present, the milking was absolutely necessary. Find someone, as soon as possible, Merle stressed, so Louise could go back to college.

"Are you working?" Merle asked.

"Of course. Always." He sounded tired. "I was going to come see you tonight. But you are not home."

"I'll be home tomorrow. Come then."

"I will try, *chérie*."

That night a knock came on the door, after dark. Merle was already in bed but Louise had stayed up, winding down from the evening milking, having a glass of red wine. Merle stood in the hallway in her robe, suspicious of visits after dark.

Two people stood on the sloping porch, a woman and a teenaged boy. The woman was explaining something to Louise who was exclaiming and shaking the boy's hand. They left the house, all three going toward the milking shed. Merle watched them through the window. As they left there was more shaking of hands. The two strangers left in a black sedan not unlike Merle's Peugeot and Louise returned to the house, smiling.

"It is your Pascal to the rescue," she said, giving Merle an unaccustomed hug. "He is amazing."

"Did he find someone already?"

"That boy, Guillaume, he is sixteen, seventeen. He can only work until the school term begins but that gives me two or three weeks to find someone else. And means I can go back to the University."

"That's great, Louise. Does he live around here?"

"Some miles away. They say Pascal did them a favor. They didn't say what it was. But I don't care," Louise said, sighing and staring at the ceiling. "I don't care at all."

THE NEXT MORNING was a new day. The teenager had already come and gone by the time Merle got up, much to Louise's joy. She had changed from a sullen, quiet girl to possibly her real self: a bubbly, smiling woman. She was going back to school, she reminded her mother again unnecessarily. Irene rolled her eyes and pouted but she was happy for her daughter, that was clear. The nurse and domestic aide arrived together from Agen mid-morning, exclaiming of their anxiety of getting lost in the hills. They were both gray-haired women and could have been sisters, especially the way they bickered about how to do things. By lunchtime Merle excused herself and went to pack her bag. She was gone by two in the afternoon, giving Louise a hug and telling her to study hard.

The Peugeot started right up, roaring to life with Merle's unnec-essary pumping on the gas pedal. She was eager to go but she didn't need to be so obvious. She drove sedately down the long drive, past Pascal's little cottage, past the goats and cows in the pastures, toward home.

Merle was parking her car in the city lot outside Malcouziac's comforting bastide walls when Madame Suchet from across Rue de Poitiers called. Merle had given Madame her phone number in case something happened while she was out of town.

Merle sank a little, seeing the number pop up. What now? She felt like she'd lost her moorings and was bouncing from one crisis to another. What about a little time just sitting in her backyard, nursing a rosé and reading a novel? Or even writing a novel? She'd gotten very little done this week, and if Merle Bennett was anything, she was a personal slave-driver. She was not a slacker. She demanded results, especially of herself.

But her neighbor didn't have a problem. She had a solution. She knew who had vandalized Merle's house, and she was ready to turn him in to the authorities.

FOURTEEN

SANCERRE

Pascal's memory wasn't as sharp as he thought. He cursed as he realized he was lost in the backroads of Sancerre, where all the vineyards look alike, row upon row of Sauvignon and Pinot grapes. Mostly Sauvignon as it made the buttery Sancerre wine, renowned around the world. From the dirt roads, all the grapevines appeared similar, their clusters nearly ripe, ready for harvest in weeks.

Workers were already getting ready, scurrying up and down the rows, squeezing, tasting, gathering supplies. Pascal would be a wine buyer again, a task he had accomplished many times over the years while undercover. It was a small miracle that no one recognized him, but there were so many vineyards in France. The chance of running across the same person in two far-flung wineries was small. And if they did, well, he was still playing wine buyer. No harm in that.

He reached an intersection where the crossroad was paved. Peering at the many small signs on a post he saw the winery he was searching for. Le Grand Vinon— to the left. He swung the BMW in that direction and drove slowly, looking for a hidden drive. He knew it was on the west side of the road somewhere. And then, suddenly, there it was.

The signage was old, easily missed. The vines themselves looked well-kept. The road was not, full of pot holes and ruts. The car bottomed out twice, the undercarriage hitting dirt. The buildings of the winery came into view as he rounded the hill, a dusty assemblage of tasting room, cave, bottling facility, and mixing room. Pascal remembered the layout now and parked in front of the main mixing room. The two-story building, more like a barn than the others, had a rough wooden door, covered with dust.

The door to the tasting room was locked. Pascal cupped his eyes to see inside but the room was dark. He wondered if they were still in business. August was a popular time for tourists to visit wineries, and locals often stopped by to fill their own jugs.

He tried the door at the mixing room and was surprised when it swung open. Wineries kept their secrets in the mixing room, formulas for successful blends and dates of changes in oak, out of oak, and the like. But Le Grand Vinon wasn't concerned about secrecy apparently. His footsteps echoed in the shadowed, cavernous space.

On one wall stainless steel vats were lined up, as tall as the ceiling, like grain silos. The other side of the space was empty, a wooden walkway leading to a control room where the read-outs of gauges from the vats could be monitored.

"*Allo?* Anyone here?"

He waited for the echo to fade. Silence. A few spotlights were on but otherwise the room was dark. The light inside the control room flickered. There was no one inside and the window that faced the mixing room was smudged. Normally cleanliness is a religion in these places. Pascal looked around and saw dirt in the corners, leaves and grass here and there, tracked in from the fields.

What was going on at Le Grand Vinon? It appeared they were still in business, but looks could be deceiving. He exited the wooden door, back into the afternoon sunshine. Turning toward the vines, he grabbed his straw hat from the back seat of his car. Full summer was upon the heartland of France, that continental heat, untempered by the breezes off the ocean. He took off his suit jacket and rolled the sleeves up on his shirt. A warm, dry wind ruffled the leaves on the vines.

The first person he encountered was hauling a cart full of assorted buckets and baskets. A young man, barely out of his teens, with black hair and a sullen expression, he stopped when he saw Pascal. He kept hold of the cart's handle while he stared at Pascal.

Pascal took off his hat and nodded to the boy. He asked if the owner was nearby. "Monsieur Delage. *Il est près d'ici?*"

The boy flicked sweat off his thick eyebrows and continued staring. Finally, he pointed at the far end of the vineyard. Then he trundled off with his cargo, rounding a stone building and disappearing from sight.

Pascal stuck his hat back on his head and walked in the direction the boy had pointed. The rows were endless, surrounding the winery in every direction. He wondered if the family still owned them all. The father had been a master winemaker but a terrible businessman, getting himself into so many financial jams that he went too far into the criminal realm. Was Léo Delage helping his son now? Was he here?

The wind died down and the heat of the afternoon hit in waves. Pascal squinted into the shimmering sky, trying to locate a human in the vast sea of emerald. He picked a row at random and walked down between the wired vines, stopping to admire the clusters of grapes. The trellises were too high to see over, so he had to wait until he reached a junction, a crossing that allowed workers to move between rows, before he could jump up and look in every direction.

In a far corner of the rows a man's head bobbed along, small and white, possibly a hat. Pascal struck out in the direction of the head and hat, looking down each row as he got closer. Finally, on the next to last row, he spotted the man inspecting vines. Pascal turned in and walked quickly toward the vintner.

Adrien Delage watched him approach suspiciously. Pascal raised his hat in greeting, trying to look nonthreatening. He greeted Delage with a handshake and introduced himself with his undercover name.

"I am a buyer for Global Vendanges," he explained, mentioning a large distributor of wines. "Exporting to the United States and Canada, also China. We heard good things about your last two vintages. Particularly last year's."

Delage doffed his white cap. The sun had aged him prematurely, with lines on his cheeks. His dark hair stuck out awkwardly. His eyes were still blue and clear but tired and wary. Even the prospect of selling many cases of wine didn't cheer him.

"It is gone. You have made a trip for nothing," he said gruffly. He began to turn away.

"*C'est vrai?* All sold? How many cases did you produce?"

Delage shrugged silently. Pascal continued. "It had an excellent reputation. I am not surprised. But disappointed of course. You have some older vintages?"

"*Non.*" He turned toward the vines and went back to work, trimming excess leaves.

"Well, the harvest is upon us, yes? When will you pick?"

"Very soon," Delage muttered. "I wait for laborers."

"Ah. Moroccans?"

The vintner shot him a look. "If I can get them. They are hard workers."

"Very true. What do you think of Tunisians? I have heard many have come as refugees?"

"If they know the trade."

Pascal stretched to look over the trellises at the acres of grapes. "You have many vines, monsieur. It will take a small army. Unless you have some employees here as well to help?"

No answer.

"Or perhaps neighbors and family? The traditional way to *vendange*?"

"*Bien sûr.* Of course."

Pascal was following him down the row now, chatting amicably as if keeping him company on this hot, tedious day in the field. "This is a family winery, correct? Many generations in the business?"

"Started by my great-grandfather after the first world war," he said as he snipped.

"How grand that you keep the tradition going. So important in this age of corporations, yes?" He cupped a cluster of grapes. "Beautiful, so perfect. Your children will help in the vendange then? Your cousins?"

"My children are very small. I have very few relatives nearby. That is why I need Moroccans."

"Families aren't the same. They move away. Just yesterday I was visiting a vineyard where none of the children professed an interest in wine-making. It made the vintner very sad, I could tell."

"I myself had no interest, I can tell you, *monsieur*," Adrien said. The meditation of working the pruners on the green leaves had calmed whatever suspicions he harbored toward Pascal and he relaxed into his tale. "I inherited this vineyard by force." He chuckled, a bit oddly.

"It was thrust upon you?"

"Difficult times. I was in the seminary. I was to become a priest."

That was a new one. Pascal wiggled his eyebrows involuntarily. "An honorable calling. It must have been a horrible choice."

Adrien took a deep breath, straightening his back for a moment. "In some ways, yes. But in others, very simple."

"How so? *Pardon, monsieur*. I find the tales of wineries, their histories, fascinating."

"My father was a passionate vintner. A genius, some would say. I continue using his formulae to this day." He went back to his task, stepping sideways down the row. "But in other ways he was— well, challenged. He was a poor businessman. It has taken these fifteen years for me to put the winery back on the right path."

"To profit, you mean?"

"To profit, to sustainability, to stability. He ruined many things when he was here. That was the easy part of the decision to leave the seminary: I was needed. Even if I knew nothing of winemaking. Which I did not. I was like the children you spoke of. I wanted a different life, in a city, helping the pious and the poor."

"It must have been difficult for you. Even though you were so needed."

"In many ways, yes. An emotional upheaval, in a way. And a physical one." He spread his calloused hands out to Pascal. "It is demanding in every way."

Pascal examined the man's hands, noting the scars. Was the time right for the ultimate question? One never knew until they asked.

"Did your father stay on and help you?"

"No. He left. Also by force."

Pascal waited a few paces down the row. "By force?"

"He is *un malfaiteur, monsieur.* A criminal. He plundered all the accounts, borrowed from gangsters. Left us destitute." He turned to glare at Pascal now, his face pink with anger. "You wonder why we have no workers here? No one will come. All the citizens here think they will not be paid if they labor for my harvest. They refuse to do business with me. I sell all my bottles before harvest, *monsieur.* You are wasting your time here. I must sell them all as advance shares so I can hire Moroccans and get the *vendange* completed, buy the bottles, the labels, all of it. Without the foreign workers, I have nothing. Nothing."

"Your wine has an excellent reputation, Monsieur," Pascal said gently. "May you have many successful harvests."

FIFTEEN

Two elderly women stood in the middle of Rue de Poitiers in the morning sun, faces close, screaming at each other. Merle paused, carrying her bag up the street. She recognized the round profile of her neighbor. Madame Suchet and the other woman were waving their hands, pointing at the vandalism, talking loudly, arguing. Her heart sunk; they were angry about her house.

They wore the usual matronly outfit of well-pressed dark dress, thick stockings, and heels. Merle could only pick out a few words: *malade, pas sympathique, mon fils, vandale*: 'the patient, not sympathetic, my son, the vandal.'

She walked slowly toward the women, hoping they would calm down. They were similar in age. Madame Suchet must be in her 70s. The other woman also had gray hair and was thinner with more wrinkles but full of vim and vigor. She lashed out at Madame S like a pro, or a lawyer.

Merle set down her bag by the padlocked front shutters, jingling her keys to distract the women from their fury.

It didn't work. Madame Suchet saw her but ignored her, looking back at her opponent, her hands on her ample hips and wagging her head. The other woman pointed a finger at her, poking it close to her face. This appeared to be escalating. Soon they would be at blows. Merle stepped up to the two and placed a hand on each of their shoulders.

"*Mesdames*, please. Whatever the problem is, I'm sure we can talk about it without shouting," she said during a pause in the ranting.

The thinner woman shrugged off Merle's hand angrily. "Do not touch me. You do not have permission to touch me."

"*Excusez-moi.*" Merle bowed her head apologetically.

"Do not speak to my friend like that," Madame Suchet spat. "She is not your inferior."

The other woman straightened proudly, eyes blazing. "And you are not my superior."

With that she turned on her heel and pranced angrily down the street. She reached a townhouse halfway down with peeling burgundy shutters, yanked open the door, and disappeared. The door banged shut.

Madame Suchet was pink from the shouting. She took a deep breath. "I am sorry, Madame Bennett. I did not expect that to happen."

"Who was that?" Merle looked down the street. She didn't know any of her neighbors on the opposite side of the street, except for Madame Suchet. "Come inside. You need to sit down."

Merle poured Madame Suchet a glass of water. She offered wine but her neighbor refused it. They sat at the old wood table, the only remaining furniture from days past. It was worn and a bit greasy, but held too many silent memories to discard.

She waited for Madame to speak. When she didn't Merle had to ask, "Was that about me?"

"No, no, madame. It— " She glanced at Merle, looking oddly guilty. "She was angry. And rightly so as I blame her son for the vandalism."

"Her son?"

Madame S nodded. "He is not well." She tapped her temple. "He comes and goes."

"I'm sorry." At least she would know who her vandal was, even if his mental state meant he would not be charged. That was fine with Merle. She'd already given up on the whole business and moved on to paint removal. "What's his name?"

"Thierry. He was a sweet boy but he is not well," she repeated. "And his mother, she does not deal with him so well either. She gives him money and then what does he do? He buys paint."

"You saw him then? Painting?"

"One of my friends saw him in the hardware store, buying spray paint. What am I to think?"

"Ah."

"I apologize. I do not wish to argue with my sister, especially so loudly out on the street. She loves her Thierry and cannot stand for anyone to say a word against him."

Merle blinked. "Your sister?"

Madame Suchet nodded sadly. "We are very close. Like twins."

As she escorted Madame to the door Merle remembered something that had hit her years ago, on her first trip to France as a college student. The entire family had traveled together to Paris, making for some memorable moments of too much togetherness. One day, Merle had gone for a walk on her own. She found a park and sat on the bench in the sunshine, much the way she did in New York when the crush of humanity threatened to overwhelm her. She was enjoying the calm when an old gentleman sat down next to her. He had a small dog on a leash and glanced at her before unsnapping it from the dog's collar and letting it run free. It was a small poodle of some kind, maybe a mix, an energetic, talkative dog. The man talked back to it, in French, and miraculously, the dog understood French. He came when he was called— in French. He stood up and begged— in response to his French command.

She felt so stupid for her surprise. Of course, dogs learn commands in whatever language their masters speak. It was one of those wake-up moments that taught her she needed to see more of the world, open her eyes to other cultures. It had taken quite a few years to get back to France but she hadn't forgotten the lesson of that dog and his master. Everyone is the center of their own story, their own life, and when you think the world revolves around you, you need to think a little harder, open your heart, open your mind.

She'd never considered, not consciously, that there would be mentally ill people in France. But of course there were in all human cultures. People whose disability was social or emotional or deeply psychotic. It didn't matter what nationality you were. France might be a drug to naive American women, all sunshine and wine and lavender, making her happy and calm— but she could hear Pascal's laugh now, telling her she was being ridiculous. France didn't cure anyone of their problems any more than a dog could speak Chinese.

Unless you were in China, then of course, they barked in Mandarin or Cantonese.

Two sisters, shouting at each other in the street. Making each other angry, pointing fingers. Two sisters who are very close, like twins; it made Merle laugh. Only someone very close would stoop to yelling at her sister in public. Or give her a slap across the face to get her to snap out of whatever was troubling her, as Merle's sister Stasia had once done. Merle could see her own sisters pointing at her, their eyes alight, laughing like hyenas, if they had heard Madame Suchet.

After she unpacked her small suitcase from her stay at Irene's and checked that the gate was still secure in the garden and that the new door shutters were working properly, Merle opened the refrigerator. It was a small one, and mostly empty. She'd left all that food at Irene's — which was fine. But now she needed to re-stock the larder.

She locked up again and walked toward the town square. She'd forgotten it was market day but the bustle of vendors and customers carried down the cobblestone streets before she had them in sight. She paused to buy a baguette and a couple croissants from a bakery stand, some green beans and a zucchini from another, and some goat cheese from an attractive display tended by an elderly man in a beret.

She picked up a small round of goat cheese dusted with herbs. "Where is your *chèverie*? Close by?" she asked, smiling at the man.

"It is not mine," he said, shaking his head. "My family has the goats. I am simply the salesman. Here, please, try a bit." He pressed a small cracker smeared with goat cheese on her.

"Do you know Irene Fayette, near Villefranche?" she asked after tasting the cheese. Maybe all goat farmers knew each other.

The man straightened proudly and grinned. "*Mais oui.* She is my cousin. You are acquainted?"

Merle launched into her best French, explaining she had just seen Irene and had been helping her while she had mobility issues after her knee surgery. He expressed surprise and dismay that his cousin was having problems.

Merle introduced herself and they shook hands. His name was Jacques. He wore the blue workers jumpsuit that Albert often sported while picking plums, and kept his black beret at a jaunty angle. He was adorable.

"These are Irene's beautiful cheeses. I am her traveling salesman," Jacques explained. "I go to the markets from here to Issigeac."

Merle wondered if Jacques had heard about the theft of the cheese money. It was probably not the time to bring it up. She saw he had a blue cash pouch with a zipper. He kept it under his arm.

She paid for three small rounds of goat cheese and wished him many sales. He lifted his beret in farewell then turned his attention to another customer with his ready smile.

Merle set the cheese on top of the vegetables in her market basket, bought some sausages, and headed home. She hoped Pascal would call, or arrive, tonight. In time for dinner, please, she thought. It would be nice to have him at her table again.

She waited until nearly nine to cook dinner but Pascal didn't show up. No call either, which was getting to be the norm. She cooked for one, cleaned the kitchen, and took her notebook to bed. Her notebook was not as much fun as Pascal in bed, she thought, frowning, as she pulled the white quilt back. She opened the shutters to let the moonlight stream into the bedroom. She'd painted this room a warm peach color and it glowed in the evening light.

With a sigh, she propped herself up on the pillows, got out her pen, and flipped her notebook open.

Time to escape to the days of the guillotine again.

ODETTE AND THE GREAT FEAR

PART FOUR

The goats were docile the day she prodded them up the hill toward the chateau. She had a desire to see it again, to see if her memory of the rainy day was accurate or she was having strange dreams of shadowy spaces for nothing. And then there was the Count himself, with that nasty scar on his face. It was intriguing to think of him in duels at royal estates, even if it was something more mundane that had maimed him. She thought she wanted to know what had happened, but maybe she didn't. She was still a bit afraid of *le comte*. Everyone in the village feared him. His temper was said to be vicious.

She trudged up the hill, holding her skirt up to keep it out of the mud. Since the rainstorm, she'd learned a few more things about the Count. He was the son of the old count but he didn't really like being a noble. He wanted to do something worthwhile, to help society, so he had gone to Paris and joined his friends at the Commune after the storming of the Bastille. He knew many fancy people, it was said with awe. Odette had no use for elites, even the ones who were now crafting the new republic out of thin air. Their hearts might have once been good but time had passed and they were different now. They had lost their focus and were fighting amongst themselves over idiotic things like men always did.

Was the count like that, she wondered, poking a bush with her stick and knocking off the last of autumn's orange leaves. She paused to admire their color against the black earth. If she were an artist she would paint them, so bright and tiny and perfect. But she was not an artist nor was she likely to become one. Her future was murky. All she knew was she probably couldn't stay on as the goat girl forever.

What did she dream of doing? She straightened and looked at the sky. It was so blue today, like a perfect lake, bottomless and clear. Was the future so endless? All lives came to an end. She must find out what she's meant to do with hers, before it was too late. She thought again of the march to Versailles, the women so dedicated and brave that she felt part of something bigger than herself, bigger than selling thread or goat-herding. Bigger than finding the next meal. But what did that mean now, when the women and men of the uprising no longer had a voice?

At the top of the hill she stopped, rounding up her goats for a chomp on the thin grass. Was this the count's land? The villagers said he tried to keep them off it for many years, or make them pay a tax to graze their animals. But the top of any hill should belong to the people. It should be for everyone, to let their spirits soar. Let the nobles have the bottoms where the rich soil grew plump grapes and golden wheat. The people would take the high ground.

She sat down on a log under a withered tree and shut her eyes for a moment. Sleep was a luxury on the farm. There was never enough of it. She felt the sunshine on her face and smiled. Where was Ghislain then? How far had he gotten on that bad leg? Had he jumped in a wagon and disappeared forever?

Something made her feel that he would be back. She wanted him to heal and come back for her. It was a wild, ridiculous thought but she was still a girl, despite all her troubles.

A shadow crossed her face, taking away the warmth of the sun.

She blinked and opened her eyes. A tall man stood over her, staring. The silhouette of him against the sun, his hat, his long coat— she stiffened, struggling to her feet. She tugged at her skirt and curtsied.

"*Monsieur le Comte*," she stuttered.

Now that she was standing she could see the Count's face better, that horrid scar dragging down one eyelid. He had no expression, not anger or revulsion or haughty disregard. He said nothing, just nodded at her. He was not even middle-aged, she realized, examining his good side that was smooth with youth. He turned slightly to hide his bad side, something he probably did unconsciously.

"*Pardon, monsieur*. I am from the Daguerre farm. I do not know the hills so well. Am I in the wrong place with the goats?"

"I remember you," he said quietly, staring at her in an intense, uncomfortable way. "That day in the rain."

"Yessir. Thank you again for giving me shelter. It was most kind."

He waved a hand impatiently. He glanced at her black and white goats, back to her, and stalked off down the hill, his hands thrust into his pockets.

What an odd man. A sad one. The villagers all thought him ugly, a monster of sorts with that scar, someone who demanded outrageous rents and taxes and had done something sinful, something against God Himself, to be so disfigured. Odette didn't think he was a bad person. Anyone could get a wound under the right circumstances. He probably was in a glorious battle of some kind. You shouldn't judge someone by their outward scars, should you? But she never argued with the villagers. They were gossips like all country people. All French people, to be sure.

Three days later, in the village, she learned more about *le comte*. A story was circulating that he was harboring a thief, a deserter wanted by the Army. The villagers also feared the Army. The new Republic was conscripting any able-bodied man, and some who were barely old enough to leave their mothers. The Army was preparing for war on all fronts, with all comers. The hated Army together with the hated Count; it was the perfect rumor.

She heard the news from Estelle who sold eggs. The girl knew someone who knew someone who'd seen the deserter at the Count's chateau, eating duck sausage in the kitchen. Odette's heart thumped. Was the deserter Ghislain? Why was the Count helping a deserter? Odette decided to tell Estelle her story. It would get around the village, she was sure, but she had to know. She whispered to Estelle that she'd found a strange man in their woods with an injury. Was it the same man? Oh, yes, Estelle was certain it was. He was a very bad man. He'd stolen from the Army, it was said, and was on the run. They would catch him soon and cut off his head.

Why didn't someone relieve the Count of the traitor? Turn him in to the Army. But the villagers were as afraid of their local noble as they were of the Army. Besides, the gossip was delicious. The stories swirled and formed, then punctured and re-formed. Why deny a favorite pleasure with unnecessary action?

That night Odette indulged in *her* favorite pleasure, dreaming about Ghislain. He climbed the rose trellis outside her window and tapped on the glass. She let him in then sucked the blood from where the thorns had cut his hands. He was grateful.

She woke sweaty and breathless.

And alone.

SIXTEEN

Elise was due in Bergerac on the three-thirty train from Paris. Merle had heard from her youngest sister a week before and was surprised but pleased about the unexpected trip. She was acting differently since the events of the spring. At their sister Annie's Scottish wedding Elise had met a Frenchman who later betrayed her rather mercilessly. To say that Elise now questioned her own judgment would be an understatement. Her denigrating self-talk was the topic of conversation in the family for weeks. Then Elise gathered her wits and moved forward. She dumped her dull boyfriend, Andrew, started jogging (of all things), began French lessons, and told her law firm that she needed better cases or she'd be gone by Christmas.

She was, according to the other Bennett sisters, a full-grown lawyer now.

So, when she decided to get a last-minute flight to Paris and visit Merle in the Dordogne, what could they say? She had vacation days and the cash to do it.

Merle was happy to have her sister, who was ten years younger and almost a different generation, come for a visit. She was getting a little lonely for conversation she could understand with Pascal gone who knows where, Tristan back home, and her French tutor forbidding her to speak in English at all. Plus, they would fly home together at the end of Elise's trip. It was time for Tristan to go to college and Merle still insisted she was needed one more time.

They would, of course, have to do some sightseeing, cutting into the decorating and writing time. But it was August, and hot. Upstairs in Merle's little *maison de ville* was a furnace, uninhabitable past ten in the morning. She was happy to walk to her new Peugeot with its dents and scratches and find the air conditioning was operable. Turning it up full blast she drove the backroads to Bergerac and collected Elise.

After hugs and exclamations of how great the other looked, the sisters piled back in the car. As they went around the roundabout for the second time (missing the turn-off the first time) Merle asked Elise about the sudden decision to come to France.

"I'm so excited you came," she said. "Just curious."

"Wouldn't anyone jump at a chance to come to France?" Elise laughed. "But, seriously, I felt a little cheated in Paris in May."

"You did get cheated. That scum Bruno."

Elise waved a hand. "I've stopped thinking about him. Really. But my last two trips got cut short. I wanted to come on my own and spend some time. With you, of course." She directed the vent to blow on her face. "Whew, it's roasting here."

They drove endlessly for the next few days, scouring the sun-bleached hills, wine-tasting at obscure wineries, and visiting chateaux on hilltops, including the abandoned one Merle had researched for her novel. They rented kayaks and paddled the River Lot. It was fun. But four days of playing tour guide to her sister left Merle with the impression that Elise hadn't entirely changed. She was still the little one who expected her older sisters to placate her, coddle her, and buy all the meals. But it was fine, Merle told herself, as she rose with the birds that morning. Merle rarely allowed herself time to do absolutely nothing constructive. It went against the grain— and the huge to-do list.

Today there was a duty to attend. Irene had called and asked another favor. This time it didn't involve the goats themselves, or nursing invalids, but selling goat cheese at the Thursday market on the Malcouziac plaza. Irene's elderly cousin Jacques, whom Merle had met, was under the weather. A new driver had been found for the week but he refused to stay and sell cheese. A neighbor in Villefranche, the driver would only deliver the cheese to the market with the table and cash bag but not stay all day. Irene was a little desperate since losing the market funds to the notorious César.

Would Merle sell cheese for a day in Malcouziac? Of course. She agreed, relishing trying out her French and the dreaded numbers. She needed to be forced to think in Euros, in strange numerals, and this would do it.

Elise would help. Together, neither of them would have to sit behind the table for hours. They could wander, shop, get coffee, and otherwise be French for a morning. They dressed in colorful sundresses and big hats, making themselves laugh as they sashayed down the street in cute sandals in the fresh glow of dawn. To have a job, a duty, in a foreign land, was a circumstance neither had ever imagined.

Merle's brain clicked into the numerals necessary for making change by about 11 in the morning. Before that, she simply let customers tell her how much change they required. Most of the cheese was € 2 or € 5 so nothing was terribly difficult. Elise brought them *café au lait* and croissants from the café in mid-morning and then salads about one in the afternoon. By then, the shoppers had thinned out.

"How long are we supposed to stay here?" Elise asked, wiping salad dressing off her chin with a paper napkin. "It's getting hot."

She did look a little sunburnt on her shoulders, even with her big hat shading her face. Merle said, "We're to wait for the driver to collect things, whenever that is." She stood up. "I'm going to get you some sunscreen. The pharmacy is right there. I'll be back in a second."

Elise smiled proudly. "I will use my best *Français.*" She began with a shout-out to cheese buyers that escalated to loud. *"Chèvre frais. Ici, mes amis!"* Merle smiled at her, then turned to cross the plaza. Elise was happy in France, that was easy to see. With her dark hair tucked up in her hat, her cheeks glowed with sunshine and contentment. She hadn't mentioned Bruno, the bastard who'd tricked her in Paris, for at least a day.

She was correct, Merle thought, in coming to France to cleanse that trauma. She was replacing it, day by day, with a pretty picture of *La France Profonde,* the deep country of traditional villages and idyllic backwaters. They made Merle happy, too, those old values, although now that she thought of it, the vandalism, corruption, and thefts in her village were hardly wonderful. Maybe *La France Profonde* was a myth, a fantasy for those who resisted change. Americans were no stranger to that emotion themselves, concocting wild stories of 'good old days' that never existed, or if they did were never very good.

Once again Pascal popped into her head, laughing at her view of France. Nothing was sacred, was it? Not a cherished belief or a time-less value. All would change with time and circumstances. Even during the 1700s, when the deep countryside of France was nearly inaccessible, chaos from Paris had reached out and affected everyone, whether a young man who was forced into the military or a Count whose holdings were under threat by the new order.

In the cool pharmacy, Merle itched to get back to her writing. The Count and Odette waited for her. She sighed. In two days, the sisters would fly back to New York. There would be no writing there. Her novel would have to wait until she returned to France.

Back at the market, Elise was talking to a short man in a wide-brimmed straw hat, clogs, and baggy pants. Talk about your *France Profonde,* Merle thought. Elise was loading the cooler with the remaining goat cheese. This must be the driver. They hadn't met him this morning. The table had been set up, the cooler stashed under it, when they arrived at 7:30.

"Ah, there you are," Elise said. "This is Antoine, the driver. We're done at last."

Merle moved around behind the table by her sister. The driver kept the brim of his hat dipped low so she couldn't see all of his face. It set off alarms in her head.

"Antoine?" Merle stuck out her hand. "Nice to meet you."

He shook her hand quickly like he was shy. His deep tan wasn't unusual in this part of the world, not among farmers. Elise was zipping up the cash bag and putting it on top of the cheese in the cooler, the way it had come. She began folding the white tablecloth that draped the table.

"Can you help me?" Elise asked Antoine in French. He took the far corners and they folded the cloth. Merle picked up the small blue cooler called *un glacière* in French. Despite the heat, the hairs on the back of her neck prickled.

"*Pardon, monsieur,*" she began politely to Antoine. She moved slowly around the table as he bent down to fold it up. "Since we didn't meet you this morning we will need some identification that you work for Irene."

Elise was staring at Merle now, incredulous at first and then suspicious of Antoine as well. He extracted a small card from his pocket and handed it to Elise. "It's a motor vehicle registration," her sister said. "It says 'Irene Fayette.'"

"May I see it?" Merle asked.

Antoine snatched it back. "Madame waits. She is very strict."

As he bent to pick up the folding table Merle stepped forward and brushed the straw hat from the man's head. "Oh, *pardon.*" She watched the hat roll on the cobblestones and was not surprised to see the face under the hat was one she recognized.

"César. How nice to see you again."

His black hair was matted with sweat and he was unshaven. He froze for a moment, glancing for help to Elise with upraised eyebrows, then back to Merle.

"My name is Antoine."

"That may be," Merle said. "But you are the man who stole Madame Fayette's money, just like you're trying to do today. And her *camionnette*. That's obvious since you have the registration card for the truck."

He lunged for the cooler but Merle jumped back, swinging it out of his reach.

"*Monsieur!*" Elise yelled. César stumbled past Merle. "*Monsieur, aidez-nous! Un voleur!*" Help! Thief!

A large man in a tan summer suit and red bow tie appeared out of nowhere, tripping César as he righted himself and tried to run. The thief sprawled face-first on the cobbles and the man put a very polished shoe on his back to hold him down. He grinned at Elise, shoulders back, neck proud.

"*Comme ça, mademoiselle?*" he said in a bad accent.

Merle felt her mouth drop open. The man in the tan suit was tall and broad-shouldered, with tortoise shell glasses, glossy blond hair, and an insouciant smirk. Who was this handsome hero?

"Exactly like that," cooed Elise, hands on her hips and pout on her lips. "Well done, *monsieur*."

IN THE GIDDY aftermath of nabbing César *a.k.a.* Antoine, Elise managed to fall under the spell of another charming foreigner. It happened in a flash of a French summer. The savior in the market was British as it turned out, on holiday with a group of friends. They had all just been to a christening of somebody's baby at the church in Malcouziac, an odd but atmospheric choice of venue. The hero's name was Stephen; he was a banker in London. He had *such* a dishy accent, Elise exclaimed. His friends, a cosmopolitan crew of young professionals who had witnessed his saving the day and Elise's gushing approval, invited the two sisters to join them at dinner that evening at *Les Saveurs*. Merle was more than happy to oblige. *Les Saveurs* remained her favorite local restaurant.

Before dinner, there was an afternoon of uproar. A public servant of some sort arrived from the *mairie* to take César into custody. He demanded that Merle and Elise accompany him to the town hall and make a statement. Merle tried to use her best French but the process was confusing and tedious. Elise insisted on telling the story her way, in her French, making the afternoon even longer. When the real driver showed up to collect the table and the cooler, he caused a minor ruckus himself.

By eleven o'clock that evening, Merle had been ready for bed for hours. But her little sister was just getting warmed up, talking animately around the large table at *Les Saveurs* to all the Brits. She focused on Stephen naturally, who eyed her as if she were a shiny object from a strange land. Merle leaned her chin on her hand, sipping the last of many glasses of wine, when the woman to her left leaned toward her.

"She seems quite taken with our Stephen," the woman said with a smile. She was wearing something flowy and orange, and had a fine English pallor. "Your sister."

"She's a very friendly girl," Merle said.

"I can see that." The woman sat back and jingled her bracelets as if finished with her innuendoes.

Merle watched Stephen and Elise talking, heads together. He was wearing a sky blue polo shirt tonight. His dark blond hair was parted precisely and he looked like something out of a 1930s sailing advertisement. No wonder Elise liked him. But, wait—

"Is he married or something?" Merle whispered to the woman. What was her name? Ah, yes, Phoebe.

"'Something,'" Phoebe said, chuckling.

"Is he— with you?"

Phoebe squinted at her with a disbelieving look. "Really?" She leaned closer and whispered, "Gay. One-hundred percent homosexual."

Oh. Of course. Poor Elise. Well, she could figure it out herself.

Stephen didn't walk them home although it was easy to see Elise was expecting it. He hung back in the safety of his friends outside the restaurant and pointed vaguely in the opposite direction as they all said good night. Elise sighed and took Merle's arm as they walked carefully on the cobblestones down the dark streets. The evening was perfect, warm and starry, and the wine at dinner didn't hurt their moods.

"Isn't he cute?" Elise said when they turned the corner. "I could just eat him up."

"Adorable."

"Hell of it is, they go home tomorrow, so I guess that's that. Fun while it lasted."

"He was very brave today, jumping to our rescue."

Elise put her head on Merle's shoulder, making walking even more difficult. "He was."

They walked the last block in silence, just concentrating on their footing while Merle dug into her purse for her keys. Elise stood behind her at the door, gazing upwards at the night sky.

The sound of the footsteps must have been disguised by the rattling of keys. Suddenly a man stood in front of them, wearing gloves, a knit cap, and a black bandanna over his lower face. He held a can of some sort in his right hand. He pressed a button and paint spewed out with a whoosh. Elise screamed. Merle turned toward her sister as the vandal giddily spray-painted Elise's dress in fluorescent orange swirls, turning her navy blue sundress into a crazy mess. Elise shrieked again, backing away as he pursued her.

"Stop that!" Merle cried, lunging forward to kick the paint can out of his hand. She missed and nearly fell over. The man said something muffled by his bandanna, then turned the spray paint on her. She cursed and yelled again to stop, holding up her hands to cover her face only to have them covered with slippery orange paint.

Elise made a grunting noise, sprang forward, and the man toppled over to the right, landing on his elbow, the paint can rolling away down the street. "Get out of here, you lowlife scum," she yelled.

He got to his feet and took an aggressive stand, arms rounded and outstretched like he meant to grab them. Merle moved back, yelling at him in French to get away, holding her keys between her fingers as she'd been taught by her father years before. The man looked around for his paint can but it had disappeared into the shadows. His eyes were glowing in the starlight, a pale blue, and he breathed noisily.

They stared each other down for a ragged moment.

"Thierry?" Merle asked. "Go home. *Laissez maintenant.*"

The man looked at her, blinking, and didn't move. Did he not understand? She repeated her demands that he leave immediately, pulling Elise's arm toward the door. She had a hand on the door knob when she said his name again.

"*Laissez ici. Allez à la maison!*"

He laughed this time, then spun and ran down the street, into the night.

SEVENTEEN

LANGUEDOC

Pascal d'Onscon adjusted the burgundy wool beret above his eyebrows for the fifth time. He felt ridiculous in this get-up as an old-fashioned farmer from the countryside, complete with blue jumpsuit, powdered hair, drawn lines on his face, and the ubiquitous French beret. He had stuffed a small pillow into his underwear, giving him a paunch, also a necessity for the elderly.

He waited in his car down the road until he'd seen the boy, the grandson of the owner of the vineyard, drive past in a hurry for his afternoon pint with his friends in the village. Pascal couldn't chance meeting up with the grandson again. They'd spent too much time together on his last visit.

Antoine-Luc Gagne had spoken to him on the phone yesterday. The harvest was due to begin next week at Domaine Bourboulenc, the grandson said. They were busy organizing workers, finding extra help, extra tools, all the necessary preparations. It would take weeks to harvest this enormous vineyard but it was done painstakingly by hand, like the old ways his grandfather demanded.

Pascal's hope was to find the ninety-year-old proprietor alone. He was nearly blind, giving Pascal an advantage in his disguise. Even if the two sons were around he was fairly confident they wouldn't recognize him either. Men rarely looked at the elderly with the same eye they gave to young women or the competition for such women, men their own age.

After Antoine-Luc disappeared in a cloud of dust in a sporty American car with blue racing stripes, Pascal turned his BMW around and drove toward the vineyard gates, finding a shady spot along the lane to park. He got out, hiked up his underpants, and began a wobbly, bowlegged walk down the lane and into the vineyard itself. His line this time was an offer of harvest workers, a special connection he supposedly had with some North Africans. Moroccans and Algerians who spoke French were highly prized. He would supply a small army for the old man, if he agreed. Finding enough workers for the *vendange* was always a struggle.

The grandson had spilled some information about illegal sales across AOC territories the last time he was here; this time Pascal hoped to get final confirmation. Selling grapes to wineries outside of the AOC, the *Appellation d'origine contrôlée,* was a serious offense but difficult to prove. Grapes didn't come with labels so wineries did much of the control themselves, to protect their reputations.

No one answered his knock on the door of the *mas,* the farm-house now tasting room where he'd been offered refreshments the last time. He walked around the old building and found an older woman picking vegetables in a tidy bed. Her tomato plants were robust, heavy with ripe fruit she was putting into a large basket at her feet. She straightened and squinted at him from under her large hat.

The proprietor was in the house, she said. She hesitated, looking Pascal up and down, then agreed to see if her brother could be disturbed. Pascal gave her a quick version of harvest workers for hire then followed her back to the house. He waited patiently in a sitting room, looking at dusty photographs on the walls of harvests past. The room was cooler than outside but still warm and musty, the shutters closed against the sun.

Finally, the old man, Henri Gagne, shuffled in, wearing a plaid bathrobe over ancient undergarments. He was bald with wiry white eyebrows and a thousand wrinkles. He and Pascal shook hands and made small talk the way people do, especially country people. It was rude to dive into business without polite chatter, at least out here in the Languedoc. The sister brought them ice water and a plate of crackers. Henri was on a strict diet, she apologized. Pascal had seen him drinking wine and eating cheese the last time but he said nothing, just bit into a stale cracker.

They sat on the upholstered chairs by a shuttered window. Dust puffed up from the seats in little clouds. Pascal explained again who he was— his *nom de guerre* was Pablo this time— and launched into a lament about harvest workers. Finally, the old man asked where he got his, offering Pascal an opening.

After a long-winded discussion on the good and bad aspects of hiring foreigners, especially Africans— Henri was as opinionated as any codger— Pascal let the conversation lag for a moment then added, "And what about trucks? To transport the grapes to market?"

"We have many trucks," old Henri said, waving a hand. "So many. My sons love the trucks. Some break down but still we have enough. You have trucks?"

"Oh, yes. We are set as well."

"Drivers though, hmmm." The old man rubbed his chin. "Last year I had to use some young ones and they got lost and barely made it home for dinner."

"Do they have to go far?"

"Oh, perhaps. Sometimes we sell to wineries a hundred miles away." He squinted at Pascal then cackled. "Don't tell *les flics!*"

Pascal laughed. "Your grapes must be in high demand."

"*Oui, oui.* Of course. They are the best *Bourboulenc* grapes in all the Languedoc. And the grand domaines know it."

"I have heard this," Pascal said. "If only my vineyard had your *terroir*, and expertise. Maybe you could send one of your sons over one day? After the harvest, to instruct me on the best practices?"

He stood up but the old man stayed in his chair, staring blankly at the opposite wall where a vase of sunflowers sat wilting. "If they remembered half what I taught them I would be surprised." He looked sad, despite crowing about his vineyard seconds before. "I pity the future. When I am gone— *pfft!* It all goes with me."

Pascal promised to call about the workers. They said 'good day' and Pascal stepped back outside into the blazing heat. He hobbled around the *mas,* running through what the old man had said. He had his confirmation but he still would need to arrange a sting of sorts where they caught the trucks on their way out of the AOC, or actually in a neighboring area. It would take some manpower to get that done.

He was looking at his phone, thinking of who to call to make this happen, as he walked slowly down the drive and turned left at the pavement. He had straightened from his elderly crouch and lengthened his stride just as the man emerged from the hedgerows.

"Look at you!" The man was laughing. "That hat! You are ridiculous."

Pascal stopped, almost to his car. The man stood between him and safety inside the vehicle.

"Can I help you, *monsieur?*"

"Can I help you, *monsieur,*" the man repeated mockingly, using an odd voice, one that made Pascal's neck prickle. He had heard this voice before. The man stepped closer, out of the shade of the tree, and Pascal saw his scar, a long vertical injury that cleft his left cheek, pink and jagged with tissue. It was hideous and made the man all the more awful. It was hard to see past his scar, to imagine what he looked like before.

"You know who I am," he said, not as a question. "You sent me to prison, back before this." He gestured at his face. "Who will you nab this time? Whose life will you ruin?"

"You mistake me, *monsieur.*"

The man stepped closer still so Pascal could feel his hot breath and smell the stink of his cotton shirt and see the spittle on his cracked lips. It was, ironically, the smell of the man that brought all the memories back, so that his reply was unnecessary. Nevertheless, it was spoken, and not in a friendly manner.

"You and me, we are enemies. I never forget— how could I? It stares at me in the mirror every day, the crime, the harm, the self-righteous vindictiveness, what you have done to me in the name of justice. There will be justice but it will be *my* justice this time.

"I will have my revenge, and I will vanquish you."

EIGHTEEN

MALCOUZIAC

"Honey? Are you there?"

Merle took the cellphone from her ear and stared at the display, making sure she was still connected. "Tristan?"

"I'm here. Can you hear me?" His voice was faint.

Merle picked at the orange paint in the lifeline on her palm. Was it some kind of a sign, that her lifeline glowed with fluorescent paint that was impossible to remove? Vandalism stained her life? She sighed and walked from the kitchen into the garden. The sunshine was bright, and very welcome.

"Yes, I hear you. Listen, there's been some new developments here." Merle had worried about what to tell him about the spray-paint attack. She'd decided to just lay it out. "You know your aunt Elise is here? Well, she and I got into a scuffle with a guy with a can of spray paint night before last. He's the one who apparently did the graffiti on the house."

"You confronted him? Mom!"

"More like he confronted us. We were coming home late and he appeared out of the dark. He sprayed paint on me and Elise."

"What a —" He cut himself off.

"I think I know who he is. Madame Suchet says he's a guy who lives down the street and is mentally ill." Merle still wasn't sure if it was Thierry or not. "The police are in the next town over now so everything takes forever to work out. Elise and I went over there yesterday and filed the complaint. But there wasn't an officer around."

"Are you all right?"

"Yes, we're fine. Just cleaning orange paint off ourselves." Merle sat in the shade of the acacia tree, on the low stone wall. "But I can't leave today. If I go now the whole thing will just get swept under the carpet. The vandalism on the house, the assault, everything. I feel like I'd be running away. And if I wait and go in a couple days it will be too late to take you to college."

"Oh. Okay." He sounded mildly disappointed.

"Elise has to get back to work and she's had enough of France for awhile." That was an understatement. She'd railed all night and most of yesterday, scrubbing paint from her face, neck, ears, arms, chest, hair, and legs. She was furious, and Merle didn't blame her.

"You're not coming back?"

"It was a tough decision. I'm sorry. But— will you be all right? Aunt Stasia and Uncle Rick can take you to college. Stasia will get everything organized in your dorm room."

"Don't worry, Mom. I told you before, you didn't need to come back from Europe just to drive me down."

"Are you sure?" Merle knew in her heart she was doing it just for herself. That Tristan didn't really need her to hold his hand, to do the big send-off which would probably include tears.

"It's cool. Everything is already in boxes and ready to go. You wouldn't believe how busy Aunt Stasia is, buzzing around like a general, giving orders and making sure everybody has every hairbrush and calculator and spiral notebook in the world. She packed toilet paper, just in case. She's even got me set up with razors and shaving cream. I still have, like, three hairs on my chin but she's convinced I'm going to need them any minute now."

"She's a dynamo." Her sister was the ultimate organizer. She probably made binders full of lists and emergency information for her daughter Willow and for Tristan. They both were going to college this fall. It was Willow's final year and Tristan's first. That they would be just sixty miles apart at their respective colleges was a comfort. The fact that Merle would miss seeing Tristan shave for the first time cut into her heart though.

"I really wanted to get you settled," Merle said.

"It's crazy to fly back for a couple days. It probably costs a fortune. We've got this dialed. Hey, how's Pascal?"

That was a good question. She hadn't heard from him in awhile. "He's busy working somewhere. I don't see him much." Which was a shame. Where was he? She'd texted him yesterday about the spray-paint assault and hadn't heard back.

"Well, tell him I've been practicing those moves he showed me and they are killer."

"What moves?"

Tristan laughed. "Ask him. I'm not telling you."

Merle talked to her son for a few more minutes then let him go. He had to finish packing and there was a party somewhere tonight. She hung up the phone and felt a little bereft. Why didn't she just go home? To hell with the police and the damn vandal. But her sense of responsibility to her property and herself, plus flying back to the U.S. then returning in four days— a crazy trip that promised killer jet lag— kept her rooted here. If nothing else she would get Thierry the help he needed. Maybe that would make up for not helping Tristan get settled in college.

She set the phone on the wall and put her face in her hands. Why was life full of so many difficult decisions? Was she being selfish by not going back for Tristan? She was, she knew it. She wanted the quiet, the writing time, the time to get things done on her house. She didn't want to spend days traveling and recovering from jet lag. She wanted to be free of distractions, of problems, of other people's lists. Even her little sister's lists. And her sweet, loving son's lists.

Tristan was going to college. Although he'd gone to boarding school for years, this last year while he lived at home had compensated for many missed moments. And yet it now made his leaving that much harder. Maybe she should have gone back with him weeks before, spent these last few weeks together. But he'd made it clear he was fine, he had all those new friends, and he didn't need her. That was what a parent wanted, right? To *not* be needed, to have done the job of growing a real boy, a man who could make his own decisions, who could study and read and laugh and love—and live!— with or without his mother.

She felt the tears run down her face. Tristan was her only child. Somehow, she had done something right, she knew that. He could be any mother's dream kid— focused, balanced, funny, and kind. If trouble came— she was sure it would, it came to everyone— they would deal with it. He would deal with it. They hadn't mentioned Harry, Tristan's father. He came up rarely in conversation these days but was in their thoughts often. He had loved his son as best he could. Harry would have been so proud of Tristan, Merle was sure of that.

"Are you ready?"

Elise was standing at the kitchen door in her travel clothes: gray yoga pants, yellow tank top, and fleece jacket with a tote bag over her shoulder. Her face was rosy from all the scrubbing and her hair was piled on her head in a messy clip.

"Yes, all set." Merle stood up and wiped her cheeks.

"I wish you were—" Elise peered at Merle. "Are you okay?"

Merle nodded. Was speaking still necessary?

"I wish you were going with me." Elise took her hand. "Thanks for an incredible week. A memorable one." They hugged. Merle felt the tears come again. Elise released her. "You can still go with me. We can work out the ticket."

She shook her head. "That train won't wait for you."

~

AFTER MERLE LEFT her sister in Bergerac, waving one last time as Elise boarded the train for Paris, she drove out of the city into the countryside, parked her car by a field of wheat, and had a good cry. Why was everyone leaving? Why did Thierry hate her so much? Where was Pascal?

She wanted to be alone— and yet. No one wants to be alone forever, to be rejected, or disliked, or abandoned. She gulped a big breath and wiped her face off with a tissue. Transitions, she reminded herself, are always hard, no matter how well-planned and well-intentioned.

She put the car back into gear and pulled out on the narrow blacktop. She thought about her job at Legal Aid, the offer her boss made before she left, to take over the fundraising arm of the non-profit. It would give Merle purpose, she knew that, and she also knew she needed that sort of validation. She was good at fundraising, at organization, at event-planning. And yet, there was nothing in the job as Lillian Warshowski did it that was very appealing. Maybe Merle could make it work for her though, work her magic and change it into something more satisfying. She could do whatever she wanted if she was in charge. She should write to Lillian and keep the offer fresh in both their minds. She made a note on her mental to-do list.

By the time she pulled into the hot parking lot next to the bastide walls of Malcouziac, her head was brimming with projects, goals, ideas, and plans. She'd called Pascal from the road and left him another voice message, asking him to call, telling him she'd decided not to go home for Tristan. She'd called the police station in Sulliac and spoken to the sullen policewoman about her complaint. She'd returned a missed call from a plumber who was to start work on the old *pissoir*, turning it into a laundry. And she'd planned out the next chapter for Odette, where she would go, who she would see.

There was a renewed sense of purpose in her quick steps as she walked through the arched gate of the ancient *ville* and smiled up at the solid, golden walls of her town.

It was like coming home.

ODETTE AND THE GREAT FEAR

PART FIVE

The letter was torn, dirty, and weeks old by the time it found Odette in the deep countryside of southwestern France. She stared at the postal scribble on the front, near her name. At least three weeks had passed, maybe four. But she had a letter from her brother at last.

Jérome was three years younger than she was. And much smarter as well. He had been sent to school where she had not because she was a girl. Odette always wondered if she would have been as clever as Jérome if she'd gone to school, learned about the world, read libraries full of books, taken Latin, and learned to fight with swords and words. But it was a fruitless daydream. Some girls were taught at home by tutors and governesses but not the merchant class like her parents. No tailor could afford a governess for his daughter. She had been working at her father's knee since she was five.

She could read however, thanks to her mother's care, so the letter was opened with excitement.

My dear sister,

Word has come finally from our parents about your situation and I am glad to hear you escaped unharmed. Paris is ablaze every night with skirmishes and drunken riots, things no girl should see. I hear you are safe and healthy and I hope it is so. It makes my heart glad.

Odette had to pause and hold the letter to her breast for a moment while her eyes cleared. She had done the same with the letter from her parents. It was so hard to think of them miles and miles away, living lives she could only imagine. Would she ever see her brother again? The next part made that clearer.

My news is complicated. I have left my college in Lyon and joined the Army. Before you cry out in protest let me tell you there was little choice in the matter. I was to be drafted within days. This way there is a possibility of a commission and thus staying out of the worst of it.

I do not delude myself; it will be bloody. But keep me in your prayers, *chérie*. I go to an unknown place, a camp somewhere, tomorrow morning. I will find out my rank, my orders, my uniform, then. I wish I could tell you to write but I don't know where I'll be. I will try to write again as soon as I can.

Until we see each other again, I remain,

Your loving brother,

Jérome.

Odette covered her mouth to contain the moan. She was sitting in the village, on a stone wall by the cemetery, under a bare tree. The sun shone through the branches onto the wet leaves at her feet.

Jérome had left his studies. He was looking at a legal career, he had a fine mind and a quick tongue, a heart for all men and women alike, all the abilities to make him a great *avocat*. And now he would wear the uniform of the French Army and take up weapons against...

whoever they commanded. It was a fuzzy war, with Spain, maybe England, perhaps Prussia and Austria, maybe with rebels inside the country itself. Yes, France was at war with itself. That perceived weakness had brought out all the old rivals, ready to pounce on the troubled state, on the royal disaster, on the chaos of the ruling class.

Where was Jérome now? Marching to Alsace? Off to vanquish 'hors de loi'— outlaws of the uprising in the Vendée? What was happening with the Queen, still imprisoned in Paris with the children? How in the year of our Lord 1793, whatever the new months were called, could the King be put on trial by commoners? It had been done already and the vote, the villagers said, even included nobles who voted for death.

The King's fate was sealed; he was dead. It was so distant from her own life. There had been rumors that the Queen was also dead, executed by the Louisette, or 'madame guillotine.' Versailles and all their fancy trappings hadn't saved them. Odette struggled to care.

She had heard someone had lost their head on the guillotine in Périgueux, the provincial capital, but nobody knew who or what the offense was. Instead she tried to remember the names for the months that had come down from the republicans. The Convention had renamed so many things, from the calendar to the clock. She reckoned it was the time of the mist, *Brumaire*, what was once late October. The old names for months were ridiculous as well. Why not rename them? She was in favor of a clean slate.

Yet, so much had changed these last few years in the nation of France. Kings gone, armies marching, nobles stripped of their riches, priests and monks thrown adrift. Here in the countryside little changed from day to day. The bell had been removed from the local church by the Army to use the metal for weapons. The priest had run off. But what else? Not much unless you counted handsome strangers arriving unannounced.

Had she run away from all the action, the important business of the capitol? She knew she had and now she wondered if her idyllic goat-herder life was really what she wanted. Jérome might be in mortal danger but at least he was doing something to save his country. He was a patriot, doing important work. What would he think of the sister who once chanted and marched to Versailles, who shook her fist at royals, who demanded affordable food and better conditions for everyone? Now she could be found with those fists around goat teats, doing the job of a milkmaid.

Oh, it was honest work. She was proud of the way she'd learned new tasks, how she'd gone from a city girl to a woman unafraid to get into the mud with goats. But part of her longed for more, for an engagement with big events. They were happening, now, but so far from here that they were invisible, as cold and ephemeral as the mistral that blew in from unseen mountains in the springtime. She wanted to find the source of the wind, to be part of its force. To help bring the winds of change to France.

And yet, here she sat, in her tattered gown and broken boots, shivering as the winter came closer. Soon it would be the month *Frimaire*, of frost. Grazing the goats on the hillsides would be cold business and she had no coat. The idea of a wool coat, or even a cotton one, filled her mind for a moment, pushing out revolutionary thoughts and dreams. A nice wool coat, heavy on her shoulders with sleeves long enough to cover her hands. Perhaps a man's overcoat. But how to find one? How to afford one?

Odette looked up and down the tiny village street, checking the citizens for warm garments. None to be seen. Perhaps it didn't get terribly cold here. But almost as she thought those words a breeze blew her hair off her neck. A cold wind that portended winter.

She stood up and tucked Jérome's letter into her bodice, next to her heart. It wouldn't be enough to keep her warm this winter but in its own way it might help her survive.

NINETEEN

Pascal knocked on the new door shutters, admiring their solid nature if not their peeling paint. It was late and he wasn't even sure Merle was home. He had driven from the Languedoc, stopping only briefly at his own cottage to pick up clean clothes, and felt the fatigue of the day in his shoulders and knees.

He knocked again and got out his phone. Did she keep her mobile by her bed? Of course she did, she was an American. He started to call then changed his mind, texting her that he was at the door and could she please let him in.

There was no reply but in a moment he heard the rhythmic pounding of feet on the stairs and across the room. Then the locks turned, including the padlock inside the shutters, and there she was. Merle stood in a pale nightgown in the moonlight, her hair a mess, arms crossed, a flicker of suspicion in her eyes. Then she reached for him and pulled him inside.

He let her re-lock the doors behind him as he flicked on a lamp. He dropped his duffle bag by the stairs. It was good to be back with her, even though it would be short and she might be angry about that. He'd been ignoring her texts for days.

She stood awkwardly by the old dining table, fingers tracing its lines. "Come here, *chérie*," he said hoarsely. He held out a hand and she put hers into it. "Look at you," he whispered. They kissed as his hands roamed over her.

She pulled back finally, to catch her breath. "And look at you. What are you wearing?"

He laughed. He was still in the farmer's disguise of blue jumpsuit and muddy boots. He took off the burgundy beret and stuffed it in his coat pocket. He still had the white in his hair. She fingered it. "Is this the real you?"

"Someday but not today. I have been undercover again. It is quite thrilling," he grinned, giving her a sample of the gimpy old man walk. "Can I use your bath for a clean up? And then we—" He pointed up the stairs. "Can you wait for me?"

Merle put both her hands behind his neck and kissed him again. "All I do is wait for you, Pascal."

Later they opened the shutters and let the moonlight wash over them. It was still hot in the upstairs bedroom, and their bodies glistened with sweat. They were silent, a little breathless with the intensity of their lovemaking. Pascal glanced at Merle and her lips were parted, eyes shut, the curve of her chin lit up by the moon. He waited until she opened her eyes to speak.

"I ran into an old friend yesterday. At the vineyard where I was playing the old man."

She rolled on her side, facing him. "A woman?"

He clenched his jaw. "No, blackbird. An old *adversaire*."

"An enemy? You don't have enemies, Pascal." She kissed his shoulder.

"Many men I have put into prison, *chérie*. This was one from fifteen years ago. I had almost forgotten him." But not now, with that scar. He would not forget that face. "He was the owner of the vineyard. Another one, not where I saw him. From an old family, he inherited the vineyard, a familiar story. He got in over his head. Took loans from some unsavory characters. Cut corners. He was guilty of fraud many times over. We caught him eventually but I was under-cover for most of that summer."

Pascal paused, picking at his cuticles as he remembered the outrage of Léo Delage at his betrayal. Pascal had worked in the mixing room that summer, hauling grapes, helping the experts, when he wasn't drinking and playing cards with Léo. His arrest came as a shock to the winery, the deception of a false friendship. The worst type of treachery, the kind with a smile and a pat on the back.

He didn't feel guilt over the operation. Delage was a criminal. But the personal deceit, the acting, the falseness— it got to a man sometimes. It made him feel dirty, as dishonest as those he put away.

"And what? He's out of prison?" Merle asked.

"He was in prison eight years then he disappeared. Left the country or something. But he returned in May, on an expired pass-port. He jumped the gates at Marseille."

"Did he threaten you?"

Of course he had. But he didn't want to worry Merle, just inform her. So he said, "Nothing like that. It was just strange. He talked of peasant uprisings and guillotines and Louis the Sixteenth. I think he's gone mad. He'd changed a lot over the years. I never would have recognized him."

He rolled to face her and set his palm on the curve of her cheek. "I shouldn't have brought him up. He is a toad of a man."

"Where were you?"

"In the Languedoc. A lovely little vineyard that grows Bour-boulenc grapes, and tries to sell them illegally outside their AOC." He smiled at her, pulling the sheet up to cover them. "Let's forget everything about him. Okay?"

She snuggled closer, burrowing into his chest. "I'm so glad you're here, Pascal. I've missed you."

He pulled her close and nestled his nose in her hair, pulling the essence of her into him. If only it could stay like this. What were they to do? "I feel very selfish. I am glad you didn't go home to see Tristan. I should feel bad about my selfishness. But I don't."

She looked up at him. "I feel exactly the same way; guilty but not guilty."

"Can a lawyer do that, plead both ways?"

"This lawyer can." She paused then asked, "Have you heard from Clarisse?"

"No. I think that is the last of that."

"But what about the boy?"

"I told you, *chérie*. We couldn't have children. *She* couldn't. She was infertile. She lied about all that." He tipped up her chin. "You believe me, don't you?"

"Of course. But, I don't know, don't you ever think maybe it could be possible? That you'd like to be a hundred percent sure? That you should get tests?"

"Paternity tests? Those are meaningless in France. The thing is, blackbird, that a woman in France can just say, 'this boy is your son,' and the courts can make you pay support for him. Neither they— nor I— can force the child to supply his DNA. Since Clarisse never even mentioned a son until that day, and never made any legal challenge, I am sure she made the whole thing up for that day in Paris. She was trying to get money out of me, any way she could. She's like that."

IN THE MORNING, Pascal showered again and packed his car. He had to keep moving. Merle didn't ask him where he was going but he could see that little wrinkle between her eyebrows asking the question. Maybe it was just the question of why he had to leave at all, although she knew that answer. Was it something about Clarisse and that horrible day in Paris? Or was it just the situation, the two of them, coming and going and never knowing when they would see each other? Whatever it was, it made him sad, that wrinkle of worry, of doubt. If there was one thing he wanted, it was to make her smile.

He pulled her into the garden and held her close in the morning sunshine that washed across the ripening pears on the espaliered tree and the golden stone of the house. The earth was torn up again, mounds of dirt were everywhere. He wished he could stay here and help her with her new laundry. And all the other little problems she had, the wrinkle between her eyebrows and especially those late night ones in the bedroom.

"I will come again soon," he promised.

"You better," she said, squeezing him against her. "Or else."

TWENTY

SANCERRE

Léo Delage hid in the rows of vines as the evening light finally left the sky. It felt strange to be back in the Sancerre, on the generational soil that had raised him and his siblings, that had fed his grandparents, and their grandparents before them. To smell the sharp scent of gunpowder in the dirt, the mint on the breeze, the heat in the clay through his shoes; memories he'd buried so deep during his years inside the prison at Chateauroux that when they returned, right in front of him, he had to blink, shattered for a moment by sensation.

The *vendange* was underway. He hadn't expected the harvest yet as the vineyard was hundreds of miles north of the Languedoc where he'd been working. They hadn't begun yet in the south but for whatever reason— poor planning, inadequate knowledge, or mere stupidity— his son had signaled the start of the harvest here at Domaine Le Grand Vinon. Léo had his doubts about his son before. Now he knew that his eldest, who had left the priesthood to rescue the vineyard when Léo was arrested, was an idiot.

It was full dark when Léo made his way through the vines to the square of light, the window in the mixing room. They would be crushing the grapes most of the night. He cracked open the door and peered cautiously inside. It would be nice to confront the idiot on his own since Léo himself was technically not allowed on the estate. His own estate, his vines, his domaine— it rankled. Still, it would be best to keep his presence quiet.

He knew this building like the back of his hand. He crept along the perimeter, around the enormous vats, listening to the machinery working in a side room. Was his son not even here? Had the idiot delegated all the important roles and was off stuffing his mouth with *canard confit* as the winery foundered?

Then he heard his voice. Adrien was speaking to someone in the control room at the far end of the building. Another man left the room and began walking toward the door. Léo pressed himself into an alcove, remembering it had once held herbs for warding off molds and odd smells when his grandmother was alive. The man walked briskly past, disappearing out the door.

Léo poked his head out. Adrien was standing outside the control room, staring at his mobile phone or something. He had aged. No longer was he the thin, bearded, head-in-the-clouds *esthète* of his seminary days. He had grown fat, Léo thought with distaste, as if the business fed him too well. He still had a small beard but it was partly gray. His hair was still brown, he was of course not yet forty, but thinning. Fifteen years was a long time to be away. Would Adrien even recognize him?

Only one way to find out. Léo walked slowly toward him, his gum-soled shoes squeaking on the cement floor. Adrien looked up, squinting. He wore glasses now, giving him a clerical look.

"Who's that? Whoever you are, you are not authorized to be in here, sir. You are trespassing. Please leave at once."

Léo kept walking toward him. Adrien was glancing around, agitated now, afraid.

"It's me, Adrien," he said at twenty paces. "Your father."

Adrien kept backing up, now standing in the control room doorway with his hand on the knob. He straightened at Léo's voice though, as if the auditory memory was dominant. He watched warily as Léo stopped at a close but nonthreatening range. "Do you recognize me?" he whispered, his voice strange even to himself.

"Of course," Adrien said too quickly. His eyes, like everyone's, fixed on the scar. "What— excuse me. How are you? Where have you been?"

"Well, that's a long story, isn't it? You only know half of it, you know about Chateauroux, *oui*? You didn't come to visit but I understand that. Times were difficult." When Adrien continued his blank stare, Léo continued. He had no wish to draw out all the years of trial and journey. The prison at Chateauroux was nothing to dwell on. "I was there for eight years. Then, South America. Have you been? It is very beautiful. The ocean, oh, yes, it is vast. Then, I am returned, back to the bosom of my family." He smiled with the good side of his face.

"But— but you can't be here, papa," Adrien said, sounding like a school boy.

"Then we won't tell *les flics*, eh?"

"You can't be here, or anywhere near. Not in the village or in Sancerre. They have been here just recently, I am sure of it. After you— your— after what happened they come regularly, I know who they are. They think they fool me with their stories of distributors and merchants but I know who they are."

"Then, if you have such a good eye, I will hide when they come."

Adrien turned a vivid shade of scarlet and sputtered, "*Absolument pas!* This is my life now. I have a wife and two children and they can't see you, ever. You must go before anyone sees you."

"You are so afraid, son? Quivering at the thought of the police? Such a child. You disgust me with your girlish fears. Where is your *virilité*? Your strength, your courage? Look at you." He frowned at the shivering jelly that was his son. "You are afraid of your own father. Is that it?"

"Papa, listen. Not two days ago a policeman was here, snooping around, asking questions, pretending to be a wine buyer. That is who

I am afraid of. Not you. Although God knows I should be. Look at your face, it is— "

Léo stepped closer, to give his son a good look. "It is what? Hideous? This is what happens when you are a man sometimes. You stand up for yourself and you take your licks. You don't shake in your boots like a little boy." He took his son's weak shoulders in his big, calloused hands. "I failed you, Adrien. I was not here. But you must pick yourself up and be a man."

Adrien flung his arms out, shaking off his father's touch. He was furious now, so angry he spit as he spoke, red to the tips of his ears.

"Don't lecture me on the proper way to live, you— you viper. Get away from me! You disgust me. Do you know the mess you left? No, that never crossed your mind. Yes, you failed me, you failed all of us at the winery. Your wife who died of shame, your poor father, all your family. But you failed yourself most of all. I can't stand the sight of you. My children will be better off thinking you are dead. Yes, that's what I told them. You are dead to me. I am the vintner now. I am the caretaker to these ancient vines. I will see them through. You are no one. Nobody."

LÉO HEARD the lock turn behind him as he left the mixing room. He stomped across the dirt parking lot, kicking weeds that had grown there. This place was dying a slow death from neglect and incompetence but he was out of it. It was not his anymore. He hated the sight of it.

He had been wrong to come here. Wrong to think there might still be something for him here, in the place where he grew up, where he raised his sons. He didn't regret seeing the back of it. It had failed him just as he had failed it. They'd gone down together, he and the winery. What could he possibly have done here but fight with Adrien?

Bon débarras, Le Grand Vinon. Good riddance. We are done.

As he reached his truck, cursing his son and the police and everyone who had wronged him, something occurred to Léo, something Adrien said.

A policeman had been here, posing as a wine buyer. Just two days before. Was it a coincidence that he'd been on the trail of the man in the straw hat at the same time? He hadn't thought d'Onscon had recognized him. But fifteen years, a stretch in prison, and a knife wound to the face would do that.

He revved the engine, grinning into the night. The game was on.

TWENTY-ONE

MALCOUZIAC

The first week of September in the Dordogne brought a welcome relief from the heat for a few days, enough to hint that autumn would come. In the countryside the grape harvest began, and with it a stirring of the old ways, a joining of hands to get the work done during long hours in back-breaking work. Merle didn't participate in the *vendange*. She was too busy trying to get the plumber to work every day, harassing the suppliers of her new washer and dryer about delivery dates, and designing and sourcing a stone countertop.

And then there was the vandalism. On Friday, the gendarme from Sulliac came to visit her finally, and take his own photographs of the mess. She also showed him the ruined sundresses stiff with dry fluorescent paint that she and Elise wore the night of the paint assault. He seemed mortified by that, and expressed his dismay and apologies to both the sisters in a nice way. But when she hinted that Madame Suchet thought the culprit was her nephew he shook his head sadly.

"Please allow us to do our jobs in the most thoughtful way,

madame," he said. He was a middle-aged man, no longer thin but trying hard. It appeared he was dyeing his hair black.

"Would you like to speak to Madame Suchet? She lives there, across the street."

"In good time, madame."

The gendarme marched smartly out of her house and down the cobblestone street without a look at her neighbor's house. It was disappointing but maybe speaking to Merle was his only duty that day. Things moved at a glacial pace in France sometimes.

She stood in front of her house, arms crossed. In the back, she heard the clanking of the plumber, working on the water lines. The electrical hook-up was delayed again. She stared at Madame Suchet's house, glanced at the ugly paint on her house again, and marched across to knock on her neighbor's door. It opened instantly.

Madame S had a worried look. She must have been watching the policeman come and go.

"What do they say? What about Thierry?" she asked Merle, wringing her hands.

"I was wondering, Madame Suchet, if you could introduce me to your sister. And maybe Thierry, too, if he's at home?"

Madame Suchet, her hair and makeup immaculate, pinched her lips together and gave a curt nod. They stepped onto her stoop and she locked up. Merle followed the older woman down the steps and they walked silently down the short street, stopping in front of the weathered stucco townhouse with burgundy shutters. The door was unshuttered, the top half of the Dutch door open, the lace curtain blowing in the breeze. From within, the sound of tinny music, something old and lively like a big band orchestra, emerged from the darkened room.

Madame Suchet paused as if gathering her courage then knocked on the lower half of the door. When no one arrived she leaned in and called, "*Coucou!* Anyone home? It's Paulette."

Madame S opened the half door and stepped inside. Merle waited outside for an invitation while her neighbor disappeared into a back room, calling the funny little 'yoo-hoo' that the French say as 'coucou.'

In a moment she heard the two women's voices and her own name mentioned. She wondered if there would be more shouting. Madame Suchet reappeared, waved her inside, and led her to a sunny parlor off a kitchen where the sister sat folded into an oversized upholstered chair, her gray hair coming loose and a scowl on her wrinkled face. She looked like she'd been napping.

"Excuse the intrusion," Merle said.

"You haven't met, have you?" Madame S said, introducing her. "This is my sister, Ninon."

The sister pushed herself up and they did the French air kiss, just twice. That seemed to indicate the gesture was strictly a formality, nothing personal. The scowl did not change.

"I should have brought you something, I'm sorry," Merle said, embarrassed to be empty-handed. "Next time." She smiled and hoped it looked sincere.

Ninon waved a bony hand. "Too many sweets. I never bake anymore. It's not good for us."

"I love a good jam," Madame S said, eyes twinkling.

"Which of you is the eldest?" Merle asked after a pause in conversation.

"*Moi. Bien sûr.*" Ninon had sat again, flicking her icy glare at her sister. "Paulette is five years younger. Why do you ask?"

"Just curious. I have four sisters myself."

"*Ooh-la-la.*" Ninon examined Merle then, head to toe.

"Is your son at home, madame?" Merle asked, eager to get on with this and out of here.

Ninon glanced at her sister. "No. He is gone."

"Oh, I had hoped to speak to him," Merle explained. "I'm not upset about the vandalism—" not strictly true— "but I wanted to see if there was some way we could work things out. Maybe there is some way I can help Thierry, and he can help me."

Ninon frowned as if not comprehending what she was saying.

Her French must have let her down again. Paulette gave a quick translation/recap.

Ninon sat forward. "What are you speaking of? He had nothing to do with the graffiti on your house. I told Paulette—" She was glaring at both of them.

"He was home with you then, on Saturday night last week, when my sister and I were attacked with paint?"

The elder sister squinted, as if thinking back to that night. "He left on Wednesday. He has moved to Bordeaux and will not be back for some months."

Merle glanced at Madame S who nodded. "Yes, I saw him off on the bus."

Thierry was gone before the attack then. "And he didn't return?"

Both sisters agreed that he had not been back to the village. So, who had sprayed paint all over Elise and Merle?

Paulette turned solemnly to Merle. "He has been very depressed. Barely getting out of bed. He is not well." In English she whispered, "I am wrong. The person who saw Thierry was wrong. I'm sorry."

ON THE WAY back up the street Madame Suchet turned to Merle and stopped, anxiety in her eyes. "I have made a mess of this. My sister is so angry with me. Thierry is a sweet boy. He has his ups and downs, like I said. But today she tells me he tried to kill himself a month ago. She only just found out and sent him to the clinic in Bordeaux for treatment."

Her voice ached with grief. Merle touched her arm. "I'm so sorry. I should never have made you go there with me."

"Oh, no. If not for you she would never have told me how bad things were with Thierry. It is better to know, yes? So one can truly help. Sometimes a little good can come from a terrible thing."

They said their goodbyes quickly, a flick of the hand. Merle paused in front of her house, frowning again at the graffiti, musing over the heartbreak of Thierry, and suddenly seeing something new. Four letters, far apart but in the same paint color, partially over-painted by the second night's work. PCRF, in dark red. And then, over there, a primitive half moon or sickle, barely recognizable. How had she not seen that before?

Inside the house she put 'PCRF' into her search engine on her laptop and confirmed her suspicion. The PCRF was a congregation of older Communist parties, the *Parti Communiste Revolutionaire de France*. If there was anything they disliked more than the 'imperial-ists' it was the European Union, NATO, and anybody who said something nasty about Stalin.

It appeared she was a victim of anti-imperialist, anti-American fervor. Somehow that made her feel a little better.

Who were these rural Communists? The case for finding them seemed hopeless. If only she'd got a better look at the man that night, the laughing painter. She closed her eyes and tried to remember his laugh, his eyes, his walk, his smell; something that would help the police find the little bastard. All she could remember was his blue eyes.

She searched the Internet for news stories about vandalism with Communist leanings. There had recently been two incidents in the Acquitaine, the large southwestern department that included the Dordogne. One had been in Villefranche, near where Pascal and Irene Fayette lived in their hilltop hamlet. She jotted down the street name from a newspaper article. Maybe next time she was in that vicinity she'd check it out. And it might be worth pointing out to the lazy gendarmes.

Oh, she didn't mean that! She apologized silently, with an eye-roll, to Pascal. The gendarmes had more to do than find her vandal. They weren't lazy, they just had priorities. Merle checked her phone for a reply from Pascal. She'd texted him four days before but nothing had come back. It wasn't unusual. She was getting used to it actually. But she sent him another quick text about the PCRF find, thinking he might know something about the group.

She sighed, wondering if she should call him. Maybe tomorrow. Instead she composed a cheerful email to her boss at Legal Aid, Lillian Warshowski. She expressed her desire to know more about the job, what it entailed, what the salary would be, when she would start. She made overtures to Lillian who might still be annoyed with her for going on leave for so long. With a quick review she hit 'send' and hoped to catch Lillian on a good day.

There was no noise from the back garden. She went through the kitchen door into the sunshine. All the work had stopped for the day. For the week, no doubt. No plumber in sight. But as she investigated she found the water line was in, the dirt trench filled, and pipes going up inside the stone laundry. When would she be able to get the washer in here? Someday she'd be able to stop hauling her dirty clothes to the laundromat behind the pharmacy.

She glanced at her watch and realized she only had a few minutes to get ready for her French lesson. She hadn't done any of the homework either. She was getting pretty lax here in France, and something about it appealed to her. The rebel in her, small as that side of her was, approved.

She would run off and do her best, and endure the disapproval of her tutor. Then it would be time for a little writing.

ODETTE AND THE GREAT FEAR

PART SIX

The skies were dark with rain, pressing low into the hillsides. Another summer had ended, another that didn't live up to the usual heat. A third bleak harvest, more rumors of famine, illness, and degradation. The villagers were on edge, sharp-tongued toward each other. Odette tiptoed through them most days, hoping not to cause notice or aggravation.

The small gathering in the *place du village* made her hesitant to move past. She put her head down and skirted the people in the town square. What were they doing? She could hear a voice above the others, chastising someone. At the edge of the crowd, holding her can of goat milk close to her chest, she stopped.

A young woman stood in front of the crowd next to a large, angry man in a dark coat. Odette craned her neck to see better. The woman looked close to her own age, maybe a few years younger. The girl's beautiful face was ashen but her large, blue eyes flashed defiantly. What had she done? The villagers were prone to citizen justice in these parts.

Neither the young woman or the large man were known to Odette. He wore dusty working man's clothes, plain and sturdy, with heavy boots. He stood behind the girl and yanked on her hair, pulling it out of its pins. She had thick hair, glossy and brown. But the man grabbed it, tugging her from side to side menacingly. He sneered menacingly. "A traitor, that's what she is. Any tramp that comes through she sleeps with him for the money. For the food. And now she sleeps with soldiers for the revolution. Men who killed the King, who chopped off his head, who paraded his head around Paris! The worst sort of Frenchman."

Odette dropped her chin to hide her expression of disbelief. She knew that royalists abounded in the countryside, even here in the Dordogne, yet she hadn't known they were so brazen, so open about their beliefs. Surely someone in the crowd will set this bastard right. Someone will tell him that the King had to go so that the people could rule themselves in the new republic. So that rights and laws were for men, not for royals.

But the crowd was silent on that point. They jeered at the girl, calling her a *putain* and an *enchantresse*. Someone pulled on her dress hem, tearing off a section and waving it over his head. Even the women spit on the girl. What was wrong with them?

Odette stepped backwards, away from the crowd. It was an ugly scene she wanted nothing to do with. And yet, that girl. Was she guilty of something? Had she betrayed France by sleeping with a soldier? Odette's dreams flashed through her mind, of Ghislain. Was he the one the girl had been with?

The big man with the awful voice brought out a large pair of sheep-shearing shears, holding the big scissors above his head. "What do we do with traitors?"

Odette set down her milk can on a doorstep. They would chop off her hair, just like that. This was too much. She moved into the crowd, watching as they egged on the big man, telling him to cut off the trai-tor's hair. The clamor grew louder as she reached the front of the crowd. The girl's head was pulled sideways, the man pulling on her long hair and dramatically displaying the shears as he cackled with delight.

"Stop!" Odette said, stepping into the clearing. "This is wrong. You must stop."

A gasp and a pause quieted the crowd. Then the big man snipped off a long hank of hair and threw it toward the people. They cheered for more.

Odette spun toward the villagers. "You must see that this girl does not deserve this! How do you know that she is a traitor? Let the officials deal with her, if she is guilty. It is not your place to condemn her."

An old man in front of the crowd began to laugh. "If it isn't the Queen herself!"

This was a bad development. Marie-Antoinette was soundly disliked by all. She sat in prison in Paris awaiting her beheading.

"I am not— I am just like you. A *paysanne*. A goat herder. But I know mistreatment when I see it. This girl has not been found guilty by anyone but a bully with a pair of shears! I demand you let her go!"

Another section of brown hair flew over the crowd. Odette turned to the odious man with the scissors and told him again to stop what he was doing.

Suddenly the hands were on her. The crowd pushed Odette toward the young woman and the bully, chanting that she was a traitor, too. "Cut off her hair," they demanded.

With a few last slashes, the bully finished with the young woman, leaving her on her knees with her hair nearly gone. The last few inches of it stuck out awkwardly from her scalp and she put her face in her hands and cried.

The crowd kept pushing Odette forward until the man grabbed her around the waist and pulled her off the ground. He crowed that she was his, a captive, and would receive the correct punishment of all traitors. Two women came from the crowd and began to pull the pins from Odette's hair. She was frantic, pushing their hands away while trying to kick the man in the shins as he held her against him.

The roar of the crowd grew as more villagers joined the show. The stores emptied, barn doors opened, horses stopped. Odette thrashed wildly, trying to free herself, getting more angry and desperate with every second. "Let me go!" she repeated as the man holding her laughed in her ears.

"She's a fine little rebel, eh? Do you hate the King, too? Do you sleep with the soldiers for the revolution?" He taunted her, building the crowd's ire.

She was tiring. The man was too strong, too tall. He could hold her off the ground for hours. She balled her fists and tried to smash his face behind her but he kept laughing. The crowd laughed with him, enjoying it all.

Her hair was loose now, a ready target for his shears. But he couldn't grab it without putting her down as his shears were in his other hand. She kept kicking and screaming and kicking and screaming. Would no one help her? She pleaded with the crowd of toothless men and scrawny women.

"That's enough." The voice carried over the crowd. Finally, Odette thought, someone has come to their senses.

Everyone turned to the south, the direction of the voice. The black hat was apparent before the rest of him: *le Comte* had arrived.

The crowd parted, suddenly silent. The Count walked forward, dour in a dark coat and riding boots. His hands were balled into fists at his sides. Everyone bowed slightly at his presence.

The man holding Odette dropped her unceremoniously. She fell into the other girl and sat down next to her in the dirt. Odette took her hand and whispered that it was all right now. She pulled her hand away and glared at Odette. Her face was streaked with tears but still her eyes were hard. She stood up and ran quickly away from the crowd, down the street. Everyone watched her go then turned back to the Count.

"Help her up," the Count demanded of the man. The bully sneered at the Count, swaggering for a moment, then dropped his shears. He leaned down and put his hands under Odette's arms and popped her up to her feet. She straightened, pushed back her hair and realized a foot-long section of it had been cut. It came off in her hand.

"Look what you've done, Toussaint," the Count said, shaking his head. "I have told you how many times now— I am the law here. Not you, not your vigilante justice. You are just a man, not the law."

Toussaint clenched his jaw and said nothing. An old woman in the crowd whispered something and the Count turned toward her.

"You wish to speak, *madame*?"

"*Oui!* You haven't the King to stand behind you anymore, *Monsieur le Comte*. Be careful."

The people shifted uncomfortably, eyeing the noble with distaste. His scar was highlighted as the sun sliced through the clouds, hitting his face. A few more gasps in the crowd.

"Thank you for the advice, *madame*. And I will remember your words when it is time to allocate the harvest from my lands." More gasps and murmurs. Odette frowned. That seemed excessively cruel, threatening the woman with starvation.

He turned to Odette. "You will come to tea this afternoon, *mademoiselle*." It was not a request. "Four o'clock." He turned back to the villagers and told them to go home and to try to behave as good citizens in the future. He watched Toussaint shuffle off. Then he tipped his hat to Odette and turned on his heel.

TWENTY-TWO

Merle stood on the tiny, sagging porch of Pascal's cottage, examining the overgrown yard for signs of life. The weeds had grown tall and lush, thistles had gone to seed, the grasses had burnt in the late summer sun. The fruit trees across the dirt road leading to Irene's goat farm had lost their spring glory and were now without any fruit at all except a few rotting apples and cherries in the dust. A pair of old leather boots she didn't recognize sat beside the door, covered with more dust.

It was obvious he wasn't here. She'd waited nearly a week since her last text to come here, to confront him if necessary, although she didn't think he was at fault. No, something was wrong. Well, maybe he was at fault. Maybe he was off with his ex-wife, or somebody else, doing what men do. Having his midlife crisis fling. It was a theory. Merle had trouble believing it, not when he was so— so *himself*, so sweet and kind and loving, the last time she saw him.

She knocked hard, pounding with her fist. "Pascal!?" No answer. She tried the door but it was locked. She rounded the house, beating at the sticky weeds and cutting grasses, to see in the windows. The curtains were drawn. She reached the kitchen door and gave it a good shake. Locked up tight. She tried each window, pushing up on the frames. The second kitchen window gave a little and she gave it a mighty shove. It went up a few inches.

Dragging over a lawn chair she stood to get leverage to winch the sash up. Finally, it was open enough to let her slip inside. She blinked in the darkened room. This was the dining alcove, a small space off the kitchen. A slice of sunshine came through the top of the window behind her.

She called his name again and for reasons she couldn't articulate sniffed the air. It smelled musty and closed-up but nothing worse. Quickly she searched the rooms and found them messy but normal. Dust everywhere. And no Pascal.

The calendar in her mind clicked into gear. It had been twelve days since she'd heard from him, or seen him. It wasn't that long, she told herself. Yet he had never gone this long before, never stopped answering completely. She pulled out her phone and looked at the gaps between texts before this one. Scrolling back she figured four days, five days at the most.

Where was he? Was he undercover somewhere, unable to break his cover to text her even once to let her know he was all right? She found herself getting annoyed, even angry, with Pascal. How could he let her worry like this? Didn't he know the way women are— at least women in, well, love? Yes, it appeared Merle Bennett was definitely in love.

She let herself out the back door, the one with no deadbolt, locking it behind her. She turned to admire the view from his back yard, the leaves turning red, the yellow grass bent from the wind. Beyond the fence, she saw two black and white goats grazing. Were they the twins she'd helped into the world? She had never completely told Irene the story of the nabbing of César at the market in Malcouziac. It was time. Maybe the old woman knew how to reach Pascal.

She found Irene Fayette out in the yard, leaning on a walking stick made from what appeared to be a well-polished olive branch topped with a tennis ball. She wore a scarf over her hair and an old sweater and was feeding three goats from a burlap bag tied to her apron. She startled when Merle approached, showing a frightened face before frowning.

"I'm sorry, Irene," Merle said in French. "I've surprised you."

"You have." She straightened and smoothed out her frown. "It's not you. I have been in an odd state since the business with César."

"Did you get your truck back?"

"Yes. That was a blessing. Thank you for helping with that."

Merle nodded. "I assume the money was long gone."

"Oh, yes. He says he sent it back to Greece, but who knows. Probably bought cigars and liquor."

"Have you found a replacement besides the young student?"

The old woman shook her head. "It's difficult. None of the young people want to do farm work. They want to get up late and party at night."

They made their way to a weathered wooden bench under a spreading olive tree heavy with ripening fruit. Merle offered to go into the house and get them refreshments but Irene wasn't interested. She sat heavily, shoulders slumped.

"Is everything all right, Irene?"

"Hmm? Oh, yes, my knee is much better. The therapist comes three times a week."

They sat in silence for a few minutes. Merle found the old woman's company oddly soothing, even though she seemed disturbed about the summer's events. As if it was just a blip in a smooth-running river of life, a rocky turn and nothing more. The water would still flow; tomorrow would still come. And all the pleasures and rituals would return.

"I came by for Pascal," Merle said finally. "But he's not here."

"Oh, eh?" Irene blinked, coming back from her reveries. "Not seen him for months."

"Really? Months?"

"Since July, I think. Where is he?"

"Working somewhere, I guess." Merle rubbed the wrinkle between her eyes. Where the hell was he? "Do you know anyone I could contact about him? A relative or a friend?"

"You mean the wife?" She said *la femme*, and Merle was unsure which woman she might mean. Did Pascal have more than one?

She bit down on her molars. "You mean Clarisse?" Irene nodded. "Do you have her number?"

They rose carefully and walked slowly back to the house. Irene was doing well, with hardly a limp. Her pace was snail-like however. In the kitchen, she rummaged in a drawer and brought out an address book, paging through it. "Here." She spun the book around on the counter to show Merle.

Under the Ps was the listing for Pascal, two phone numbers then one for Clarisse and another one labelled PN. "Is this his *Policier Nationale* office number?" she asked. It was. She wrote all four numbers down in her spiral notebook and tucked it back in her jeans. She was eager to leave now, to dial all the numbers. To find him.

But first Irene wanted to have tea. Merle put the kettle on for her, found the loose tea, dumped it in a teapot, then waited for the water to heat. Irene had planted herself in a large flowered chair, her favorite spot, she declared. She put her feet up on the matching ottoman, laid her head back, and closed her eyes.

Merle went through the motions for tea, gathering cups and milk and sugar on a tray. When she presented it on a small wooden table near where Irene sat, she realized the woman was snoring. Merle poured herself half a cup, clinking the china dishes needlessly. Irene kept snoring, a soft kitten-like purr.

Finally, Merle wrote out a note for Irene, telling her thank you and *à bientôt*— 'see you soon,' then slipped out the front door. She sat in the Peugeot and stared at the numbers. Where to start? That was simple; you always start at the first on the list. That's what a list is for.

The first number was Pascal's mobile. She recognized it and dialed it anyway. Maybe this was the moment he would answer.

Instead it went immediately to voicemail then announced the mailbox was *'terminée.'* Did that mean full or dead?

She dialed the second number. It rang about twenty times and she hung up. Clarisse was next. She picked up before the third ring: *"Allo, oui?"*

In a burst of imagination Merle decided to be a bill collector from the fictional *Banque du Sud-Ouest.* "I am looking for Pascal d'Onscon."

"He's not here," Clarisse said coldly.

"When will he return? It's very important."

"Never. Is that good enough for you?" She hung up with a bang.

Merle stared at the phone number. Was this Clarisse's mobile? Because Pascal said she'd moved all over Paris in the last years. And why would he give Irene his ex-wife's mobile number? Was she still his emergency contact? Had Clarisse lived here with Pascal? Did Irene know her?

Merle sighed. She was getting anxious— yes, jealous— about a woman he swore he didn't care about, whom he said was a little crazy. Just stop, she told herself. *Be a grown-up.*

So the grown-up got serious, took a breath, and called the *Policier Nationale.* It seemed to be a Paris number. In her best professional French, she asked for Pascal, then his supervisor when he didn't answer. She ended up talking to a woman who was the supervisor's assistant. She tried to explain that she was searching for Pascal, that she was his special friend, that she hadn't heard from him in weeks and was worried about him. After asking for her name and address, the assistant was curt with her. Maybe many women called, looking for the handsome Pascal, so many women that his personal life bored and annoyed her. For whatever reason Merle was shut down.

We do not give out information on our officers, madame. Au revoir.

～

BACK AT HOME, Merle's phone rang later that night. Irene Fayette was calling to apologize for falling asleep during teatime.

"You need to rest, Irene," Merle told her. "Give your leg time to heal."

"Yes, yes," the old woman said impatiently. "That's what they tell me. But life is waiting for me, yes? I don't have decades ahead. I must get up and act now."

She sounded like she was giving herself a pep talk, a tactic Merle was familiar with. Irene continued, "Have you seen Jacques at the market?"

Merle tried to remember. "No, I don't think anyone sold *chèvre* at the last market. Do you want me to sell again?"

"Perhaps. But I am worried about Jacques. You met him, yes?"

"At the market about a month ago. He's your cousin?"

"*Oui.* He lives by himself, like I do. On the other side of Malcouziac, out in the country. Do you have time to check on him? It's not far."

"Of course." Merle wrote down the directions to the old man's house, somewhere to the north of her village. There was no street address, as happens in the middle of the hills. She promised to get back to Irene in a day or two.

She hung up the phone. Out in her garden the purple twilight soaked the sky in velvet. A cool breeze made her shiver. Autumn or lost souls? Was finding people her new profession? She didn't like it. She wanted her people known, found, and safe.

Calculating the time in Connecticut, she called Tristan on his cell phone. He would be eating lunch or in class. But she needed to hear his voice.

"Mom! Hang on," he said, his voice muffled with what must be lunch. Sounds of chattering and laughter, dishes and silverware. Then he was back, his footsteps in the background. "Okay, sorry. It's too loud in the cafeteria."

"How are you? How are your classes?"

"All good. Physics is a bear but I'm getting some help on that."

"Did they set you up with a tutor?"

"An upperclassman. He's super smart, and cool, too."

They chatted for a few minutes then he had to run off to another class. He was taking six classes right off the bat. Merle worried it was too much, but if anybody could do it, Tristan could. She hung up, watched the stars come out, and sent him a wish for happiness and success across the ocean.

Tristan was good. One of her people was safe and sound. She could sleep a little better tonight.

TWENTY-THREE

Late the next afternoon, after supervising the unloading of the washer from a truck and the careful hauling of it up the alley and through the garden gate, Merle grabbed her purse and walked back to the parking lot outside the city walls. She had a vague idea where Jacques lived but wanted to leave herself enough time to get lost.

And lost was what she got. There were many small hamlets in the countryside north of Malcouziac, most of which had no names or identifying marks. Some were like Pascal and Irene's, somewhere on a dirt road, hidden in the trees. Others were a collection of buildings along the pavement, once one farm but now converted to holiday homes. She stopped at an intersection with two direction signs, one back to Malcouziac and the other toward Issigeac, and called Irene for a consultation. The phone rang and rang. She must have been outside with her goats.

On either side of the road, wheat fields had been cut and harvested. The sun was setting behind a forested hill to the west. Remembering Jacques had mentioned Issigeac she put her car in gear and headed toward the town. Maybe someone knew him there.

The town was a beautiful old village but no one seemed to know this particular Jacques. She got all sorts of stories about a Jacques who was a small boy, another who was a priest, and a third who died last year. After a quick dinner in a bistro built in an old train station where she asked one last time if anyone knew Jacques, the *chèvre* salesman, Merle headed home. She was a little disgusted with her person-finding skills at this point. Both Pascal and Jacques were nowhere to be found.

She called Irene in the morning, early, at six. The phone rang ten times then finally she answered. Merle explained her wild goose chase of the day before and got better directions for another try. Apparently, she had been close, just not close enough.

"Does he have a telephone, Irene?" Merle asked.

"He did. But when I call it now it says it is not in service."

"How do you communicate with him?"

Irene let out an exasperated sigh. She hadn't had any communication with him for weeks apparently, since he'd called and said he was sick and couldn't work. She'd tried to call but either he didn't answer or the phone was disconnected.

Merle frowned. This wasn't good. Anything could have happened to old Jacques. "Have you called his relatives or the police?"

"I *am* his relative," Irene barked. "The only one nearby. Can you try again today please?"

Merle promised to give the search another round and hung up. At least Irene had her daughter to check up on her, and the therapist was still coming three times a week, she'd said. Was there a penalty for stubborn independence?

Merle was making espresso in the tiny kitchen when someone knocked on the front door. Her plumber, she hoped, to hook up the washer. Or maybe the electrician who had been MIA for weeks. She opened the door and unlocked the shutters. A policeman stood outside with a stern look on his face. It was the same gendarme who had come by about the vandalism.

"*Madame*," he said formally, nodding. "I am here to tell you that we are making progress on the graffiti on your house." He looked up, frowning.

"That's excellent news, *monsieur*." She waited for him to elaborate but he continued squinting with distaste at her house. "Did you notice those letters?" She stepped outside into the street and pointed. "There: P, C, R, F. The Communists. And over there, the sickle."

He didn't look surprised. "*Oui, madame.*"

"And there was similar vandalism in other villages around here. I found two from the news."

"*Oui, madame.*" He squirmed a little then spoke again, in a slightly harsher tone. "I have had word from the *Policier Nationale* that you have been calling them. About— about a certain officer." He raised a small notebook, tucked into his palm. "Pascal d'Onscon?"

"Yes! He's a friend." Merle's heart leapt. Pascal must have checked in with headquarters. "Have they heard from him?"

"*Madame* Bennett. I am here today to inform you that you are to please stop contacting *Nationale*. The officer in question is undercover and cannot be disturbed. To give you information about him would jeopardize his safety. Please, *madame*, try to control yourself and refrain from calling him or his supervisors. It is a matter of national importance. We are counting on your discretion even though you are not a French citizen."

He jiggled his head for a second at the end of his pompous little speech, gave her a squaring of his shoulders and a touch to his cap, and spun away on his heel. She watched him march down the cobbled street, looking into windows right and left, swinging his left arm wide. He turned the corner without looking back.

Merle stood fuming, appalled by the *gendarme* and more than a bit mortified. The day before she had called the headquarters of the national police in Paris four times. She kept hoping to get one of Pascal's fellow officers, somebody who had sympathy for her situation. Someone from the Wine Fraud Division. She tried to find out the name of the man he'd put in prison years before, the one whom he'd met again a couple weeks ago. But her calls were routed back to the same assistant supervisor who apparently had her fill of Merle Bennett and her so-called love life.

How embarrassing. To have a gendarme come around and tell you to quit bugging people about your boyfriend. A man you might *think* was your boyfriend but obviously, *madame*, you are delusional.

She covered her eyes. *Stop!* She was thinking like a teenager now, undermining her own confidence.

Still, she went inside, pulled out her notebook where the story of Odette was unfolding, and made a list of all the kind, sweet things that Pascal had said or done, searching for a few *bons mots* in texts and emails, and her previously amazing memory. It wasn't a short list, she had to admit. It ran to thirty or thirty-five or forty, from the way he called her 'Blackbird' to singing snatches of Beatles songs while dancing under the stars. The weekend they pretended they were at the beach, holding hands in lounge chairs in the garden. Helping her sisters. Saving the wine, and herself. The weekend in Brantôme. Meeting her in New York and Scotland. The nights they'd made love. She embarrassed herself by counting how many times there had been over the last three years.

Then, because she was a lawyer after all, she made another list of the times he'd lied to her or hurt her. Then added the reason for those incidents. According to Pascal, because he cared too much. So those got transferred to the first list.

She fixed herself another espresso and went back to the heavy dining table and stared at her lists. With a gulp of caffeine she ripped them out and crumpled them up, angry with herself. She threw them in the trash can then stared out the kitchen window at the garden and gave herself a lecture.

"Enough, Merdle. He is missing. What are you going to do about it?"

TWENTY-FOUR

ousin Jacques lived in a tiny stone house, nestled near two similar ones with tile roofs, blue shutters, and weedy yards. Merle stood at the door of the one to the right of Jacques's and spoke with an old woman with bright eyes and a red bandanna around her gray hair. Finding the cottage was harder than Irene thought but Merle had persevered, asking everyone she met to point out the way. It was only five kilometers from Issigeac but hidden in the hills.

"Oh, yes," she said, "Jacques has been on the road for some time, selling the cheese. He goes away, goes from *marché* to *marché* all over the Dordogne and part of the Lot."

"Yes, I've been sent here from his cousin, the *chèvre* maker."

The old woman, who had merely introduced herself as Mignon, squinted at Merle. "But you are not French, *madame.*"

"No, American. But I am a friend of Irene Fayette, Jacques's cousin. She is concerned that she can't reach him. Irene had surgery recently and can't drive."

"But Jacques still drives. He has an old Renault, one of those *camionnettes.* He painted it red so everyone would know when he was in town."

"Do you have a telephone number for Jacques while he is out of town? In case there is a problem with his house? Irene gave me one but maybe there's another?"

The mention of Irene's name seemed to reassure Mignon. Her shoulders lowered and she sighed. "I will see. Come in."

Mignon's cottage was small and tidy with the smell of garlic in every corner. The old woman limped over to a telephone on a small cupboard. Opening the doors, she extracted a threadbare address book and leafed through it. She limped farther, to the kitchen table where she'd left her glasses, then sat down, staring at the book.

"Here then." She read out a number. Merle was ready with her pen and tiny spiral notebook, scribbling it down.

Outside Merle checked the number that Irene had given her for Jacques. The same number that Mignon gave her, which she knew was disconnected. Still she punched it in, standing on the front step of Jacques's cottage, listening for a ringing inside. There was none.

Jacques had left his shutters open. Merle walked through the weeds as she'd done at Pascal's and peered through the windows. It was a small place, barely four rooms. The only room she couldn't see thoroughly was the bathroom. What if he had fallen on the floor of the bath, or in the tub? She tried the front door. Locked. She tried the back door and was surprised when it opened and she almost fell inside.

"Jacques? *Es-tu ici?*"

The back door led directly into the kitchen. It had been cleaned, the dishes in the strainer by the sink, the wooden table wiped of crumbs. She ran a finger over the table. Dust. She located the bathroom door and opened it cautiously. But it was empty.

She decided to leave the old man a note, telling him she'd been to visit and to call his cousin Irene immediately. She set it on the kitchen table and let herself out the back.

In her car she called Irene with the news, technically no-news, of

Jacques. Irene was disappointed. "I think you should report him missing, Irene," Merle said. The older woman muttered something nasty about '*les flics.*'

"Irene," Merle continued, "speaking of the police, do you remember when Pascal arrested somebody doing wine fraud many years ago? One of his first cases? He might have talked about it. I think there was a public trial."

"Hmmm. That one in the Sancerre?"

"Maybe. Do you remember anything more?"

"He was quite proud of his work, I remember that. A bit of a peacock about it, you know these *flics*. But he gave me no details except where it took place. He never talked about his work very much. But I remember Louise was nine years old that year, starting in a new school. It was the year my husband died. We were all still reeling from that. Pascal took Louise into the village to school a couple times. He was very kind to her."

"What year was that, Irene? When Louise was nine?"

"Let's see, she's what—? Twenty-four now? So, fifteen years ago."

Merle thanked Irene and scribbled it all down in her notebook. Sancerre. Fifteen years ago. Would it be difficult to find in old newspapers?

"One last thing, Irene. You gave me his ex-wife's number, right? Clarisse?"

"Yes?"

"Did she live there in the cottage with him?"

"Oh, yes. Pretty girl. Not much work for her around here. She wouldn't work with the goats."

"What happened with them? He's never said much."

"He says she ran off with her piano teacher. Somebody from Bergerac or Cahors or somewhere."

Merle sighed. "I see. Thank you. I'll keep looking for Jacques if you tell me where else to look."

But Irene had no more ideas. She didn't know any of his friends and all their relatives lived far away, in Paris and Normandy. Merle urged her to call them, ask if they'd seen him. If they haven't, she should call the police.

This time Irene said she would.

THE PUBLIC LIBRARY in Bergerac was large and well-staffed. It was a modern *mediatheque*, with rows of computers along with books. All the computers were busy when Merle arrived so she decided to inquire with a librarian about searching old newspapers. She wished she'd brought her laptop but maybe the staff would give her direction on searching when she got home.

Newspapers were not online, she was told. They were housed in a backroom on microfiche and compact disks. The staff librarian who looked barely out of college told Merle they were digitizing the entire collection but it wasn't complete yet. Merle asked for the year in question, 2002, and was relieved to find they were on CDs. She was set up at a desk with a computer reserved for newspaper searches and left on her own.

Inputting terms 'Sancerre' and *'vignoble'*— vineyard— brought up a huge list of articles. She tried several times to add other terms to narrow the list down but ended up starting at the beginning of 2002 and going through every article. It took hours. Most were puff pieces about wineries and winemakers with projections on prices and reports on weather, from *Le Monde, Le Figaro, Le Parisien,* and other, smaller regional newspapers.

At the very end of the list, in December, she hit gold. The summer before a *vignoble* had been discovered to be importing Spanish wine and bottling it as Sancerre, a serious crime. The investigation had apparently been announced in January 2002 but it hadn't come up in her searches. By December, however, the trial was underway in Paris. She squinted at the blurry text, trying to scribble it down, word for word. In the old days, she used to make photocopies of microfiche but the librarian hadn't mentioned a hard copy option today. She continued in her notebook, page after tiny page, writing out the French to make sure she got it correct. She scanned ahead for a name, a perpetrator. He was not named.

One thing was clear, however. The name of the winery was Domaine Le Grand Vinon.

WHEN MERLE PARKED outside the old walls of Malcouziac, it was late. She'd eaten *steak frites* in a greasy bistro in Bergerac while writing out a translation of the article from the library. She felt alive, on the hunt, in a way that shouldn't have thrilled her as much as it did. Pascal was still missing but she was on her way to finding him. She knew it.

She had coffee after dinner for the drive home. There was no chance she would sleep tonight, not with her discoveries and her worries and the caffeine. She gave up about midnight, lying in bed, hoping for a miracle. She turned on the light. She looked at her cell phone and calculated the time in New York. Which sister could she call? Annie was no doubt busy with Callum, Stasia with her family. Her two single sisters, younger than Merle, were Francie and Elise. Elise had just been here, she might not be ready for more French intrigue after the spray paint incident.

Francie answered right away, indicating she must be home. "Hey, Merle. *Comment ça va?*"

"*Ça va bien.*" All is well. "How are you? What's going on?"

Francie began a litany of complaints about her partners in the law firm, her stupid clients, the bad calls by judges, and her inconsiderate neighbors who held huge, drunken football parties every weekend.

"I completely forgot about football," Merle said when Francie finally ran out of complaints. "One of the nice things about France."

"Oh, everything is nice in France." She sighed. "Well, almost."

Francie had some bad experiences in the country the year before. She rarely talked about them though. And Merle didn't want to bring up the "cheese business," a scheme to import exotic cheeses from France that her sister seemed to have forgotten.

"Elise had a good time here," Merle said. "Did you talk to her?"

"Uh-huh. She said you got robbed."

"Well, an attempt, yes. But here's the thing. Coming back to France exorcised her demons from the spring. It was her idea, and it worked, I think."

"Except for being sprayed with fluorescent paint."

"Yeah, right. Okay, France isn't perfect. Pascal and I had that discussion." She paused after saying his name, the ache in her stomach tightening. Where was he? "I haven't seen him in awhile. I'm kind of worried."

"What do you mean? Did you break up?"

"I don't think so. The last time he was here it sure didn't seem that way. He just doesn't answer my calls or texts. Francie, I think something may have happened to him while he was undercover."

"Like what?"

"He said some guy he'd arrested years ago had talked to him, or threatened him, or something. He was strange about it, like he didn't want to talk about it."

"Because—?"

"He didn't want to scare me. I've called his office and they are completely stonewalling me. They even sent the local cop around to tell me to mind my own business."

A rustling of papers sounded. Francie said, "Are you by yourself? What's your schedule?"

"I've got a couple more months here. I'm scheduled to come back for the holidays."

Francie swore under her breath. "You know it's only September. Okay, look. I can come next week if I move some stuff around. I don't have any court dates or actual dates or anything."

"What? No, you don't have to come over, Francie. I wasn't suggesting... I was just, you know, grousing."

"And you never grouse, Merle. I'll call you back in the morning. Go to bed."

Merle leaned back against the pillows. Francie was coming, even though she hadn't asked her, or even needed her. Francie, who was braver than Merle and at least as brave as Annie. Together they would figure this out.

Her head was still buzzing, even with the relief of knowing she'd soon have a sidekick to help her. Merle grabbed her notebook and pen and set down her phone.

She needed the distraction of a faraway time.

ODETTE AND THE GREAT FEAR

PART SEVEN

Odette took a last look over her shoulder at her goats, tethered together on the side of the hill facing the chateau. She would not be long, she promised them silently, hoping no fox or boar came along and got them tangled in a frenzy. She crossed her fingers behind her back and knocked on the heavy wooden door.

She had learned something back at the Daguerre farm, that the Count was once a priest. He was the second son and had gone into service to the Lord while his older brother was groomed for inheritance. When the revolution broke out he had cast off his robes and joined the friends of Robespierre who were fashioning the new laws of the Republic. His brother had died last year of cholera or something, the rumors varied, and now the second son had the half-ruined chateau and the inheritance.

The footsteps approached. This section of the manse was intact as always, according to the Daguerre's, but they recounted with relish the destruction to the chapel and adjoining wings after the first flush of the revolution. Someone had set fire to it, and the ensuing bonfire was a cause for much celebration. It was while fighting that fire that *le Comte* had been badly burned, the cause of his disfigurement.

Odette straightened, queasy with anticipation. The Count was a terrifying figure, with or without his scar. The maids at the farm had peppered her with stories about his cruelty. It was all idle gossip. Surely. He was stiff and formal but he didn't scare her. Not much.

The heavy door swung open and an elderly man escorted her into a drawing room off the main hall. She was told to sit. A large clock ticked off the seconds and she became restless. How long was she to sit and wait? Her flock could be in distress. She went to the window, pulling back a musty drape. The view was stunning, the sun piercing the gloom, the orange of the autumn leaves set a glow. But her goats were somewhere in the mist, out of sight.

"*Mademoiselle*," a voice behind her said. She turned to see the Count, now without his long coat and top hat, standing just inside the door. "I'm glad you could join us. If you would come this way—" He gestured toward the hall.

He led the way to the dining room, a grand room that had seen better days. Wallpaper peeled from the upper edges of the high walls, near the ornate carved ceiling where a sooty chandelier hung. The table itself was elegant with curved legs and twelve high-backed chairs. Odette followed the Count down the left side, admiring the silver and candlesticks and white linens. When she was halfway down the table she registered the presence of someone else, a man, sitting at the end of the opposite side. She faltered at the sight of Ghislain, upright and seemingly healthy. And as handsome as ever.

"*Mademoiselle*," he said, nodding. "You will forgive me for not standing. My leg is not as it once was."

She blinked, flustered, muttering something inane. The Count pulled out a chair opposite Ghislain for her then seated himself at the end of the table. A maid appeared with a tray, carrying a silver teapot and china cups. Odette was grateful for the distraction of pouring and stirring.

After introductions where she learned Ghislain's surname was Leclair and he learned her full name, the Count sat back silently, sipping his tea. It seemed he had arranged that the two of them would meet again. He seemed quite pleased with himself.

"*Pardon, monsieur,*" Odette said finally. "Have you been here all these weeks? Since you appeared in the woods near the farm?"

The Count spoke then. "One of my workers found him. Half-dead near the river."

Ghislain smiled. "Half-dead but half-alive. The Count has been so kind as to allow me to stay here and mend."

"Anything for a soldier of the revolution," the Count said. He stood then, set down his tea cup, and walked to the door. "You will excuse me. I have matters to attend to. I will return shortly."

As soon as he left, the maid returned, refilled their tea cups and offered a plate of shortbread biscuits. It had been two years since Odette had tasted such a delicacy. She dipped them in the hot tea, closed her eyes, and savored the melt of the biscuit on her tongue.

"He feeds his people well," Ghislain offered, watching her.

"I see that. It has been too long. I'm sorry— I—" She blushed then, which only complicated her feelings.

"No need to apologize for enjoying the finer things." Ghislain was clean-shaven now and ruddy, the color back in his cheeks, his dark hair clean and combed over his collar. He didn't wear his uniform but a green jacket and white shirt with a stiff collar, like he might have borrowed from the Count. Of course he had, she thought, smoothing the skirt of her muslin gown, washed so much it was almost transparent.

"No? You have been converted to the noble cause?"

He laughed then, his eyes crinkling and his white teeth flashing. "No, *mademoiselle.* Just eating their food. Besides, the Count is on our side. He was in Paris with Robespierre. He did well to leave though. Things are bad in the city. The new government is chaotic and vengeful."

Odette listened carefully. "You were there, in Paris lately?"

"In the summer." He looked away, his brow darkening.

"Before you deserted?"

His gaze spun back. "Why do you say that?"

"Because you're a soldier and you're not with the troops. *Pardon, monsieur.* It seemed obvious."

His shoulders sunk a little in defeat but he didn't answer. He stared into his tea cup instead. Odette felt she had insulted him but didn't know how to make it right.

They ate in silence. When the maid returned she took away their dishes. Odette dabbed the fine linen napkin to her lips. "Is he returning? I should go see to my goats."

"Don't go," Ghislain said desperately. "Please."

Odette's eyes widened at the emotion in his plea. "But I must, *monsieur.* I have duties."

"I'm sorry, of course." He held her gaze and she felt her stomach turn over. "Of course you must go. But will you come back? Another day, not too long in the future? The Count is very solicitous to all my needs but I keep thinking of you by the fire. It was so cozy and warm. I liked it better there but I couldn't stay. You see that, don't you? Say you understand."

"I understand the food is much better here, and there are servants to see to your wound, I suppose. You must have a large room with feather pillows and a grand view." She leaned closer to him and whispered. "Are you in hiding?"

"Until my leg is strong and I figure out what to do. I may go south, to Spain. The republic is hard on men. Many will die in these wars."

"The Spanish are fighting near the border. It would not be safe."

"Then Bordeaux and the sea perhaps. Safety is elusive, *Mademoiselle Odette.*"

He said her name with such gentleness, she wanted to cry.

"Of course I will come back to see you, *Monsieur Leclair.* If you wish."

"I wish one thing, that you call me Ghislain."

"All right— Ghislain. It sounds like the name of a gallant knight." She smiled into his eyes.

His voice was as soft as a breeze. "Just a man, *mademoiselle*. Just a man."

TWENTY-FIVE

DORDOGNE

Francie Bennett flounced off the train in Bergerac, wearing skin-tight flowered jeans and a t-shirt that didn't hide a thing. She threw her arms around Merle and they hugged there at the station for a long minute. Francie exclaimed, "God, it's good to be back. Look at you, all relaxed and tan. It's still so warm here. I'm starving. Let's get lunch."

As usual, Francie talked a blue streak, exclaiming over everything from Merle's dented Peugeot to the salad in the café to the workers in the vineyards, bent over their harvesting tasks. Francie was a loud enthusiast of almost everything and being with her was overwhelming and cheering for Merle. You didn't have the energy to worry and mope when Francie filled all the space with her chatter and enthusiasm.

It was only three days since they'd talked on the phone yet here she was. Francie didn't like waiting to do things she wanted to do. She had broken up with her latest fling, a lawyer in another firm in Greenwich, because he wanted her to move in with him. "Too much, too fast, even for me," she said, smiling over her glass of Champagne at the outdoor table. "Oh, these bubbles. You were so right, Merle. Coming back to France cures everything that ails you."

Merle opened her mouth to tell Francie what Pascal had said about that but her sister was already off on another topic. They discussed the family, Tristan at college, Willow doing some senior project about Twitter, how their father was doing health-wise (good), and more. Merle realized she had missed Francie, even though she always said Francie wore her out. Now her larger-than-life presence was so appreciated.

They were in the Peugeot, halfway back to Malcouziac, before the topic of Pascal came up. Francie had paused in her ramblings and a seriousness fell over them.

"So. Pascal. Where the hell is the cad?"

Merle shrugged. "I wish I knew." She told Francie about the winery in Sancerre where Pascal had arrested a vintner fifteen years before. "I think he's the one that threatened him."

"What's his name?"

"I don't know. The owner of the winery is Adrien Delage, I looked that up on their website, but I don't know how long he's owned it."

"Then tomorrow, we fly. Two detectives, armed with their wits and their law degrees." Francie patted her shoulder. "Don't worry. We'll find him. Wherever he is."

"But first," Merle said, glancing at her sister, "we have reservations at a very special restaurant tonight. It wasn't easy to get in. It's only open to the public for two weeks a year."

"Sounds marvelous." Francie lay her head back on the seat. "Oh, France you lovely country, I couldn't quit you."

BY NINE O'CLOCK THAT EVENING, nestled in a cozy corner of the restaurant's stone townhouse, the two sisters had to stop talking and eat. The food at *La Petite Étoile* was the stuff of dreams: colorful, inventive, delicious to the point of ecstasy. The delicate, mouthwatering *amuse-bouches*, smoked *foie-gras* with various colored salts, the *noix Ste-Jacques*— scallops— with citrus notes, the lamb, the strawberry melange, the deconstructed cheesecake, the homemade ice creams; it was too much and absolutely just right.

The drive home was lit by stars— appropriately— big and small. The moon rose, nearly full, as they rounded the last hill and Malcouziac came into sight. Merle sighed in relief as she locked the Peugeot, shouldered one of Francie's bags, and led the way through the city gates. It was good to be home, and with a sister at her side she felt optimistic about her projects. Especially the main one, locating her missing boyfriend.

IN THE MORNING they sat in the garden, drinking espresso, and called Pascal's cell phone again. According to her own phone Merle had called him twenty-two times in the last two weeks, not too bad considering how anxious she was about him.

"It goes straight to voicemail." Merle set her cell on the table that had replaced the stolen one. It was similar, green metal, but didn't have the patina of the vintage one.

"So he's turned it off," Francie said. "Because he's undercover."

"I've tried all times of day, early morning, the middle of the night, lunch time. It's the same, Francie. His phone is dead and he hasn't bothered to plug it in?"

"Maybe he lost it."

"Okay, sure. But he didn't get a new one? He's a cop. That's how he communicates."

"Maybe the people he's investigating took it."

"Same as losing it. He gets a new one."

Francie adjusted her wide-brimmed hat. She was fair and freckled and worried constantly about her skin. They'd all reached that age, Merle mused. She turned her back to the morning sun, feeling it warm her neck.

"So, what do you think? His phone is dead and he's— what? Injured? Tied up? Unconscious? Even— dead?"

Merle tensed. That was exactly what she was thinking. But hadn't wanted to give that possibility a voice. "Is that too whacky? Paranoid?"

Francie frowned. "What about his family? Doesn't he have sisters? Maybe they've heard from him."

"I don't know their names."

"Then let's go break into his house. Come on."

The plumber arrived as they were leaving, causing a delay as he pointed out a potential problem in hooking up the hot water to the laundry. After much discussion Merle okayed a plan to buy a small water heater for the laundry. What was the price for clean undies? Pretty damn high but worth it.

It was past noon when they arrived at the hilltop hamlet where Irene and Pascal lived. Neither sister had been hungry after the enormous meal the night before so they subsisted on espresso. Pascal's cottage didn't look any different than the last time, still dusty, quiet, and empty. Francie proclaimed it quaint and began tugging on door knobs.

"I went in through the window last time," Merle admitted, pointing out the kitchen window she'd used before. "But I locked it."

"Well, that was smart," Francie said, looking around the yard. She marched over to a wood-pile and grabbed a log. At the back door, she hacked at the knob, breaking it off. She put her shoulder to the old door and they were in.

"Do you do this often, *mademoiselle?*" Merle said, eyes wide at Francie's command of house-breaking.

"Only in emergencies. This is an emergency, right?"

They split up to search the cottage. Merle wondered why she hadn't done a more thorough job before. She'd been tentative, worried about Pascal's privacy, but she was over that now. She pushed up the mattress and looked underneath it, stripped the sheets, used a broom under the bed in case something was hidden there. Meanwhile, Francie was tearing up the kitchen. They met, empty-handed, in the living room. Small as it was, with only two chairs, a television, and a few side tables, there was still a chance to find an address book, an old letter, something from his relatives.

A few minutes later Francie crowed, "Ah-ha!"

"What is it?"

"Mail in the trash." She dumped the small wastebasket upside down in the middle of the rug.

"I think I saw this on 'Murder She Wrote,'" Merle said as they began pawing through envelopes.

"Or was it 'Columbo?'" Francie said, peering closely at a torn envelope. "What's this? I can't read French writing."

Merle took the envelope and stared at the return address. The script was ornate and tiny. "Looks personal but I can't read it either." She stuck it in the pocket of her jeans. "Keep looking."

They sifted through old magazines, bills, and solicitations, the same sort of junk mail that Americans got. Francie held up a birthday card with a big frog on the front. "Someone wrote: *Felicitations, oncle*. Does that mean uncle?"

Merle took the card. It appeared to be from a nephew of Pascal's. There was more writing that would need a magnifying glass before she could read it. Merle had no idea what sort of children his sisters had, how old they were, or how close they were. It was just like his parents. She had so little curiosity about his family, his past, and felt miserable about it. What was wrong with her? Why had she never asked? On top of everything, she'd somehow missed his birthday. When *was* his birthday? June? July? Something like that.

She pulled the envelope out of her pocket. The card fit perfectly in it. "Bingo," Francie said.

Merle took Francie out to see Irene's goats before they left. Irene was out in the pasture, walking with a cane, talking to her animals.

They waved at her and she squinted back, uncertain apparently who they were.

"Just a second," Merle told her sister, clambering over the fence.

Francie followed. Irene's frown broke into a smile as Merle got closer and said her name.

"Ah, Merle," the older woman said, kissing her cheeks. Merle introduced her sister and said they were still looking for Pascal. And Jacques, of course.

"These men," Irene growled. "They run off and never tell us where they are."

"Have you heard from either one?" Merle asked.

Irene hadn't. She had called the police to report Jacques missing but they didn't seem particularly interested in an old man who didn't answer his phone. His vehicle was also missing, she'd told the cops, and that at least was something to go on.

"What does his car look like, Irene?" Merle asked.

"An ancient Renault, once red but now not so much. He told me the young Brits are always trying to buy it from him. Do you think they stole it?"

The Bennett sisters admitted it was a possibility although how that related to finding Jacques was still a mystery.

"Those nasty Brits," Francie laughed as they made their way back to Merle's car. "They'd probably throw an old Frenchman out on the street to get their hands on a collectible old beater."

Merle laughed. She knew a few nasty Brits but also some nasty Americans and French. Nasty knew no boundaries.

Even in *La France Profonde*.

THEY HAD PLANNED to go find the winery in Sancerre today but the lead on the envelope and possible relative changed that. They returned to Malcouziac and by five were seated in Albert's garden under his plum tree. It was chilly with the sun gone but the tea he brewed for them helped.

Merle hadn't seen her neighbor in awhile. She'd been busy, or running around the countryside. Now that she had her own vehicle she didn't have to borrow Albert's Deux-Chevaux. But she felt bad about not checking up on him. What if he disappeared one day like Jacques? She made a promise to check on him at least every other day for the rest of the time she was in France.

Merle grabbed the old man's hand. He squeezed it, a thin smile on his face. "How have you been? I'm so sorry I haven't seen you in awhile."

"Oh, I was in Paris," he said. "Valerie had a concert. She plays the violin in a student orchestra."

"I would have loved to have heard her play," Merle said. She got out the card with its envelope. "This is strange. But I can't seem to locate Pascal. We found this in his house and were hoping you could help us read the address."

Albert pushed his spectacles up on his forehead and brought the envelope close to his face. "Eustace, Avenue Fumier, nineteen, Victoire. There is a postal code as well."

"Where is Victoire?" Francie asked.

Albert shrugged. "After the Revolution many small towns changed their names to Victoire, Liberté, Marat, and so on."

"What is Marat?"

"One of the first martyrs of the Republic."

"We'll look up Victoire," Merle said. "Now the card."

He squinted at the inside of the card where the greeting was written. "'Congratulations, uncle. Fifty is a good number on you. Thank you again for the check at Christmas. I bought a—' What is 'Play-Station'?"

"Video game player," Francie said.

"Ah. 'I bought a PlayStation and have been shooting many police on it, ha ha. Don't worry, I won't shoot you. Have a nice birthday. Jean-Louis.'" Albert curled his lip. "What is this, a joke?"

"The teenage boy version of a joke," Merle said, taking the card back. "He's just playing games, Albert. I doubt he means any harm."

Francie was anxious to leave. They thanked Albert and Merle promised to check in the next day. "You have my mobile number, right? Call me for any reason."

They crossed the alley and through the gate into Merle's garden. Francie grabbed her arm. "Pascal is fifty! Who knew?"

"Not me," Merle admitted. She had thought him much younger. Didn't he say his sisters teased him about their age difference? Was that a joke on her?

The plumber was wrestling with the water heater in the laundry, trying to wedge the little unit into a corner. They listened to him curse for a few minutes then went inside.

"What should we do now?" Merle asked.

Francie was sitting at the dining table with Merle's laptop open, tapping on keys. "We know the little fucker's name and town. We'll find Pascal's sisters, or one of them."

In a moment they were looking at the French Facebook profile of one Jean-Louis Eustace. They were pretty sure it was the right one since he stated his school was Lycée Bellevue in Victoire, a town in northwest France, not far from Rennes.

"He looks like a real peach," Francie said, staring at his profile picture. He had Pascal's dark hair but otherwise was a greasy mess with sunken cheeks, heavy eyebrows, and a sneer.

"Teenage boys all look sketchy," Merle said. "How old is he?"

"Fifteen, I think."

"Awkward year. Now how do we find his mother?"

Francie clicked something on the page. "Well, we could call him."

"What do you mean?"

"He seems to be asking girls to call him. Look at that— a photo with his phone number."

Jean-Louis stood with a poster in his hands featuring a phone number. He made a little 'call me' gesture with one hand, and smirked.

Merle wasted no more time. She dialed the number in the photograph. The boy answered with a gruff: "*Oui, allo.*"

In fast French, as fast as she dared, Merle explained she was looking for Pascal d'Onscon who she'd been told was his uncle.

"*Comment?*" He switched to English. "Who is this? Speak English."

With a sigh of relief she said, "My name is Merle Bennett. Your uncle, Pascal, is a friend and I am trying to find him. He is missing."

After more arguing she got the boy to give her his mother's telephone number. He hung up unceremoniously.

"Got it," Merle told Francie, waving the slip of paper.

"Call her. Quick."

Merle was already half through the number. "Madame Eustace? My name is Merle Bennett. I am a friend of your brother, Pascal." She spoke in a slower French now, trying to calm herself.

"Ah, dear Pascal. How is he?" The woman sounded sweet and motherly.

"I hope he's good. But that's the thing. I haven't heard from him in weeks. I'm worried. Has he been in touch with you?"

"No, no. Not for some time have we talked. Who did you say this is?"

"Merle Bennett. Pascal's friend from America?"

"Oh, yes! Merle— the blackbird! *Bien sûr!* It is so nice to make your acquaintance at last. You are in New York City?"

"No, I'm in France now, in the Dordogne where I have a house. Pascal has been here to visit me a few times, and I've been to his house, but now— nothing, no replies for three weeks or more. I was hoping you might know where he could be. A friend's house, another woman perhaps, another relative?"

Madame Eustace— first name unknown— had no idea where her brother was. The other sister who lived outside of Geneva, Switzerland, had called only that morning and said nothing about Pascal. A half-brother who Pascal had never mentioned to Merle lived outside the country. Their relationship was not a strong one. Madame apologized, got Merle's number in case Pascal turned up, and rang off.

Francie stuck out her lower lip. "No dice, huh."

Merle sat down with a thump. "I guess they're not very close. Or maybe Pascal is secretive with everyone, just like he is with me."

"You think he's secretive?"

"A little. It comes from being undercover, I think. He's opened up a lot more to me lately but for a long time I didn't even know where he lived."

Francie was looking at the laptop with sudden interest. "What's this? *Odette and the Great Fear.* Is that your novel? Oooh." She made to click on it and Merle jumped up, pushing the laptop away.

"Oh, no, you don't."

"Come on! I want to read it." She made another attempt at the computer.

Merle snatched it away, closed it, and put it under her arm. "It's not ready. Or finished. Lots more to go. And— and I'm not sure anyone's going to read it. Ever."

"Oh, pooh, party pooper. Hey!" Francie brightened. "Got any wine?"

TWENTY-SIX

The first thing Pascal felt, before anything else, was the cold. His entire body was stiff and whatever he was lying on— face-down— was hard, slick, and frigid. He twitched, aching. He couldn't feel his hands, or his feet. He twisted one shoulder up off the surface and found he couldn't move his arms.

He opened his eyes, blinking into a darkness that revealed little. He lifted his head, peeling his cheek off the stone. It was a floor where he lay, a cold, polished stone floor. To his right a blue ray of light sliced the darkness.

Struggling to a seated position he confirmed his fears that his hands were cuffed behind his back. He tried to wiggle his fingers, get some blood flow in them, but he couldn't even feel that. He moved his feet inside his boots, the pain and numbness battling. At his back a stone wall rose two or more stories. He could barely make out an ornate wooden ceiling, its arches meeting in a high dome.

He was panting with the effort of sitting up. He blinked hard, clearing his head, shaking it until the action proved a mistake. His head hurt on the left side, above his ear. What the hell had happened? Where was he?

The last thing he remembered was Delage holding the gun on him, an old double-barreled shotgun, the kind farmers used on crows. Where was that? Somewhere south of Sancerre, in a barn. Pascal remembered the hunger, the sips of water, but little else about how much time had passed there. Was that Léo Delage who had fed him the bits of stale bread, or someone else? His memory refused to say.

He brought his mind back to here, now. What had happened over the last days was immaterial. Now he needed to get free, get away from here. Wherever 'here' was. He shivered violently. An old chateau? A church? Somewhere in an old building, a solid structure with an ornate roof.

He estimated the room to be twenty feet across. Shadowy, unidentifiable hulks sat at intervals and a glass-fronted case stood close by, to his left.

Another shiver racked his chest. If he didn't get out of here soon his blood would freeze. He moved his legs up and down. At least they weren't bound. One of his boots was missing. He looked right and left for it but couldn't see it. The foot in a sock was numb. He rubbed it on his other leg, trying to get some feeling back. How could it be so cold in September? Was it still September? Was he still in France?

Thinking made his head pound. He had to stop thinking and move.

He got one knee under his body and pushed himself upright, teetering with the effort and the dizziness. He bent at the waist, waiting for his head to clear, breathing hard. His stomach felt hard, knotted, and without warning he gagged. Nothing came up, nothing was there.

He lurched to the window. It was at neck level, a high, stone sill. Why was the outside so blue, he thought, then realized it was stained glass. Was this a church after all? He squinted up at the pattern in the glass. Mostly blue, there was a design high over his head. Something round? Didn't seem religious.

He knocked his forehead on the glass, succeeding at little but making the ache in his head increase. He cursed and turned back to the room. At least cursing felt good. He focused his breathing, trying to concentrate on what was at hand. What could help him escape.

The cuffs cut into his wrists. His own cuffs, he recalled, the memory coming back with a flash. The glove box of the BMW, the shotgun blast that opened the lock. His shock that caused him to be too slow to react to Delage.

The reflections of the blue window on the glass-fronted cabinet caught his eye. He squinted, trying to discern what was inside. It would give him information, a clue as to where he was. He dragged himself over to it, laying his forehead against the cabinet panes.

Toys? Miniatures? His mind refused to categorize the objects. Tiny guillotines? They were twenty centimeters tall, up to knee height, a collection of killing machines, the national razor as they once called it. How macabre. He frowned, disgusted. Who would collect such objects? He dimly remembered something about a fascination with the guillotine during the Revolution to the point of small replicas used by children. Or sociopaths.

Where was he? Was he being held captive by dangerous criminals, sociopaths, or worse? Was Delage in league with gangs, with the Mafia? Had he, Pascal, been sold to a criminal organization, or worse, to a psychopath? But why leave him alone here, unconscious but alive, to freeze on the stone floor? Was he really alone? Who was here? Was that footsteps? He held his ragged breathing for a moment to listen.

Silence.

His attention shifted back to the cabinet. He'd never seen a guillotine in person. It was last used in the '70s to execute a prisoner but was widely hated. No one had been executed in France by any means for decades, let alone by a symbol of abuse of power during the First Republic. An unexpected prickle of fear ran up his spine, just looking at the miniature guillotines and their tiny, sharp blades of death.

He blinked hard, bringing his thinking to the now. *Focus.* Must get these handcuffs off.

Somehow.

TWENTY-SEVEN

SANCERRE

The goat farm stretched back from the road, encompassing barns and pastures and a store where cheese was sold, fresh or aged. Francie had read about this place and demanded they stop on their way into the Sancerre winemaking region, near the Loire River. It was only nine o'clock in the morning but at a goat farm work had been going on for hours. A herd of brown and white goats grazed in the distance as they parked. Merle couldn't complain; she could use the place for research for *Odette.*

After sampling and purchasing several *chèvre frais* varieties they took advantage of the offer to roam around, poking their heads in the *chèvrerie* and admiring small goats born that spring but already nearly grown. They were the playful ones, prancing around the grassy pasture.

Back on the road the sisters passed miles of vines on both sides, the hillsides terraced steeply with grapes as far as the eye could see. Winemaking was the thing here, obviously. They'd chosen a small village near Le Grand Vinon where Pascal had uncovered the fraud scheme years before. The winery was close to Sancerre, the main town in the region, but Merle thought being in a small village people were more apt to gossip about a winemaker. And gossip, rumor, and identities were what she was after.

The tiny two-chamber bed-and-breakfast they'd found online was part of a vineyard, tucked into the rafters of the old house. It wasn't fancy but both Bennett sisters were satisfied. They would be close to the winemakers, guests in their home. Questions could be asked about Adrien Delage easily, they hoped.

The hosts were as friendly as they hoped. A young married couple with a baby, they were incredibly busy however, with the winery, the harvest, the guests, the tastings, the employees, and, of course, the baby. There was little time to gossip and it was too early in the day for wine-tasting. The sisters took a quick look around the winery, admiring the modern equipment, then went into the village for lunch.

"This is the place," Francie said, consulting her guide book about a bistro. "It says all the local winemakers hang out in here."

"Prospects!" Merle exclaimed, parking the car on a side street.

"Gossipy, drunk prospects."

The bistro in the *auberge* Francie picked out was the main building on the tiny village street, taking up most of a block. The sun shone bright on the stone facade and the 1950s plastic signage. It looked like it hadn't changed in fifty years, which Francie declared an excellent sign.

The restaurant was packed with men and a few women, many of them on the business of winemaking, or so it appeared. A large table at one end seemed communal, grizzled old men with scarred fingers lined up on either side, feasting on olives and bread. The rest of the room was groups of four or six, serious as they examined the color of wine in their glasses or poured over papers.

The sisters snagged one of the last tables, near a window overlooking a side garden. The flowers were dormant, trampled by sun and rain over the summer. Merle took a seat next to the window though, just for the sunshine. Francie read through the menu like her life depended on picking the best, most exotic local tastes.

After they ordered Sancerre *blanche* and *quenelle de brochet* (pike dumplings) and beef cheeks in red wine— Merle let Francie order for both of them— they sat back and examined the room.

"See anyone you want to strike up a conversation with?" Merle asked quietly. "An English speaker. That narrows the playing field."

"Yeah, none of those vineyard workers, I guess." Francie nodded toward the communal table. She squinted, catching the eye of an attractive man in a blue suit who raised his glass to her. She nodded coyly and looked away. "Does he look British?"

"He looks single, at least for today."

"Who am I to judge?" Francie sipped her wine delicately. "Is he watching?"

"Reel him in." Merle glanced over at the man, who was dark like Pascal but more refined and slender with a precise haircut. She'd never seen Pascal in a suit of any kind, let alone a sleek-fitting one, in a shirt with French cuffs and an orange tie. He sat facing them. Sitting across from him was another businessman in a gray suit.

Francie crossed her legs. She had very nice legs and wore red espadrilles. Then she tipped her head back and laughed at nothing at all, loudly, throaty, a sort of movie star move. She had a nice neck, Merle had to admit, and was well practiced in the ways of mating. Her V-neck sweater, also red, was cut down to there. Merle laughed, too, for the heck of it.

"You minx," Merle said, grinning. "Here he comes."

But before the man in the blue suit could stand up and button his jacket, the waiter stepped between them, carrying two glasses of buttery white wine. "Compliments of Monsieur Tallerand."

He gestured toward an elderly man seated at the bar. He was short and hunched over, wearing a navy blue beret. He doffed the beret with a grin and bowed toward them.

"Oh," Merle said, returning the nod. "Tell *Monsieur merci beaucoup.*"

The waiter vanished, leaving the path open for the man in blue. He looked a little chagrined at their luck with free wine, and at himself being empty-handed. Merle and Francie sipped their new glasses of wine, even as their original ones were more than half full.

"Delightful," Francie said, eyes sparking.

"You're going to have to do something to get that guy to approach now," Merle whispered. She looked at Monsieur Tallerand at the bar, still looking at them, a little sad now. "I've got it. I'm going to thank the old Frenchman."

She rose and took the new wine glass in one hand, smoothing her skirt. "Be back in a few."

"Work it," Francie whispered.

Merle glanced again at the man in blue. He'd sat down again, jaw tight. She paused on her way to the bar and caught his eye. His chin rose, his eyes flicked back to Francie. Mission accomplished.

Feeling like a *femme fatale* in a *film noir*, Merle approached the old man, setting her glass on the bar. *"Merci beaucoup, monsieur. Pour le vin. C'est magnifique."*

He was as wrinkled as a prune, his skin like leather. When he smiled, waves of skin rose on his cheeks and under his watery blue eyes. His eyebrows, tangled gray affairs, lifted comically. She smiled and stuck out her hand. *"Bonjour. Je m'appelle Merle Bennett."*

He grabbed her hand and pulled her in for cheek kisses. They were as juicy as you might expect from an old lecher. He told her to sit down— please.

"I saw the two most beautiful women in this bistro and I said, *ooh-la-la*, they must taste the best wine in the region. My own wine of course."

He tipped his head coquettishly, making her chuckle. "It is like butter, *monsieur*. Lovely." She sipped it appreciatively. "What is the name of your vineyard?"

With such an opening the old man fell in with enthusiasm, regaling her with stories in colloquial French about his winery named — she thought— Domaine Tallerand, begun in the 19th Century by his grandfather or someone, wiped out, down to the ground, three times and replanted. The Nazis were mentioned with loathing then the topic moved on to his grandson who now ran the vineyard. He was very smart, very capable. *Monsieur* was very proud and now he could spend his days here in the bistro, drinking the fruits of his labor, literally.

They chatted for awhile, Merle letting the old man ramble while she sneaked looks over her shoulder at Francie. The man in blue was talking to her but not sitting down. Why didn't he sit down? He was being polite, she supposed.

After ten minutes Merle cut to the chase with Monsieur Tallerand. "Do you know the winery, Le Grand Vinon? We might go there for a wine-tasting. Is it a good winery?"

The old man stared at her, hurt. "Why not Domaine Tallerand?"

"Oh, we will go there now that we've met you, of course. We're planning a little tour, several places. I'm making a list. Is Le Grand Vinon worth a visit?"

He shrugged and twirled the stem of his wine glass. "They've had some good vintages."

"But...?"

He sighed. "There is still a cloud over them. Their reputation."

"From what?"

"Franck's son, he would now be an old man, not as old as me, but old. And he was bad. Went to prison." He glanced at her. "You never know about people. But this one, Léo, he was evil. He smelled of it."

Merle flinched inwardly. It was rare to hear someone baldly called 'evil.' "Is that Adrien Delage's father?"

The old man nodded and gulped his wine. "Adrien is a good boy. Not a good winemaker though. He doesn't have the passion. His wine leaves me flat."

Merle gulped the wine. She'd had enough. "Which way to Domaine Tallerand? Maybe we will see you there."

The old man blinked and gestured to the south. "On the hillside. You can't miss it. The best-tended vines in the region."

She thanked him again and turned back toward their table. The man in the blue suit had disappeared. Francie sipped her wine, a cat-like smile on her face.

"So?" Merle asked.

Francie shrugged. "He got my number. I told him I couldn't possibly see him later but he insisted."

"Is he British?"

"Oh, no, madame. He is very, very French," Francie purred.

Merle laughed. "Something comes over the Bennett girls in France. They get positively lovestruck."

She told Francie what the old man had said about Le Grand Vinon. The current owner was definitely the son of the man Pascal arrested.

"What do we hope to find out there? What's our mission possible?" Francie asked.

Merle looked out the window. "Something to help find Pascal. Anything."

"Do you think this Delage has done something to him?"

Merle shivered. "I hope not."

TWENTY-EIGHT

lthough the afternoon was a scorcher the Bennett sisters headed over to Domaine Le Grand Vinon with their new information, anxious to see what, if anything, could be gleaned. They had a name: Léo Delage. Francie had downloaded a photograph of Delage she found on the Internet. His arrest and trial had made a splash in local newspapers and someone had taken a decent photo of him as he walked into court in a suit and tie.

"He looks pretty respectable," she said, showing it to Merle on her cell phone as they parked under a spreading tree outside the entrance to the vineyard. Merle took the phone and squinted at the photo.

"Looks are deceiving."

Francie pulled down her wide-brimmed hat and adjusted her sunglasses. "That they are."

The heat came off the dirt road in waves as they made their way to the tasting room. On either side of the narrow valley the hillsides rose steeply, acres of vines accessed only on foot. Dozens of terraces, a row of vines per terrace, stair-steps to the top where workers bent low, baskets at their feet, carefully picking grapes by hand.

Merle paused, shading her eyes to look up the hill. "I was going to suggest we offer to help with harvest."

"Oh please. I have a manicure."

Merle swatted her. "Come on, Fancy Francie." They continued up the drive as it rose and sweat broke out on the sisters' brows. "What was that guy's name? The one in the blue suit?"

"Jean something. Jean-Joseph. Why do the French have so few names?"

"I think it's a family thing. His father is probably Jean-Marie or something."

"And why are men named Marie? That's silly." Francie puffed to a halt, taking off her hat and waving her face. "Hey, did you ever find out who spray-painted your house? And Elise and you, of course."

"The cops say they're looking into it. I'm more worried about Pascal."

They tried to not enjoy themselves in the tasting room but it was deliciously cool, smelled like wet stone, oregano, and lavender, and was jammed with people clamoring to get a taste of Le Grand Vinon *Sancerre blanche* and its equally renowned (according to a British couple) Pinot Noir. The crowd had not heard, apparently, about the cloud of suspicion that hung over the winery. The sisters tasted a small glass of white then moved on to a rosé and the Pinot. By then they had almost forgotten they were supposed to be sleuthing out the winemaker.

"Let's go look around," Merle whispered, taking Francie's glass from her as she pulled her out the door.

In the yard, they stopped to reconnoiter. "What we need to find is some old guy who remembers Léo." Merle took her sister's arm. "Come on."

As usual the sight of Francie in her short skirt and red shoes caused a few heads to turn. A couple younger workers carrying baskets of grapes into the mixing room stopped in their tracks. Merle waved at them.

"Hey, can we look around in there?" she said in English then caught herself, repeating it in French. The two young men looked at each other and shrugged. Merle and Francie trotted over and introduced themselves. The men weren't all that young, maybe 30 or 40, and Francie played them like a fiddle, flashing her smile and her cleavage. Soon they were inside the cool, dark mixing room where huge stainless steel vats sat along one wall. The set-up reminded Merle of the winery where she'd given tours near Malcouziac. And they both were places where wine scams abounded.

"Ask them about the scandal," Francie said as they wandered behind the men down the center of the room. "About Léo."

The darker of the two men turned back toward them. *"Comment?"* He looked startled. "You know about Léo?"

The other man whispered something in the vein of 'shut up.'

"Is the scandal a secret?" Merle asked. "I don't want to get you in trouble."

"It's no secret," the first one said. "Why do you want to know?"

"Tell them you're writing an article," Francie hissed in English.

"I'm a writer. I write about wine," Merle explained to them in French. "I was curious how something like that gets going, and how nobody finds out until it's too late."

"Everybody knew about it," he said. "Just like everybody knows he's back."

The second man blanched and spun away, walking rapidly toward the control room at the end of the room.

"He's afraid of the boss but I'm not. I saw him. I saw the old boss." The first guy puffed out his chest. So bold. "He doesn't scare me."

Francie looked at Merle who asked: "Is there something scary about him?"

"He is just an old man, and an ugly one at that." He straightened. "Now, ladies, I must get to work."

On the way back to the car, Merle said, "So Pascal was here, and Léo Delage was here. This was where they met, where Léo confronted Pascal— it must be. That's the first real lead we've had that we're on the right track."

"Too bad we didn't run into the son," Francie said.

"I doubt if he would have told us anything. His reputation is already tarred by the business with his father."

"Right. Oh, man, all that wine! Merle, stop! I need to pee really bad. I'm just going to sneak into those bushes."

Before Merle could look around for passersby Francie plunged into the tall grass, through some shrubs, and behind a tree. Merle unlocked the car and aired it out while she waited. In a moment her sister emerged with a big grin on her face.

"Look what I found," she said, setting a burgundy French beret on her head. "Isn't it a kick? I feel *très Français!*"

Merle smiled then stepped closer. The hat looked familiar. "Is that— Let me see it." She held out her hand.

"Finders keepers," Francie said, dancing backwards.

"Seriously, Francie. I don't want to wear it, just look at it."

"Look at your mean face. Oh, all right." She handed it to Merle.

Merle turned the beret over and looked inside. There, in a messy ring on the inside band, was a trace of sticky white powder. She touched it with her finger and pulled away a gob of it. She put her nose inside the beret and breathed in.

Merde. The scent of Pascal.

THEY TOOK the beret home the next day. They got no more leads in the Sancerre but both Francie and Merle vowed to come back for more winery tours. It was a beautiful area, like so many in France, that demanded closer examination and a leisurely drinking plan. Another summer for sure.

The food— especially the goat cheese— was amazing, Merle thought, still in a rich haze from the dinner the night before, another extravagant feast. Francie had actually stopped eating through the third course, a real sacrilege. Merle cleaned her plate down to the last smear of sauce, in the local manner. They both refused dessert and were served them anyway.

"How do you stay so thin? I think I gained three pounds," Francie moaned, throwing her suitcase into the house. "I need a nap. I read that taking naps helps you lose weight."

While her sister slept upstairs Merle watered the plants in the garden and checked on the plumber's progress. He was nowhere to be found but had finished much of the work, from hooking up the washer to installing the water heater and connecting the drain. Merle had concocted a plan to use the gray water from the washing machine to water plants, now that the cistern was gone. That wasn't in place yet as it involved installing a large drum outside the laundry building to hold the water. The plumber assured her he knew all about it; he just hadn't gotten around to it.

She set Pascal's beret on the mantel. Where the hell was he? Why was his hat in the bushes? Where was his car? She dialed his number again. Straight to an overstuffed mailbox.

Francie had emailed her the photograph of Léo Delage. Merle downloaded it to her phone and stared at it. How had he changed? Why did the field workers call him '*affreux*.' She looked up the word to make sure she correctly understood it. Yes: 'frightful', 'horrible.' But in what way? She opened the old photograph on her laptop and blew it up large. M. Delage looked normal, respectable, broad-shouldered, with a large nose and dark hair, like a million Frenchmen. How had he changed in prison?

She did a search on his name again. Zip. He'd been in custody and out of the country for fifteen years. If only she'd had more time to question that guy at the vineyard.

A knock on the front door startled her. She saw the gendarme's uniform before she opened the door. It was the same one who had lectured her about bothering the *Policier Nationale* and she straightened her shoulders for another onslaught of French *mansplaining*.

He glared at her seriously, his hand on someone else's arm.

"*Monsieur le gendarme*," she said, peering out to see who else had arrived. It was another man, younger, maybe twenty-five or thirty. He wasn't happy.

"*Madame.*" The gendarme had gotten a haircut, very short and militaristic. It made him look a little fascist. "I present to you— your vandal."

TWENTY-NINE

The young man being held by the gendarme frowned at Merle. He turned back to the cop to sneer at him. Merle crossed her arms and stepped outside, closing the door behind her.

"Is that so?" She pointed to the front of her house, still a riot of colorful paints. "This is your handiwork?"

He didn't answer. He wore baggy black pants and a ripped blue t-shirt. He had longish hair that was a greasy brown with a low widow's peak in the front. She had to admit he looked the part. What she remembered of the vandal were his muscles and his height, both of which matched. Oh, and his eyes. Blue: check.

The gendarme shook him. "Answer the lady."

He glared at them both silently. Merle said, "Are you a Communist?"

The man curled his lip in disgust. "No."

"But you did this? Why?"

"Why not?"

"You sprayed me and my sister. You ruined our clothes. This will cost me thousands to clean off my house."

The gendarme shook him again. "Apologize. You will help clean her house or you will land in jail."

The man's dark eyes flicked nervously between them now. Finally, he said in a low voice, "I am sorry, *madame*."

Merle wasn't sure she believed him. "What's your name?"

The gendarme shook him again. "Claudio, madame," the man said. "Claudio Droz."

"Let me see your hands, Claudio," Merle demanded. He glanced at the cop then spread his hands, palms up. He had apparently given up at this point, sneer or no sneer. "There, just like mine." She pointed to fluorescent orange paint in the deep creases of his palms. "It's hard to clean, isn't it?"

The gendarme explained how the cleaning of the paint off her house would work. A citizen volunteer would supervise Claudio but only the guilty party would actually do the work. He would arrive each day at nine in the morning and work until the volunteer agreed to stop for the day. At least three hours per day, the gendarme reminded Claudio.

"If you work longer, you are done sooner. But you must show up every day until it is done. *Every* day." The cop pulled Claudio to attention. "Starting tomorrow. He works whether you are here or not, rain or shine, *madame*. The volunteer will arrive with him, and approve all the work. *Bonne journée.*"

Merle stood in the street and watched the gendarme half-drag Claudio away. How had they found him, she wondered, then realized it didn't matter. Justice, in the form of cleaning the facade of her house, would be hers. She wondered how long it would take.

Was Claudio spending the rest of his time in jail? She didn't know how work-release or restitution or whatever they called it worked in France. And who would be the volunteer to keep Claudio on task?

∼

AT 9:05 the next morning, as Merle and Francie left for Bergerac to meet the train, they found out. They stepped into the street among ladders and buckets and scrubbers on long poles. And there was Albert with Claudio.

"Albert!" Merle cried. "Are you the volunteer?"

The retired priest was bright-eyed with a stern, schoolteacher's expression as he spoke to Claudio in a low voice. He kept talking for a moment, making sure his point was taken, then turned to the sisters. Claudio moved to a ladder and began to stand it up against the house.

"Yes, I am," Albert said proudly. "It is one of the things I do for the village." He stepped closer to Merle. "This is the first time I have been called upon. I am a bit nervous."

She patted his arm. "Call me if you need me to back you up." She glanced at Claudio and remembered his cackle as he sprayed her and Elise in the dark. "Be stern."

Madame Suchet stepped out of her house. She watched the commotion for a moment then stepped down to talk to them. "Is that Claudio Droz?"

"*Oui, madame*," Merle said. "He has confessed to the vandalism and is working off his sentence by cleaning it."

"Very good," Madame S said approvingly then went to talk to Albert.

The sisters drove the farm roads to Bergerac, going slowly to take in the last of the *vendange*, the grape harvest, and various grains being cut as well. They were quiet, even Francie.

At the station Merle waited on the platform with her sister. "What will you do?" Francie asked. "About Pascal."

Merle shook her head. "I've run out of ideas."

Francie looked distraught. She hugged Merle tightly. "You'll think of something. Keep pounding."

Driving back from the train station was as usual Merle's lowest moment of the week. But at least her house was getting cleaned by the vandal himself and she didn't have to pay for it. But what about

Pascal? She couldn't think of another angle. Where was he? Why didn't he call?

Maybe it was time to take a break, think about something else. Like the French Revolution and a goat herder. What *was* that girl going to do?

ODETTE AND THE GREAT FEAR

PART EIGHT

The day Ghislain lost his foot Odette was high in the hills, kicking grasses and poking under alder trees for truffles with her walking stick. Her mind was in the clouds, musing about the Revolution. The word had come to the village a few days before that the new guillotine in Périgueux, the provincial capital, had been kept busy. Three men, one of them a judge, had reportedly been subjected to the blade of the *Louisette*. Rumors swirled about other beheadings in cities and towns all over France. A newspaper engraving showed nobles in Paris with ribbons around their necks to celebrate their connection with someone who had lost their head. Like it was a fun excursion or a costume ball and not a beheading.

The news was disturbing. The gossips said *le Comte* was next. That he had collaborated with nobles like Robespierre. Odette had thought Robespierre was a young patriot, a fine, decent gentleman, but the tides turned against him.

She looked up as the sun broke through gray clouds. Below, the chateau was shrouded in fog, vapor coming from the river on this chilly day. She pulled her long coat tighter. It was a gift from the farmer, Monsieur Daguerre, for days when she had to be outside in bad weather. It dragged the ground as she walked. It was a losing battle, trying to keep the olive wool out of the mud. She would have to clean it again tonight.

When she returned to the farm with the goats that evening the talk in the kitchen was loud and animated. It took her a moment to realize the maids and cook weren't discussing the Revolution at all.

"I saw him myself," the youngest housemaid cried. "Hobbling through the woods with a crutch."

"It's only justice," said another. "He fought for the royals, they say."

"Who?" Odette asked. "What are you speaking of?"

The four stared at her. "Where have you been, girl?" asked Cook. "It's the soldier. He's been at the Chateau all these weeks."

Odette tried to look surprised. "What?"

"Oh, yes, you won't believe it, Odette."

"He lost his foot!"

"Not 'lost,' you fool. It was cut off by the butcher. He was the only one with a knife big enough, they say."

Odette sat down hard. "That poor man."

"Get her some wine, child. The cold's gone clear through her."

Perrine handed Odette a small tumbler of sour wine. The fire felt warm against her shins. She had been to visit Ghislain only once since the day the Count invited her for tea. It had been two weeks before and she had no clue that his foot was bad. Although, now that she recalled, he hadn't risen to his feet on either visit.

She listened to the idle kitchen chatter. Ghislain LeClair had lost his rosy complexion; he looked pale and thin. But he had been just as solicitous and eager for her regard. And she had felt drawn to him as if fate had set them on this path together. They sat in the drawing room, in the sunshine, and talked of dreams. He wanted to raise horses for the Army, he said, if he could no longer serve. He described his home in Brittany as lush with grass, perfect for the best horses. There was a view of the sea across the downs. He had wanted to be in the Horse Guards because he knew the animals so well, but the Army had other ideas. He kept a blanket across his legs but she thought he had both feet intact. Now— oh, she hurt for his loss. For a man— anyone— to lose a limb was too cruel.

Where was he now? Back in the woods where she'd found him before? It was nearly winter and cold. Should she go search for him?

"Where did you see him— the soldier?" she asked Perrine.

"Near the road. Running across the neighbor's orchard," she said vaguely.

"Running? With one foot?" Odette pressed.

"With a cane. Have you never seen anyone run with a cane?"

Not lately, Odette whispered into her wine.

"Will you run away with him now, Odette?" another maid snickered. "Odette and Lieutenant One-foot, a story of true love."

The maids all laughed until the cook told them to be quiet. "She's the one who found him, if you remember." Odette looked up. She'd never told anyone about putting Ghislain in the fruit store. "I heard you two talking one morning. I think you saved his life, Odette. I really do."

Odette shook her head. "No. I—" The loss of him felt like a knife. Where was he?

"We all helped him back to health for those few days. And the Count, too, if you believe what the gossips say. But you're the one who found him, who started him on that road."

Why hadn't she gone back to see him? It had been a busy time on the farm and she'd been pressed into duty, milking goats, carrying cheese, sorting apples, loading wagons. It was a large farm and there weren't enough men. Still, she should have gone. She could have snuck away. She could have helped him get away from the Count, if that's what he wanted.

The maids said something about le Comte and she raised her head to listen.

"They say Toussaint is very angry. That the Count humiliated him and he is out for revenge."

Odette turned toward them. "Toussaint is a bully. He cut off the hair of a girl in the village. He is reckless and cruel."

They all turned toward her. "Pierre Toussaint?" Cook asked.

"You must know who I speak of. The big man."

"He is my cousin. Do not speak ill of my family, Odette. Remember you are not from here, and you are only a goat-herder."

The maids crossed their arms haughtily. Odette stood up, straightening. "I don't care if he's the King's cousin. He tried to do the same to me. He cut off a piece of my hair. Just for speaking up for that girl. The Count stopped him from taking it all. Toussaint had no right. None at all."

The silence in the kitchen was broken only by the crackling of the fire. Odette glared at the cook who glared back at her. The maids began to snicker behind their hands. One whispered, "Goat-herder, goat-girl. You smell like *merde*."

"You and the Count should be careful, Odette," the cook warned. "Very careful."

THIRTY

Delage left, cackling.

The sound of the door slamming echoed off the stone floor, the arched ceiling. Pascal heard the lock turn and the bolt being thrown as the room was plunged into darkness again. He felt a mild surprise that the winemaker had shared his bottle of red with him then left him again without so much as a kick in the gut. His torture was the slow variety, Delage had explained. The kind that gives you hope then crushes your soul as it slowly trickles away.

Pascal had lost track of the days. His head swam and the stars that floated in the darkness were inside his head. He was dying of starvation, he knew that much. His hands and feet had come back to life only to submit to the cold and lack of water again. He felt cold into his bones.

The bitterness of the wine clung to his tongue. It was just like Delage to serve him the most vile vintage he could find, especially when water would be better. Much better. He squinted up from his place on the floor, slumped against the tall killing structure. On top of the glass-front cabinet with its miniature execution devices sat a plastic two-liter bottle of water. Out of reach.

Torture, indeed.

If Delage had meant to scare him with the old guillotines, big or small, the nicks in the rusty blades where bones had chipped the steel, he was disappointed. Pascal had ceased to care. In fact, a swift death might be preferable. He understood the motive now, the reasoning behind the awful invention, *madame la guillotine*. He could use a little mercy, in death or whatever.

Delage knew the history of each guillotine here. Two were from near here, wherever this was. They had decapitated priests mostly. There were three full-size models altogether, possibly the last ones in France. Most, he knew, had been cut up and burned. Why had these been saved? Surely not for Pascal d'Onscon.

His hands were still cuffed behind his back. He had given up trying to escape the cuffs days ago, or weeks— who knew. He was too weak now to even think about escape. All he could think about was water. Delage had laughed when he placed the water bottle up there. He found himself very amusing.

Pascal listened for the sound of a vehicle. Was Delage gone? Did he live here? Pascal made an effort to count, to one-hundred, five-hundred, two-thousand. Then he scooted across the stone, too weak to stand, toward the cabinet.

The cupboard was heavy and old, made of thick oak with ball feet like melons. He nudged it with his shoulder and it didn't move. How was he going to do this? He shook his head to clear it, to think. More stars circled his vision. He breathed hard, gasping.

With a grunt he turned his back to the cabinet. There was no way to get leverage near the floor. He would have to stand.

It took a monumental effort. He tried to get his feet underneath him, then get up on his knees when that failed. Finally, he got one knee up, his foot on the floor. He leaned against the cabinet, panting. He was dizzy with hunger. Past hunger into another realm. A place of pure survival.

He took another breath, holding it, then pushed up on the knee, getting his other leg under him. It was numb and barely responsive but if he didn't put too much weight on it, it might function. His head banged against the stone wall. It barely hurt. He used the wall for balance, stretching upright. Finally, he turned his back to the cabinet, grabbing the side that faced the wall with both hands. He moaned, pulling on it.

The toy guillotines rattled, their little blades clinking.

He leaned against the wall again, gathering his strength. The blood seemed to return to his limbs now, as he was upright. His blood still worked, he marveled, despite the lack of fluids. He counted to twenty, grasped the cabinet again, and again only managed to jostle the miniatures.

Pascal looked up at the cabinet's rim. It was easily twelve feet tall. He needed to be higher if he was going to pull it down. He could open a low door and stand on a shelf. But when the cabinet toppled he would be pinned, or worse. No, there had to be something else. He looked around the dim room for something to use.

He stumbled over to the nearest guillotine. The blade was lowered for safety reasons, he supposed, but its size and heft was impressive. The rest of the apparatus was fixed. The only moving parts were the blade and the cross-bar it was attached to. He turned to the rest of the room.

The two other guillotines, slightly smaller, were similar and of no use. He squinted at something by the door. Shuffling closer, careful not to fall, he came close to the fireman's box, set into the wall behind a glass door. Inside was a fire extinguisher and an axe.

The only way to get inside the box was to pull the fire alarm set in the frame at the top. He tried to reach it with his forehead but wasn't quite tall enough. He stood on his toes, but no. He slumped against the wall, breathing hard from the effort.

He set his forehead on the glass door, his breath fogging it. He clenched his jaw. There was no choice. He stepped back then lunged at it with all his force, slamming his forehead into the window. It shattered, cutting his nose.

"*Merde*," he gasped, feeling the blood run into his mouth. He flicked it off and backed up to the fireman's box, feeling for the axe. In a moment he'd wrenched his shoulder— again— but clasped the wooden handle and pulled the axe free.

It was heavy with a large metal head. He dragged it across the floor to the cabinet. He struggled to lift it, to get it in the crack behind the cabinet but it was too heavy and too awkward from the back. It could work, if he wasn't handcuffed.

One of the smaller guillotines was displayed with the blade halfway up. The apparatus was still large, at least as tall as the cabinet, maybe fifteen feet tall. The blade was fierce, heavy enough to sever a head from its shoulders in one whack. Pascal eased up the side of the guillotine, over the ropes that kept the curious back. The blade hung at seven feet, just over his head. At the receiving end was a curved wooden slotted stop to cradle the neck.

He turned so he could work the elaborate knot that held the rope that in turn held the blade. It took some time, working blind. He began to sweat. Finally, it was free. He tugged on it but nothing happened. The blade wiggled but stayed aloft.

There was, of course, a second rope on the other side. He clambered over the flat platform where the prisoner would lie prone before the execution and found the rope on the other side. He ducked under the blade and worked on the rope. Suddenly it was free and the blade fell with a metallic thud, deadly and swift. Pascal fell backwards in surprise, letting a few more curses fly. He bent over to catch his breath.

The second time the blade made its journey he was ready. He raised the blade then wrapped one end of the rope around his foot. He placed his handcuffs carefully with only the chain in the blade's path, and jerked his foot free. Leaning forward, hands behind him, too weak to be terrified, Pascal closed his eyes and said a small prayer. He felt the blade whiz by. And heard the metallic crunch.

He pulled his hands from behind his back. It had worked. His hands were free.

He picked up the fireman's axe, his arms burning with fatigue.

He swung it over his head, catching the lip of cabinet. Stepping back, he jerked the axe handle once, twice. The cabinet rocked forward, hit the wall, rocked again. Then finally a third pull did it: the cabinet tipped forward, crashing to the floor.

Pascal found the water bottle wedged under the guillotine. He drank the water greedily then remembered to slow down and let his thirsty body adapt. He gagged but kept the fluid down. Leaning against the wall, he sat on the floor amidst all the glass and sipped.

THIRTY-ONE

Merle set her notebook aside and checked the time. She'd been up early, in the dark, when Odette had called to her from deep inside her story. The tale was winding up, she felt it, and she was already mourning the loss of these characters. Was that normal, to feel sadness for imaginary people? It was so far from the nuts and bolts, the hard realities, of law. But it must be true.

She blinked, surprised to see the sun shining in the garden. It was later than she thought. She stretched and made herself an espresso, a ritual she could almost do in her sleep now. Cup in hand she grabbed her cell phone and stepped into the morning sunshine. It was chilly, reminding her that summer had passed. How was she going to stay warm until Christmas? She consulted her to-do list in her head and mentally moved "wood stove" to the top. She'd better get busy on her list.

At the hardware store in Sulliac, later that morning, she examined all the options: electric, wood, gas. Her house had no gas line so that was out. Maybe a couple small electric heaters would make-do until a more permanent solution reared its head.

As she handed over her credit card to the clerk she got a text from Francie.

Home safe and sound. Any word from Pascal? Maybe show people that old photo of Léo? can't hurt. xo

It seemed hopeless. Nobody knew Léo Delage around here. Did they? She frowned, finding the photo on her phone. Oh, well, it can't hurt, according to Francie.

"*Excusez-moi,*" she told the clerk, a young woman with pink hair. "I was wondering if you've seen this man around here lately?"

She hadn't. But the task lit a fire under Merle. Her new mission. She'd been awake the night before, worrying about Pascal. Before she returned to her house with the electric heaters she stopped into two bars in Malcouziac, the gas station, and the little market where everything was overpriced. No one had seen Léo but nobody laughed at her either.

Back at her house Albert was still supervising Claudio, holding the ladder as he scrubbed the stone of her house with a big old-fashioned brush. It was messy work, intensive, and she was glad she wasn't doing it herself. Progress had been made, at least a little. Enough to give her hope that the house's facade might someday be clean.

"*Bonjour,* Albert," she said, setting down the box of heaters. "Just a quick question. Have you by chance seen this man around here?" She showed him the photo.

"*Dommage, non.* Who is he?"

"His name is Léo Delage. He may know something about Pascal, where he is. Pascal arrested him years ago."

"What has he done with Pascal?"

"I don't know. He doesn't answer his phone. We talked to his sister and she hasn't heard from him either."

"Maybe he loses the phone?"

Of course it was possible, as everyone posited, that Pascal had simply dropped his phone in a river. But she didn't believe it, and neither did Francie.

After lunch Merle showed the photograph of Léo Delage all over Malcouziac. If he was around it would probably get back to him. Maybe she would flush him out. She stopped in at the café on the central plaza, her favorite restaurant, *Les Saveurs*, the tiny library, the church, the *tabac*. She accosted a couple old ladies at *La Poste,* who were very kind. She asked Madame Suchet and her sister too.

No one recognized Léo Delage, or claimed to have seen him. Merle returned to her house, dragging her feet. Albert was sitting on a folding chair in the shade, looking as tired as she felt. Claudio was headed down the ladder with the bucket in one hand. The job was more than half done. At least something was getting accomplished.

"Are you done for today?" Merle asked, pausing in front of the old man. "You look tired."

"Oh, I'm fine. I'm not working, not really." He looked at the phone in her hand. "Did anyone recognize him?"

"No. I guess Léo Delage hasn't been to Malcouziac. It was a long shot."

The loud clatter of the ladder coming down stopped the conversation. Claudio set it on the cobblestones and joined them. "Let me see," he told Merle in French.

She raised her phone for him. "It's an old photo. Before he went to prison."

Claudio leaned in, squinting. "He doesn't look like that anymore."

Merle startled. "You— you know him?" She was so rattled she didn't follow the rush of Claudio's guttural French. "*Comment?* Albert, what is he saying?"

"Some nonsense." Albert pushed himself up and grabbed Claudio's arm. "Don't play games," he warned Claudio. The young man spoke rapidly back to him. "He says he knows this man. I don't know if I trust him, Merle."

"Tell me, Claudio," she implored. "Tell the truth. Where did you meet him?"

"At the bistro, the one that stays open late, he says," Albert interpreted. "Delage asked him to do something. Paid him money."

"To do what?" Merle demanded.

Claudio looked up at the house and shrugged. "Not the first one, that was someone else. But after, yes. He gets the idea. He pays me to scare you off."

Merle stared at him.

"I got that boy, the one who's not right in the head, to buy the paint. I think, no one will find out it was me. No one knows this Delage."

Albert sneered. "Someone always talks in this town."

"And now it's me," Claudio said, unconcerned about betraying confidences. "He doesn't pay after the second time, the one where I spray you and your sister. So— pffft. To hell with him."

"Where did you meet him?"

"In the parking lot. He pays me for the painting and tells me do more, to attack you with the paint."

"And you just— " Merle stared at him. "Did you enjoy it? Frightening us like that?" She bit her tongue to keep from calling him a name.

Claudio rolled his shoulders. He didn't look the least bit ashamed. "He said he would pay."

Albert spit out a few curses, surprising Merle. Claudio glanced at him, running a filthy hand through his hair. "He looks different. Not like that."

Merle looked at the photo on her phone. "Like what then? His hair is gray?"

"No, *madame*. It is the scar," Claudio said. He switched to English: "It is a big fucking scar."

THIRTY-TWO

Merle stared at Claudio. The man had widened his eyes and traced a line from his left eye down his cheek to his chin. Albert gasped then chucked the man on the shoulder.

"Don't lie, boy," he repeated. "You want to go back to the jail?"

She swallowed hard and glanced up at the sky.

The man with the scar. She'd seen him, more than once. She'd used his disfigured face in her novel, appropriating his likeness for her own purposes. Could he be the one who— ?

She grabbed Claudio by the arm. "Tell me everything about him. Where does he live?"

"He didn't say, *madame*." Claudio squinted at the old priest. "Don't lecture me, *père*. I am not your student. I know the truth. I have no love for the ugly man."

"What kind of automobile did he have?" Merle demanded.

Claudio shrugged then said, "Green? Blue? It was dark."

"Green?" Merle's voice was going up an octave. "A green BMW sedan?"

"Who knows?"

Albert bumped him again. "Think, boy. This is important."

"Is it? To who?" He glared at them both.

"To me," Merle said, trying to modulate her voice. "He's kidnapped someone I love. Someone who owns a green BMW. Do you know what a BMW looks like?"

"*Bien sûr*," Claudio scoffed. "No, it was something cheap. A Fiat? A van sort of thing. Something small and rusty."

"Did you see the license plate?"

"*Non.*"

"What else can you remember? Try to remember anything he said, a place, a name."

"That's it. Oh, your name, *madame.*" He made a gesture like spraying her with paint, and laughed.

"Don't *madame* me," she hissed under her breath.

Albert argued with Claudio for a few more minutes but they'd gotten what they could out of him. The younger man packed up his supplies, picked up the ladder, and carried it down the street on his shoulder.

Albert looked upset, almost as distraught as Merle felt. "You saw him, didn't you? The man with the scar?"

She nodded. "Twice."

"You couldn't have known who he was." Albert patted her arm. "Come. We will have a glass of wine and talk about it."

"I— I have to make some phone calls, Albert. I'll see you a little later. Or I'll call." Merle gave him two cheek kisses and unlocked her door. She watched as he waddled down the street to the corner, feeling unneighborly about putting him off. But the anxiety inside her was building. She had to call the *Policier Nationale* again. And this time she had to get through to someone.

STANDING tall in the garden she gathered her wits as the line rang in Paris. When a man answered she asked for the Wine Fraud Division. It rang more at that end. Finally, someone picked up.

Slowly, carefully, in tortured French, Merle explained that the known criminal, Léo Delage, had been seen in the area and that their officer, Pascal d'Onscon, may be in danger. She tried not to overplay her hand or be the hysterical female. Just the facts, *madame.*

The officer listened idly until she got to the part about Pascal. Then he interrupted her and put her on hold. Finally, she thought, someone was listening.

A man with a baritone introduced himself as Etiénne Marcau. "You are American? Who am I speaking to?" he asked in English.

"My name is Merle Bennett. I am a friend of Pascal d'Onscon. I recently met someone in my village who was paid by Léo Delage to vandalize my home, to scare me away."

"Is that so. You are sure it was Delage?"

"The vandal himself told me. He met Delage here in the village on at least one occasion."

The policeman paused. "And when was the last time you saw Monsieur d'Onscon?"

"Two and a half, nearly three weeks ago. I haven't heard from him. I can't get through to him. Have you—" She stopped, biting back the worry. "Is it possible to report a policeman as a missing person?"

"Of course, *madame.* But first, let me make some inquiries. I have your phone number. You have called before, yes? Thank you for your call."

"But— wait. Can't you tell me anything?"

"I am sorry, madame. This is a police matter. Please allow us to do our jobs."

Merle hung up, cursed, and threw her cell phone in the dirt. She was sick to death of being told to let somebody else handle it when obviously no one was.

Where was Pascal? Were they finally worried at headquarters? She tried to remember everything he'd said that last time he was here. Where had he seen Delage? Was it in the Sancerre? No, he said it wasn't at the family vineyard but somewhere else. She sat on the green garden chair and put her head in her hands. Where?

They were in bed, she remembered that. Then it came to her: the Languedoc. A vast sea of vineyards on the flat plains that stretched to the Mediterranean.

Too many vineyards. He could be anywhere. Pascal mentioned a type of wine grape though. All she could remember was it started with a 'B.' She dusted off her phone and searched the Internet for types of grapes. A long name, unfamiliar to her. Was it Bourboulenc?

She said it out loud in a whisper. "Bourboulenc." It had sounded like 'Bo-bo-link' when Pascal said it. That had to be it.

She searched again for vineyards in Languedoc with that type of grape. That went, well, all over the place. She tried again, adding 'AOC' to the search. The fancy appellations like Châteauneuf-du-Pape popped up. They put the bourboulenc in their wines apparently. She scanned the Wikipedia page and stopped on a name: Domaine Bourboulenc. Could it be this one? How could she tell?

She groaned and set her forehead on the garden table. This was endless, this searching. Yet what else could she do? Where else could he be? Where was Delage?

She was itchy, ready to get out of here, go somewhere, anywhere. She couldn't sit here doing nothing. What was Pascal doing? Was he alive even? Her throat nearly closed. No, don't go there. She felt the adrenaline in her veins, telling her this was 'fight or flight' time—or both?

When her cell phone rang she nearly jumped out of her skin.

"Hello? *Oui?*"

"Madame Bennett? This is Director Marcau. We spoke a minute ago?"

"Yes?" Merle stood up, flashes of bad news crossing her mind. She shut her eyes.

"I want to tell you that we have found Monsieur d'Onscon's vehicle. We haven't found him yet but it is a sign."

"That was quick."

"It was registered as abandoned a week ago. Found in a small town. But we have only now looked at the records."

"Where was it found?"

"A village near Beziers." A rustling of papers then: "Champartier. Very small."

"And—? What are you doing to find him?" To hell with voice modulation.

"We have a unit coming in from Narbonne." He cleared his throat. "We will be in touch, *madame*."

Merle stared at the screen of the phone. What could she do? She was going out of her mind. Was that a good state to drive in? But what else was there?

She took a deep breath to calm herself. First things first, she must find out where the village of Champartier was. She ran into the house and opened her laptop. In a moment she had a map of the region, far in the southern Languedoc-Rousillon region, along the Mediterranean. She looked at the statistics of Champartier. It was very small, as the policeman had said, perhaps a few hundred people. A wine-making village not unlike the one in the Sancerre where she and Francie had visited. Farms, goats, sheep, and grapes.

On the tourist sites she scanned the village history as a Roman site where a fort had stood. Parts of the old walls around the village remained. 'Champart' was a tax in medieval times, a portion paid by farmers to the landowners. Like in her novel, she mused. 'Champartier' was a tax collector— maybe.

She didn't have time to search for everything. She had to do *something*. Find Pascal. Was he there, in Champartier? To keep herself from flying out of control she flicked through another website of the village. There were wine tasting rooms, several of those. A golf course. There was a museum nearby, an obscure one only open during the summers. It sat on the outskirts of town, in an old chateau. It was a collection of relics of the French Revolution called *Musée de la Paysan*. Her interest piqued even as she knew she should be *doing something* about Pascal. Her nerves were shot. She needed to settle down and think. She bit her thumbnail. Maybe there was a detail here she could use in *Odette*.

She clicked quickly through photographs of the exhibits. There were items of clothing like '*sans-culottes*,' the baggy pants peasants wore, objects recovered from royalty, engravings and pamphlets and posters. And guillotines. Real ones. Complete with blades.

She stood up, her heart racing. Guillotines. Pascal had mentioned them when talking about the man who had confronted him. She'd just been writing about guillotines, and had tried to find one in Paris. The crazy guy who mentioned Louis the Sixteenth, the last King of France, sent to guillotine in Paris. There weren't supposed to be guillotines on display anywhere. They had all been chopped up and burned. But here they were. Big as— life.

She snapped the laptop closed.

Now. It was time.

THIRTY-THREE

It was nine o'clock and pitch dark when Merle stopped at the outskirts of Carcassonne. The fairy tale castle with its round towers was lit up against the inky sky, a dream made of stone. She was tired and hungry but needed to keep moving. She got gas and asked about a café or bistro for a quick bite. The attendant was unusually cheerful and sent her to his uncle's establishment three blocks down the side road.

She glanced at her phone while eating a bowl of cassoulet, a particularly good one rich with sausage and duck. The uncle was as amiable as his nephew, scurrying to her make her happy when she told him she was in a hurry. *"Pas de vin?"* She shook her head: no wine. He shrugged and made her an espresso.

No word from the *Nationales*. Or from Pascal. The only call was from Irene and she had left no message. Sipping her coffee, waiting for her check, she called Irene.

"Ah, Merle, there you are," Irene said. "I thought you too had gone missing."

"No, just driving. How are you? How's your knee?"

"They say there is progress. Who knows? But I must tell you—Jacques has been found."

"Oh, good. Where was he?"

"Well, it is not a pretty story, or a happy one. You are not driving now, are you?"

"No. I'm in a café." Merle set down her cup. Bad news was coming.

Irene sighed. "He ran his car off the road somewhere. He was stuck inside, can you believe it? He couldn't open the doors. All he had to eat was goat cheese for days."

"Oh, no."

"This goes on, I don't know, maybe four days. No one sees his car. It is a ditch or something. But heaven help him, the goat cheese saved his life."

"He's okay?"

"He doesn't remember much of anything. He was out of his head, delirious, when a farmer pulled him from the car. Didn't know his name. He's been in a hospital in Agen all this time."

Merle scribbled her name on the credit card slip, waved to the uncle, and stood to go. "I'm so glad he's alive, Irene. Listen, I have to run. I'm still trying to find Pascal. Have you seen anyone at his cottage?"

"Still dark as a tomb over there."

Worry ate at her. Back on the A61 she almost missed the turnoff to the north toward Champartier. French road markers assume you know every byway. She took the third turn on the roundabout and headed into the hills.

She slowed and still almost missed the next turn-off onto an even narrower road, barely wide enough for two vehicles. She passed grapevines lit by moonlight, and crept through sleeping hamlets. The village of Champartier was also sleeping, its windows dark. The fabled city wall was a pile of rubble lit by a tourist sign as if it might be fascinating to night people.

What now? She had no plan. Just 'find Pascal.' He had to be here.

It wasn't even that hard to admit, her "planlessness." What did that mean? She had learned to follow instincts at last, to go with her gut? Even as she pondered that new wrinkle she rejected it. And yet, here she was, looking for her Frenchman without a plan.

She pulled into the town square parking area under some mulberry trees. Where were the police? It was after midnight, the streets deserted. She rolled down her window and strained to hear sounds of sirens, boots, anything. A bird called from the forest beyond the village. That was all.

Did Pascal have business here, investigating local wineries? He said he was working in the Languedoc but if he said where she couldn't remember. His BMW was found here. That had to mean he was nearby. It was the only clue they had.

She stretched outside her car, looked at the dark houses and starry sky in each direction then began wandering the narrow *rues* of the little village, up one street and down another. It was built into the hillside and the streets were steep above the central plaza. It seemed abandoned, with no lights in buildings and very few streetlights. Where did the people live?

When she reached the eastern side of the village she saw faraway lights in farmhouses, tucked into vineyards beyond. The air was warm here, the Mediterranean climate. Even in October the smell of harvest and the last of summer's fruit clung to the air. Somewhere a dog barked, a door slammed, an engine started.

When she turned to go back into the village a large hulking structure caught her eye, above the village, in the trees. There was at least one spotlight on it, highlighting a tower. Was that the former chateau, now museum? She found the website on her phone again. It had a link to a map. She oriented herself to the north, holding the phone at the right angle. That had to be it.

The chateau, or museum, or whatever, sat high on the hillside, a shadowy presence. She found the road to it after a number of wrong turns, and began to climb. The forest that blanketed the tops of the hills began here and the moonlight faded into shadows. Piles of fallen leaves lined the roadsides. It smelled of pine now, and leaf mold. The dark deepened, setting her even more on edge as she walked slowly, peering into the trees for things that go bump.

At last she rounded a bend and came to a high wrought iron gate. Beyond the gate sat the chateau. There was a sign: *Musée de la Paysan: fermé. Ouvert Avril à Septembre*. It was open April to September. Now, in October, it was closed, padlocked with a huge chain across the opening of the gates. Merle rattled them for good measure and threw out a curse to the dark manse. It rose three stories of chilly nobility, all gargoyles and gothic windows. The spotlight she saw from the village lit up the tip of a four-sided tower.

She sighed. This was ridiculous. She was in the middle of nowhere, on a wild goose chase. She could see far into the valley from here. The trees must have been removed for the gentry to have a better view of their fiefdom. The village of Champartier was a dark mass. She looked out over the vineyards. From the south headlights approached, at least three vehicles. Then, out of the silence, the *doo-wop* wail of a siren. It blared then abruptly stopped.

The police? She should go talk to them. She was turning back to the museum for a last glance, in case she had to use a spooky old chateau as a setting, when the sound of glass shattering broke the silence. She startled. Where was it from? Then more glass, the clink of it hitting slate, sliding to the gravel, muted by distance. Somewhere inside the gates, she couldn't tell where. She couldn't see any movement or broken windows but the moon had gone behind a cloud.

"Hello?" she called, rattling the gate again. "Is anyone there?"

Another hail of glass was the answer.

She called again. No one replied. Was Pascal in there? With the guillotines? Was the whack-job in there too?

She examined the padlock, wondering if she could break it. The lock was shiny and new, although the chain it held was black with rust.

She cursed again, turned back toward the village, and ran.

As she turned the last corner, skidding to a stop in the central plaza, the police were shining a large flashlight into her car. There were three of them that she could see, two in navy *gendarmerie* uniforms and one in jeans and a sports jacket. They straightened as she approached in the dark, on guard.

"*Arretez!*" one yelled at her: Stop!

She put her hands up, fear making her shiver. Would she get shot here in Nowhere, France? "*Excusez-moi. Je m'appelle Merle Bennett.*" That elicited no response. She switched to English: "I called *Nationale*. Are you here to find Pascal d'Onscon? I am his friend. Someone is breaking windows up in that museum and I think it might be him."

By now several villagers had stepped outside, watching the action. One plump, older man in a dressing gown waddled over and announced that he was the mayor. "*Qu'est-ce qui se passe?*" *What's happening.*

The plainclothes cop, a solidly built, close-cropped man, obviously in charge, told the mayor they were looking for a missing person. He gave the mayor Pascal's name and a general description. It apparently meant nothing to the white-haired gentleman just out of bed. The cop gave him the usual spiel, to call if he heard or saw anything about the man. The mayor turned to go back inside.

"Wait!" Merle yelled. "*Attendez!*"

The mayor nearly tripped in his slippers. "*Comment?*"

The head policeman began to speak but before he could say two words she called out again in her halting French: "Who is in charge of the museum? Who has the keys?"

The mayor stared at her, confused. In the pause another man came out of a doorway. Tall and lanky he stepped under the streetlight like his moment in the sun had come. He said in a booming voice: "I am the caretaker. I have the keys."

MERLE RODE with the plainclothes cop in his car, the caretaker in the back seat. "Do you know Pascal d'Onscon, *monsieur?*" she asked the cop.

He nodded, his face grim. "We have worked together, *madame.*" He glanced at her. "We will find him."

"Before it's too late," she said in a whisper as she crossed her fingers.

"He is very experienced, *madame*. One of the best."

"He is," she whispered. "One of the best," she repeated like a mantra, trying to breathe.

They parked at the gates and the caretaker attempted to open the padlock with his many keys. None of them worked. He shouted about the padlock, demanding to know who had changed it and why he hadn't gotten a key. The policeman motioned to one of the gendarmes. "Up and over," he commanded. "Give him the keys."

Reluctantly the caretaker turned over his key-ring. "Which one for the front?" the gendarme asked. Armed with that information he used the caretaker's shoulders to climb onto the stone pillar that held the gates and drop down inside on the grass. He grunted and rose with a limp. The policeman urged him on.

"Can't we all go over the wall?" Merle asked. "Is it safe to just send one gendarme?"

The policeman squinted at her. "*Non, madame*. You cannot go."

"Send the other gendarme. He might need help."

The second gendarme was a young, soft-looking fellow, barely tall enough to qualify for the corps, and carrying some extra pounds. He looked alarmed when the policeman motioned for the caretaker to push him over the pillar as well. It was an even less graceful entry, complete with somersault on the lawn.

"Get up, man. He's in," urged the policeman.

The first gendarme had unlocked the front door and was looking back, waiting for his comrade. They hesitated, then stepped inside the museum. In a moment they were back out.

"The power's out."

"It's shut off for the season," the caretaker said.

"Use your flashlights," the policeman suggested helpfully.

"Tell me," Merle said, tugging on the caretaker's sleeve. "Is there a room with lots of windows? Not on this side. I heard glass breaking."

The tall man furrowed his brow in thought. "The old chapel? It has stained glass windows. It's where we keep the *Louisettes*."

"The what?" the policeman asked.

"Guillotines," Merle explained. "Tell them to check the chapel. What's it called now?"

"*Soulagement Béni*. The Room of Blessed Relief."

The policeman and Merle both stared at him, hoping they heard that wrong. "I did not name it, *madame*."

"Call them," Merle urged the cop. He made the call to the gendarmes who sounded like they were bumbling around in the dark. "What floor is it?" she asked.

"First. West end on the back," the caretaker said.

"What does that key look like?"

"There is a pass key for all the rooms. It has a little green spot on it."

The information was relayed to the gendarmes. The three outside the gate waited anxiously, some more than others. Could it have been a bird? Beer bottles? Or her imagination? She laid her forehead on the iron bars, trying to breathe.

They heard a noise, like a muffled crash, through the open door. "What was that?" Merle asked.

The policeman pulled a gun out from under his jacket while staring at the entrance to the museum. Merle was both relieved and shocked by the sight of the weapon.

"Go behind the pillar. Both of you."

Merle and the caretaker stepped to the right, behind the wide stone pillar. Merle stood in front with the caretaker looking over her shoulder toward the museum. He patted her back kindly. "*C'est okay, madame*."

Not much consolation, a rangy janitor at her back. What was

happening inside? There was another sound, then the clatter of foot-steps. The policeman raised his gun as a figure emerged. It was gendarme number one.

"There's a man in here. He pushed Silvio down the steps."

"Where is he now?"

"He's got a twisted ankle—"

"The suspect."

"Ah, he went toward a side door." He pointed to the west. "That way."

"Go upstairs and find Officer d'Onscon. Find the *Salle de Soulangement*. You have the keys?" The gendarme nodded and disappeared inside. The policeman glanced at Merle. "Stay here, behind the pillar. Both of you."

The policeman eased away from them, walking carefully along the fence, stepping over bushes and around trees. The western wing of the museum was not long and from this angle it appeared small. But in the purplish dark it was difficult to see anything.

The policeman melted into the forest. Even the glint of moon-light on his firearm faded. Merle shivered. "Are you cold, madame?" the caretaker whispered. "Would you like my jacket?"

She shook her head. "You're very kind, *monsieur, mais non.*" She couldn't keep her languages apart and didn't even try. Where was Pascal? What was happening?

A ruckus erupted inside the building: footsteps, shouts, doors slamming. Men's voices, loud. She couldn't make out any words.

Another door slammed, closer. From the east side of the building, opposite from the direction the cop had gone, a figure emerged from the shadows, limping toward them. Merle peeked out then shrunk back in the safety of their shadow. The caretaker grabbed her shoulder and pushed her against the pillar.

He was at the gate. Merle didn't dare look at him. She knew who he was anyway: Léo Delage. He was unlocking the padlock with a key, that was obvious. It was also plain neither she nor the caretaker were going to tackle him. Would he get away? Calling for the policeman would only call attention to them. She could feel the care-taker breathing in her hair and the tremble in his hand on her shoulder. She willed them both to stay still.

"Hey!" someone yelled from the museum building. "You— stop!"

Delage slipped through the gate. The overweight gendarme half-ran, half-limped from the front door, slamming through the gate and pausing to look around. Delage had vanished into the shadowy forest.

"That way," Merle shouted, pointing into the woods. The gendarme took off, crashing through underbrush.

The gate hung open. "Come on," Merle said, pushing it wider and motioning to the caretaker. "Hurry. Show me the way."

In the upper hallway the caretaker led the way to the end of the corridor where the taller gendarme stood, fiddling with the keys. He looked up helplessly and the caretaker grabbed the key-ring, quickly locating the pass-key and inserting it in the door. Everything seemed to be happening in slow motion to Merle. The tinkling of the keys, the distant shouts, the shadows in patterns on the walls. She watched, waiting, as finally the door swung open.

The interior of the room was dark and cluttered with glass and debris. A huge cabinet lay flat on the floor. Moonlight streamed through the high broken windows. Merle stepped inside after the gendarme, her shoes crunching on broken glass. The gendarme shined his flashlight around, the beam glittering on the glass. The room was in chaos, furniture down, broken things everywhere.

"Pascal?" she called tentatively. "Are you here?"

The gendarme pointed his light at the tall wooden structures and muttered a curse before he crossed himself. She stared at the horrible guillotines with their gruesome blades. Her stomach lurched and she gasped. But no blood there. No bodies. "Pascal! Where are you?!"

They heard a low moan. The gendarme rushed toward the sound, in a corner behind a fallen cupboard. "Here, *madame*. He's alive."

Pascal lay sprawled, slumped against the wall, his face bloody and lips cracked. His dark beard had grown in, making him look like a stranger. He opened his eyes halfway at the sound of her voice but they were dull, almost lifeless. He made no other movement. She touched his cheek. It felt cool to the touch but not too cool. He was alive. She kept saying that to herself: *He's alive.* Only then did she realize she had steeled herself for the worst after weeks with no word from him. She squeezed her eyes shut and banished the thought.

Tears fogged her vision. He would recover. He would be all right.

"Oh, my love." She grabbed his limp hand and put it on her cheek. "We found you, *chèri.* It's over. We found you."

THIRTY-FOUR

LANGUEDOC

An ambulance took Pascal to the hospital in Beziers. It took nearly an hour for the emergency vehicles to arrive: ambulances, more police, even a fire truck summoned somehow by the museum's alarm system. An alarm system that hadn't done Pascal much good, Merle thought, frowning as she followed the ambulance down the winding road to the main highway. She drove as fast as she dared, trying to keep it in sight, but when they hit the A61 they took off like a rocket.

When she finally found him again in the Emergency Room, the nurses kept her outside in a corridor. He was critical, they said, from dehydration. Merle slumped onto a chair next to an old man who looked as worried as she felt. She bit her lip and tried not to cry. Pascal was here, getting help.

Two hours later a nurse woke her. They had transferred Pascal to a hospital room and he was improving. The IV fluids were doing their job, she said, giving Merle a slip of paper with the room number and a pat on the shoulder. "You can see him now," she said.

Merle spent the next day by his bedside, holding a straw to his mouth every ten minutes so he could sip water. He was painfully thin, the muscles in his shoulders gone. He was weak as a kitten until the next evening when he squeezed her hand.

"*Embrasse-moi,*" he croaked. *Kiss me.* His voice was scratchy, barely a whisper. She leaned down, touching her lips to his sore ones. He flinched then squeezed her hand harder. "It's okay."

"Wait." She rummaged in her purse for lip balm. Smiling at his expression of horror she smeared the balm first on her lips then on his. She dabbed them carefully. "Better?"

WHILE HE SLEPT Merle texted her sisters, giving them the good news about Pascal's rescue and downplaying the state of him. Francie wanted a photo, demanded one, but Merle ignored her. He wouldn't want that sort of pity.

The policeman who had helped with the search of the museum visited the next day. He hung his head at seeing Pascal, to keep his shocked expression from being seen. Whether Pascal noticed, Merle couldn't tell.

"*Bonjour, François,*" Pascal said, his voice getting stronger.

"Pascal. *Comment ça va?*"

"*Tout va bien,*" Pascal said, laughing. *All is well.* He could smile now without his lips searing with pain, thanks to many applications of lip balm. "Thank you for your help."

The policeman brushed that off and gave them a report on Léo Delage. His van had been found in the woods, unoccupied. There was a bulletin out on him now, with an arrest warrant. He would be found shortly, François promised.

"Slippery devil," Pascal said.

François looked sheepish. "Director Marcau says he feels responsible. That they should have found Delage before he did this."

"He warned me. There is not much more he could do."

"Headquarters has given you leave for two months. More if you need it."

Pascal glanced at Merle. "I will use the time well."

She squeezed his hand. "Try to behave," she whispered with a smile.

MERLE SLEPT in the recliner in his room, bathed in his tiny shower, and stayed by his side for four days in the hospital. On the third night, she woke in darkness. The light from the hallway glowed from the edges of the dark door. She had been dreaming. But what? Something that woke her from a deep sleep.

She checked on Pascal, touching his hand. It was warm now. His eyes were shut and his breathing was regular. The IV had been changed recently. Nothing to do. She curled into the chair and pulled up the blanket. Closing her eyes she tried to go back to sleep.

Then the dream came back in technicolor. The hallway door opened— in her dream— and Harry walked in. Her late husband looked as he did in life, pudgy, short, with impeccable clothes (a tailored suit) and a smirk on his face. He said something to her and she rose out of the chair.

"Why are you here? This is Pascal's room." She was talking, or thinking, at Harry in her dream. Hard to discern.

He looked at Pascal, his expression unreadable. Harry seemed to glow in the darkness. He was a ghost after all.

With a flash she realized she could say the things to Harry that she'd never had a chance to in life. "I should have been there for you," Merle sputtered. "When you had your heart attack. When you were dying all alone. All those nights we spent apart." A sorrow she had buried racked her chest. "I'm so sorry, Harry. I wasn't there."

Harry turned toward her, his eyebrows wiggling and the smirk in place. "But Merle, how could you be with me? I died at work, just as I lived at work."

"But I gave up. On us. On you."

"Not before *I* gave up on us," Harry said. "You aren't the guilty party. You always want to make it about you, don't you? You were always like that. Silly woman."

He stepped closer to her and she could see he was— insubstantial. Transparent. Nearly gone. "Live your life, calendar girl. Not in the someday. Not in the past, worrying about things you can't change. Live in the now. Live your life the way you see fit. The way that makes you happy. You— alone. You know that's what I did."

SHE OPENED her eyes in the dark room. Tears streamed down her face. Was that really Harry? Or some part of her that couldn't let go of him? Her husband had been gone two years but it seemed much longer. Why was she dreaming about him? Was he giving her permission to forget him, to move on, to forget the mistakes she'd made, that he'd made?

Or was she giving herself that permission?

She wiped her cheeks with the blanket. Something bloomed, just a little, inside her. Something good and true, like hope. She didn't believe in an afterlife, not like that. Not one where the dearly departed come back to haunt you. This was something else, something inside her. Something she hadn't been able to forgive herself for— for giving up on their marriage. What had she said once to one of her sisters after Harry died? "He was already dead to me."

She was so ashamed for not loving him. She was deeply flawed as a human being, as a caring partner. There was no denying it. It was heartbreaking to a driven perfectionist to admit. But maybe accepting those flaws was the purpose of Harry's appearance.

She sighed deeply, trying to exorcise the dream from her consciousness. She was getting the second chance Harry never had. She would live on, without him, not because she had to— but because she wanted to. He'd abandoned her, and ignored Tristan. He'd made his choices, had his secret family, worked out a way to be happy. Was that so bad? If you weren't happy, you should find a way to be happy, right?

"Blackbird?" Pascal said softly in the dark. "Come here, please. I need you to lie here next to me."

Merle gathered herself, wiping her eyes as she took her blanket to his bed and lowered the side rail with a clatter. "Shhhh," Pascal said, his eyes dancing.

Oh, God, his eyes were dancing again.

Making herself as small as possible, she scooted onto the bed and tucked herself under his arm. He adjusted the blanket over her shoulder and held her against his side. With her nose on his ribs she felt a warm bath of love pass down her body, and her heart began to mend.

She draped an arm over Pascal's body, lightly, with care, feeling his lungs move the air in and out.

This, she whispered. *This.*

THIRTY-FIVE

Pascal stayed in the hospital in Beziers for a week. Toward the end of that week, Merle got a hotel room nearby although her sleep was still not the best. She worried about him— was he eating enough, or too much? Would he recover his strength? How could she take care of him— she who was a lousy caretaker of others? Would they bicker and fight? Would his sisters swoop in and assume control?

She'd called his sister in Victoire the day after the rescue. Like with her own sisters Merle downplayed the seriousness of his condition. She told the sister that Pascal was dehydrated. That wasn't a lie, although the doctors told Merle he probably wouldn't have lasted another day or two without water.

Pascal recovered enough to tell the tale of his abduction, as much as he remembered. He'd lost track of time in the *musée* and had no idea how long it had been. Two weeks at least, she figured. He used his last bit of strength to push Léo into the chapel window. Then he'd passed out. It would be much later when he finally told Merle about using the guillotine to cut off his handcuffs. He would tell her that he was ready to lose a hand, and that he couldn't believe it had worked.

The *Policier Nationale* had a new mobile phone delivered to the hospital. Pascal called his sister to give her the new number and tell her he was fine and not to worry. Within an hour he got his first call on the phone. It was Clarisse.

Pascal answered before checking who was calling, then held the phone away from his ear. He rolled his eyes at Merle. He listened to his ex-wife rattle on and finally reassured her he was okay and hung up.

"She called my sister. Believe it or not she was worried about me," he said. "She said nothing about that boy, *chérie*. And she didn't ask for money either."

"A miracle."

"Yes, I am. Come here. Give your miracle a *bisou*."

AFTER A FEW DAYS in the hotel to make sure he could walk and eat, Merle drove Pascal back to Malcouziac for his convalescence. She wanted to make a bed for him in the living room but he insisted he could handle the stairs. That became part of his rehab plan, up and down the stairs, four times a day. Well, at first, once a day, then finally two and three and four.

Merle attacked his recovery like a four-star general going to war. She cooked constantly, making his favorites like *coq au vin* and *cassoulet*. She researched ways to gain weight and get muscle back, bought vitamins and cookbooks and new pots. She became that mother-figure who is never happy with the amount of food you are eating, always urging one more bite.

Pascal wasn't terribly worried about regaining his weight and strength. He began doing sit-ups and push-ups in the garden by the end of the first week at home. He gloried in the definition in his abs, pointing them out constantly and laughing. Merle started trying to record his laughter, for those someday times when she might need to hear it again.

Then she stopped herself.

Harry's ghost had told her not live in the future, or the past. To enjoy the moments now, fully. She knew he was right. Pascal was here now. *Don't get between the moments you want to live in by over-thinking them. Succumb to the joy.*

She had to write that down in her notebook. She had little time for writing at first, but slowly, as Pascal got back to his old self, strong and capable, she stepped back a little. First she let him cook, mainly because he was much better than she was and knew all sorts of French dishes without using a recipe. His sisters had taught him well.

Then after weeks of her taking him on walks to build up his stamina, he announced he would start jogging and took off alone. And he survived, mostly.

Albert and Madame Suchet came by often to give Pascal special treats. Albert recounted his troubles supervising the vandal and proudly pointed out the clean facade of Merle's house. He raised his beret and showed them his new hearing aids. Lately when he'd seemed a little lost, he was just not hearing well.

The house itself felt more alive than ever with Pascal in residence. Merle couldn't believe her luck, finding this Frenchman in her bed each morning and in her garden each afternoon. She still looked at the list of chores she'd brought with her from home, many items crossed out now, but many not done. She was running a finger down the list one evening as Pascal cooked *Soupe à l'Oignon Gratinée*, the classic French Onion Soup with cheese and bread slices on top, when she found something on her list that looked simple. She had yet to name this house.

Wandering into the kitchen where he stirred copious amounts of onion Merle watched him for a moment, savoring the scene and the scents. "What is the French word for 'lucky'?" she asked.

Pascal glanced up. "Hmm? Oh, *chanceux*. Or, *heureux*. Like 'happy.'"

"*Chanceux*," she repeated. "*Je suis très chanceux.*" Pascal leaned in for a kiss and went back to his onions.

Merle opened her notebook and wrote down the new name for her house in France. Then she called back to Pascal: "Is this right? *Maison de Chanceux?*"

"No, *chérie*. The Lucky House would be *Maison Chanceuse*. *La maison*: the house is feminine."

Of course the house is feminine, she thought. It was *her* house. She looked at the chipped white vase with its dried blooms from summer, at the colorful blanket thrown across the horsehair settee, at the antique cupboard she'd found to replace the one that had been ruined by the thieves. She was a simple, functional house, but a lucky one. She had survived so many disasters and still warmed and sheltered with all her might.

Merle scratched out what she'd written and started again.

Maison Chanceuse

∼

BY THE FIRST week in December Pascal announced himself cured. He did look fine, his muscles returned to their state of grace, bulging under his black t-shirt, his lung capacity was worthy of a three-mile run, and his weight settled just under what it had been before.

"I am going a little bit crazy without work, *chérie*." They were in the kitchen, stirring a bisque on the stove. He put his arms around her from the back and pulled her into him. "You understand?" he asked, nuzzling her neck.

Merle felt sad that their time together was over. Was it over? She blinked into the soup. "But—?" She put down the wooden spoon and turned to face him.

"But what?" He kissed her nose. "You think I am not ready?"

"No, not that. You look ready to me. But what about— us?"

He stepped back and looked at her seriously. "I have thought about that endlessly, blackbird. But you have your lawyer job in New

York and I have my police job here. How can we figure it out? I can't move to New York, *chérie,* it is not possible."

She laid her hand on his chest. "I want—" She swallowed hard.

He whispered: "What do you want, my love?"

Her stomach lurched. What was he thinking? What did *he* want? But that wasn't the question, was it?

"I want to quit my job." The words stuttered out of her, scaring her but all true. "I don't want to go back to the city. I want to stay in France."

He paused, staring into her eyes. "Are you sure?"

She nodded, her throat in a clot.

"Shall I rent out my sad little cottage on the internet?"

She threw her hands around his neck. "And make a small fortune off crazy Americans and other animal lovers."

He rolled his eyes. "I should throw in goat cuddling? Is that what you call it?"

"It will go viral."

"What do they say on MTV? That would be sick."

THAT NIGHT MERLE composed an email to Lillian Warshowski, breaking the news that she was quitting. Not taking that very complimentary raise. It was a hard letter to write. She was not one to turn down offers, to walk away with no plan in place. About ten o'clock she stretched, still not finished, and clicked on her inbox. She hadn't been online much. Her sisters only texted these days and her parents and Tristan called her when necessary. Her inbox was stuffed with appeals for politicians, weight loss remedies, and cocktail recipes. A note from her friend Betsy; another from Tristan's counselor. He was doing fine, the counselor said, replying to a "hovering mother" letter Merle had sent a week back.

And there it was: an email from Lillian.

Merle froze. She'd never heard back from her boss, she realized, after she'd written to discuss the new job. Too much had transpired, and she'd completely forgotten that Lillian had been silent. She squinted at the date: one week had passed since Lillian had written.

Now Merle's finger hovered over the key, apprehensive. Lillian had replied.

It was short and not-so-sweet, a reflection of the author. Lillian had decided not to retire after all: hadn't Merle heard? How silly it was that the news hadn't crossed the ocean!! In Lillian's world, in the Legal Aid and New York lawyer world, it was front page, above the fold, top drawer gossip.

Lillian Warshowski realizes she is indispensable. Huzzah.

Merle stared at the screen. Lillian had changed her mind. Lillian had not bothered to tell Merle. Wait— she scrolled through her inbox, checked her spam, looked everywhere. Nope. Nothing from Lillian until this.

There were tidbits in the email about the young lawyer who had taken Merle's job temporarily. It sounded like Lillian was stalking him. Ugh.

What a—

Merle blew up her cheeks and let out a big breath. *Stop.* She no longer had to reject Lillian because she'd been rejected instead. She should be happy— right? She didn't have to break it gently to Lillian, to tell her that working with her was a moral and ethical quagmire and that she never wanted to drink with another white-shoe lawyer for the rest of her life.

Merle stood up and shut the laptop. She walked out the kitchen door into the garden, lit by a few neighbors' lamps and the moon. It was a sliver of new moon, a crescent, silver and bright, with the dark, shadowed side a deep midnight blue. But it was there, obviously, that dark side. Was it telling her to look beyond the bright and shiny? That there was more to life than the obvious? Was it telling her— here is the whole picture? Not everything is seen. In fact, very little is as it seems. Waiting for you is the rest of the story. The unknown. The future. What's coming.

She shivered. It was cold in the Dordogne in December. Not unexpected, even by Americans abroad. The wood stove was to be installed last week, but of course there had been delays. This week? Maybe. In the meantime, there were blankets and those tiny space heaters. At least the laundry had been finished. It sat dark and quiet in the garden, the newly-painted blue door reflecting the moonlight. Strange how having a laundry made a woman feel complete. She smiled at her silly, womanly self, at her feminine *maison*. Her *Maison Chanceuse*. She looked at a star and made a promise to never forget how lucky she was.

The sound of the window latch, then the hinges creaking. She looked over her shoulder at the bedroom window. Pascal was leaning out, his forearms on the sill, his face cut through by shadow from the moonlight. He was smiling down at her.

"*Chérie?* Are you coming to bed?"

ODETTE AND THE GREAT FEAR

PART NINE

Days passed, cold and rainy, full of the deep mist of the mountains that chilled to the bone. Odette took her goats far, searching for Ghislain in caves and along riverbanks, in abandoned *bories,* the beehive stone shelters for sheepherders. She looked in them all and sometimes napped there, out of the wind that blew down from the Alps.

The days were long because of her wandering and she often returned in the dark, exhausted. It was easier too, to avoid the maids and the cook who had taken against her. They were no longer friendly since her comment about the cook's cousin, the horrible Toussaint. She knew her days were numbered here. She also knew there was no one to replace her and the goats would suffer without grazing.

One morning she slept late, too tired to rise for the communal meal and too despondent to care about a tongue-lashing. The kitchen was deserted when she arrived. She poured hot water into a cup and rummaged for some herbs to make it seem like something decent. A single crust of bread lay on the sideboard. She dipped it in the water she called 'tea' and ate quickly.

Outside in the yard Margot from the milking shed stood with her hands on her hips, talking to a man. His back was toward Odette and she didn't recognize him. While Odette grabbed her coat he turned and was gone by the time she stepped into the chill. She caught up with Margot inside the shed.

"Ah, good, you can help me today. I am so tired I could fall asleep against these beasts." Margot handed her a bucket. "Take Eloise for me."

Odette didn't argue. Her goats could wait a bit. She fixed her stool next to the big nanny Eloise and set to milking. In a moment though she had to ask: "Who was that man? The one you were talking to?"

"Oh, just now? Someone from the provincial government. They're looking for that soldier, the one you rescued from the woods." Margot stuck her head out from behind her nanny goat. "You haven't stashed him away somewhere, have you?"

"Me? No. I haven't seen him at all."

"Is that a fact?" Margot went back to her business, the sound of liquid hitting the pail a clatter in the background. "Because the word is that he's been seen in these parts."

Odette startled and stopped squeezing teats for a moment. "Oh?"

Margot poured the goat milk into a tall can. She put her hand on Eloise's rump. "Don't you want to know where?"

"I can see you want to tell me," Odette said.

"All right then. It was near here all right. In the woods, some-where. Vague, a bit. No one ever gets directions in the woods correct. But it sounded like where you found him in the beginning of all this."

Odette said nothing, just finished milking Eloise. She felt her heart race. When she was pouring the milk into the can Margot stepped up beside her, taking the pail from her trembling hands.

"That's enough for today, *mon amie*." She gave Odette a knowing grin. "*Sortez d'ici* — get out of here."

The goats found him.

It was past midday and warm in the sunshine. But the goats needed grass that still grew green and thick under the alders so Odette let them wander. She was not very attentive to the goats. She had one thing in mind, finding Ghislain.

And then, with a shock of recognition, near the tree where she'd found him months before, there he was. He lay on his side, his great coat wrapped around him, clutching a wooden staff. She crouched beside him quietly. His eyes were closed, his head resting on his arm. Was he asleep— or? She raised her eyes to the sky, sending up a prayer. When she looked down at his kind face again, his eyes looked up at her.

She couldn't speak for a moment. He reached out with a trembling hand and she grasped it tightly. "Are you all right?"

"Help me up," he said in a weak voice.

She helped him sit up, leaning against the tree. He looked exhausted. "Have you eaten? Do you have water?"

"Until yesterday," he said. "Or the day before."

"Wait here. I will fetch you something."

She began to rise and he caught her hand again. His face contorted. "Don't leave me."

"You must have food. I will return very soon. I will leave my goats here to protect you."

Odette brought back a hunk of cheese, two apples, and a bucket of water. No one on the farm looked at her twice. She walked slowly through the yard, then broke into a run when she neared the woods. She raised the pail to Ghislain's lips and let him drink. After he had eaten the apples and the cheese and quenched his thirst, she sat back and looked him over.

He was wearing both his fine leather boots, and the same clothes he'd worn the first time she'd seen him at the Count's chateau, the green jacket and the white starched shirt now filthy with road grime. His dark trousers were torn and dirty. No wound was visible.

He closed his eyes again, leaning his head against the tree trunk. She let him doze. When he opened his eyes again they looked brighter, the brilliant blue she remembered.

"What are you doing here, Ghislain?" she asked quietly. "What happened?"

"They came for the Count. You know he is a friend of Robespierre?" She nodded. "An angry mob arrived late one night with torches, ready to burn the rest of the chateau. They accused him of harboring royalists and being a traitor to the Republic. I know, it makes no sense but in these times, nothing makes sense."

"But I didn't hear— did they take the Count away? Did they take him to the guillotine?"

Ghislain shook his head. "He talked them out of it. At least for now. All the nobles will suffer, that is a certainty. He will lose his land to the people, and who am I to say he shouldn't? But he was good to me. He helped me as much as he could, to mend and be well."

"The Count told you to leave?"

"He was a friend but now I am a liability. I had to go. Being his friend was not going to help me in the end."

She glanced at his leg. "How are you mending?"

"It was bad for awhile, Mademoiselle Odette. Before you came to see me last a contamination set in. Fevers, chills, the wound was poisoned. The people there, the Count's people, they worked hard and pulled me through. It is better but not healed."

"There is a story going round that you lost your foot."

He grinned then and Odette felt her heart lift. "Feel it." He wiggled toes in both boots. "Go ahead." She squeezed the toes of each of his boots.

"I am so happy for you." They stared at each other for a moment. In that pause in conversation she knew she wouldn't go back to her garret in the Daguerre farm, tonight or any other night.

Odette took her goats back at the usual time and ate her soup in silence with the maids. Everyone was quiet tonight, no gossip and chatter. Someone said that the wheat prices were good but only because there was so little wheat. The domestic help knew nothing of grain prices so that ended the conversation. When Margot got up to leave Odette followed her outside.

"Helping with the evening milking, are ya? Can't get enough of the teats?" Margot said, tucking her hair under her cap while striding toward the milking shed.

"Wait," Odette said, taking her arm. She dragged Margot into the barn. "I found him."

Margot held up her hands. "I have no idea what you're speaking of. Do not tell me, Odette."

"I want someone to know. I leave tonight."

"Again." Margot put her fingers in her ears. "I don't have any idea who took the horse."

Odette blinked, glancing behind her at the stalls. A small black horse had his head out over the gate, nickering at them. She jerked her head toward him. "Yes?"

Margot bit her lip. "I must go." She hugged Odette. "Blessings and godspeed."

The moon had not yet risen when Odette led the black horse out of the back of the barn, through the sheds and the orchard, and into the woods. She picked up windfall apples, stuffing them in the feed sack she'd purloined. How long could one live on apples? They may have to find out.

Ghislain was standing when she returned, holding onto the tree. He had heard the horse coming and was ready for a fight. When he saw Odette he groaned and fell into her, holding her tight. She stiffened, unaccustomed to so much hugging. Then Ghislain let her go, mumbling apologies, embarrassed. He tugged his forelock. She pulled him back to her. It wasn't her first kiss but it was the first one that meant something. The first with a promise.

"Can you mount the horse? He is not so large and they say very gentle."

Odette led the horse to a fallen log and with help Ghislain stepped onto it then swung up on the horse. There was no saddle, only a bridle and a blanket, but he declared it fine.

"He's a good one, Mademoiselle Odette," he said, stroking the horse's neck. "He will carry us far. What's his name?"

"I don't know. What would you call him?"

He reached for Odette's hand on the reins. "*Chanceux?* Because tonight I am the luckiest man."

EPILOGUE

The holidays came hard and fast upon Merle Bennett, as usual. No matter where she was or what she was doing, she was never truly prepared and often in a state of panic. This year in particular everything was chaos. Reining in the mayhem took every ounce of her prodigious planning abilities.

The email that she eventually sent to Lillian Warshowski was not too hard to write. She simply turned in her resignation. She hadn't been getting paid these last few months anyway. Her vacation days had run out weeks ago. Merle hadn't figured out what she'd do for income yet but her sister Annie was starting a new consulting business and they'd been discussing working together. Nothing could be better than working with her favorite sister.

Merle and Pascal would return to the States for two or three weeks. She wanted a specific return date but he convinced her to be flexible. She might want to stay longer, get her house in order, put things in storage, find a renter, do whatever it might take to make the transition less stressful. Tristan might need her. Her parents might demand her time.

He was right as usual. But before they left she wanted to visit

Irene Fayette. It was frosty in the hills of the Dordogne, with mistletoe growing in balls high in trees and holly sporting red berries. Pascal needed to arrange some work to be done on his cottage as well, to get it ready for use as a rental. He already had several reservations for later in the spring. So, they traveled south to the hamlet on the hilltop a few days before they were scheduled to fly west.

Irene had told them Louise was going to be home for the holidays so they weren't surprised to see three cars in front of the low-slung stucco farmhouse. They parked Pascal's green BMW, recovered and running like a top but in need of a new glove box, in the dry grass and knocked on the door.

Louise greeted them warmly, giving them air kisses and thanking Merle profusely for all her help this year. Irene was getting around very well now with only a slight limp, hardly noticeable. They found her in the kitchen, cooking as usual. The smells of garlic and butter filled the air.

"And look who else is here," Louise said.

Jacques, Irene's elderly cousin with the mischievous smile, raised his beret in greeting. *"Bonjour! Joyeux Noël!"*

Irene, dressed in Christmas red, turned from the range and gave everyone hugs. Her cousin, she told them, had come to live with her. There was no point in him getting lost again. He was good company and a little help around the *chèverie* even if she didn't let him drive farther than the goat shed. He had found her someone to milk the goats, and another person to sell cheese at markets. He had many friends.

Pascal was pressed into telling his story of abduction and rescue over a not-so-simple lunch of *hachis parmentier,* a sort of delicious shepherd's pie with layers of mashed potatoes and lamb, served with crusty baguettes and olive tapenade. Wine flowed, as is the French way, then came the *crème brulée* for a sweet finish. Jacques told his tale of survival by goat cheese as well. Everyone enjoyed the drama and offered many compliments for the chef.

As they left Merle brought out a print-out of *Odette and the Great*

Fear, loose pages wrapped in a rubber band. She pressed the stack on Louise and asked her to translate it for Irene.

"Nothing fancy, just in front of the fire some night, tell her the story."

Louise's eyes widened. "You wrote this?"

"There are goats involved," Merle said. "And a handsome stranger."

Louise pressed it to her chest. "I will do my best, Merle. Thank you for the honor. My mother will love it."

In the car as they buckled themselves in the seat belts and waved to Irene and Louise on the porch, Pascal said, "What a meal, *mon dieu.* So delicious. She did us such a courtesy. It was like my mother's cuisine, full of love and respect. You know what this means. These are your people now." He touched her shoulder. "Our people, blackbird."

Merle smiled. "*Our people.* I like the sound of that."

READ MORE ABOUT ODETTE

The full story of **Odette and the Great Fear** will be available as
an e-book.
Look for it wherever books are sold.

Coming this Christmas
The Bennett Sisters French Cookbook

READ ALL THE BENNETT SISTERS MYSTERIES

Blackbird Fly
The Girl in the Empty Dress
Give Him the Ooh-la-la
The Things We Said Today

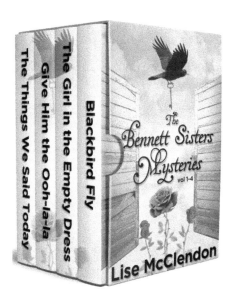

I hope you've enjoyed **The Frenchman.**
Sign up for the newsletter to hear about new releases, giveaways,
contests, and more
Click here
or copy and paste into your browser:
http://eepurl.com/A6bsD

~

Visit online at
www.lisemcclendon.com

ACKNOWLEDGMENTS

A special thanks to Helen Mulroney for checking my French like the pro she is. If I called a lawyer an avocado, it's on her though. 😉 Let's go to France again, *mon amie!*

Thanks as well to Kipp Webb who understands my love of France as well as my love of him. To Evan and Nick, love always, and to Kate and Abby and Zoe and Kira, may we all have many adventures together. Love you.

To my readers who have inspired me to keep writing tales about the Bennett Sisters: thank you for reaching out and keeping in touch. To everyone who sent me a correction about an accent or a pronoun: *merci.* It helps to know there are perfectionists like Merle in the world!

ALSO BY LISE MCCLENDON

The Bluejay Shaman

Painted Truth

Nordic Nights

Blue Wolf

One O'clock Jump

Sweet and Lowdown

All Your Pretty Dreams

as Rory Tate

Jump Cut

PLAN X

as Thalia Filbert

Beat Slay Love

ABOUT THE AUTHOR

Lise McClendon is the author of fifteen novels of crime and suspense. Her bestselling Bennett Sisters Mysteries is now in its fifth installment. When not writing about foreign lands and delicious food and dastardly criminals, Lise lives in Montana with her husband. She enjoys fly fishing, hiking, picking raspberries in the summer, and cross-country skiing in the winter. She has served on the national boards of directors of Mystery Writers of America and the International Association of Crime Writers/North America, as well as the faculty of the Jackson Hole Writers Conference. She loves to hear from readers.

www.lisemcclendon.com

CPSIA information can be obtained
at www.ICGtesting.com
Printed in the USA
LVHW051647201021
700977LV00013B/506